African American Literature and the Classicist Tradition

African American Literature and the Classicist Tradition

Black Women Writers from Wheatley to Morrison

Tracey L. Walters

palgrave
macmillan

First published in 2007 by
PALGRAVE MACMILLAN™
175 Fifth Avenue, New York, N.Y. 10010 and
Houndmills, Basingstoke, Hampshire, England RG21 6XS.
Companies and representatives throughout the world.

PALGRAVE MACMILLAN is the global academic imprint of the Palgrave Macmillan division of St. Martin's Press, LLC and of Palgrave Macmillan Ltd. Macmillan® is a registered trademark in the United States, United Kingdom and other countries. Palgrave is a registered trademark in the European Union and other countries.

ISBN-13: 978-0-230-60022-5
ISBN-10: 0-230-60022-0

Library of Congress Cataloging-in-Publication Data

Walters, Tracey Lorraine.
    African American literature and the classicist tradition : Black women writers from Wheatley to Morrison / by Tracey L. Walters.
            p. cm.
    Includes bibliographical references.
    ISBN 0-230-60022-0
    1. American literature—African American authors—Classical influences. 2. American literature—Women authors—History and criticism. 3. Mythology in literature. I. Title.
PS153.N5W335 2007
820.9'9287096—dc22   2007011353

A catalogue record of the book is available from the British Library.

Design by Scribe Inc.

First edition: October 2007

10 9 8 7 6 5 4 3 2 1

To my husband, Dean
For my daughters, Amouri and Tori

Contents

Acknowledgments

I am eternally grateful to Julia Cohen and Farideh Koohi-Kamali. Thanks for supporting the project and seeing it through until the end. Rosemi Mederos, I appreciate all of your hard work and your unwavering patience. I am indebted to the following individuals who read the manuscript at various stages of completion: Dr. Ann Kelly and Dr. Jennifer Jordan, a special thanks for your critical eyes and continued encouragement. Dana A. Williams you are a lifesaver! Thanks for stepping in at the fifth hour to read my last chapter. Natasha Gordon-Chipembere, I cannot thank you enough for taking time to read my chapter while churning out your dissertation. Adrienne Munich, Daniela Flesler, Cherron Barnwell, and Eugene O'Connor thanks for reading early chapters.

I must give special acknowledgment to Michele Ronnick, Patrice Rankine, and Shelley Haley. Thank you so much for sharing your time and your scholarship. Your work in the area of *Classica Africana* has inspired me and I am looking forward to contributing more scholarship to the groundbreaking work you have each produced in this significant field of study. To my colleagues and friends at Stony Brook University, I am grateful for your encouragement.

To my parents, siblings, and friends (Allan Walters, Elaine McEwan, Sandra, Claudette, Dion, Sharon, Randal, Jordan, Randy, Peaches, Jason, Ange, Tara, Rissa, Tracee, Chad, Rosha, my stepfather Herman, Ana, Ethline, Courtney, Ron and Emma Nelson), I appreciate your unyielding love and support. To my husband and best friend, Dean Edwards, and my beautiful daughters, Amouri and Tori Edwards, thanks for understanding that in order to complete this project I needed to disappear for hours on end. This book is a gift for you. And to the most high, thanks for teaching me that with faith and perseverance all things *are* possible.

Introduction

Writing the Classics Black:
The Poetic and Political Function of African American Women's Classical Revision

African American Literature and the Classicist Tradition: Black Women Writers from Wheatley to Morrison is a study of how and why African American women writers appropriate Greco-Roman mythology. In addition to discussing how eighteenth- and nineteenth-century women writers such as Phillis Wheatley and Pauline Hopkins established the tradition of African American women's classical revision, I investigate how twentieth-century African American women writers Gwendolyn Brooks, Toni Morrison, and Rita Dove apply both modernist and postmodernist approaches to classical mythmaking. A comparative reading of Brooks' "The Anniad" (1949) and "In the Mecca" (1968), Morrison's *The Bluest Eye* (1970), *Song of Solomon* (1977), and *Beloved* (1987), and Dove's *The Darker Face of the Earth* (1994) and *Mother Love* (1995) uncovers the diverse nature of their appropriation of classical myth. In order to demonstrate the development of Black women's classical revision, the respective authors and their works are discussed chronologically.

Classicists define scholarship on African Americans and their contributions to classical discourse as *Classica Africana*. *Classica Africana* became a recognized sub-field of classical studies during the the 1990s. Classicist scholar Michele Ronnick, who coined the term, adapted the phrase from Meyer Reinhold's *Classica Americana* (1984). Reinhold's text examines the role of classics in

America during the eighteenth and nineteenth centuries. Ronnick explains that the "new subfield of the classical tradition, *Classica Africana*, explores an area overlooked by Reinhold and examines the undeniable impact, both positive and negative, that the Greco-Roman heritage has had on people of African descent in their creative and professional endeavors" (Ronnick 5). *Classica Africana* focuses on three main areas of investigation.

First, scholars study the contributions of African American classicists past and present. Ronnick, who has undoubtedly proved to be one of the most committed scholars of *Classica Africana*, has created "12 Black Classicists," a traveling exhibition of early notable African American classicists. She also edited *The Autobiography of William Sanders Scarborough: An American Journey from Slavery to Scholarship* (2004), followed by *The Works of William Sanders Scarborough: Black Classicist and Race Leader* (2006).[1] In both works Ronnick uncovers Scarborough's significance as one of the earliest and most successful Black classicists of the nineteenth century. Scarborough served as chair of the classics department at Wilberforce University and published *First Lessons in Greek* (1881), "a text that according to his obituary in the *New York Times* made him 'the first member of his race to prepare a Greek textbook suitable for university use'" (Ronnick 6). Ronnick reports that Scarborough's affiliation with the American Philological Association (APA), publications, and command of classical languages helped refute the nineteenth-century belief that Blacks were intellectually inferior. Scarborough, like many of the early writers in this study, regarded the classics as his passport to equality.

According to Ronnick, Scarborough viewed the APA as an inclusive group that treated its Black members respectfully. In a letter, Scarborough noted when he first joined the APA he found that "the men and women of those days thought more of scholarship and less of prejudice; the color of a man made no difference with them. It was his standing as a scholar and as a representative of American scholarship that counted" (Ronnick 266).[2] In addition to Scarborough, Ronnick has also written about other Black writers who have been inspired by the classics such as sixteenth-century poet Juan Latino, eighteenth-century Jamaican poet Francis

Williams, and nineteenth-century African American sculptor Mary Edmonia Lewis. Along with Ronnick, Shelley Haley is another classicist who has produced numerous innovative readings about African Americans and the classics. Haley's work on nineteenth-century African American female educators and scholars, for example, establishes a connection between classicism and female and racial empowerment.

In addition to studies on African American classicists, there is also a large body of early scholarship produced by classicists who study Blacks in antiquity. Frank Snowden, a former chair of Howard University's Classics department, produced *Blacks in Antiquity: Ethiopians in the Greco-Roman Experience* (1970) and *Before Color Prejudice: The Ancient View of Blacks* (1983), two groundbreaking studies about the Black presence in antiquity and the Greco-Roman perception of Blacks. Leo Hansberry's historical research on Blacks and the classics was published in Joseph Harris's edited volume *Africa and Africans: As Seen by Classical Writers: The William Leo Hansberry African History Notebook Vol II* (1977). Other works on Blacks and antiquity include Ivan Van Sertima's *Black Women in Antiquity* (1984), and Martin Bernal's *Black Athena* (1987). Bernal's text is one of the most well known, though not necessarily well-respected, books on the subject of Africans and antiquity. In *Black Athena* Bernal argues for recognition of the Afro-Asiatic roots of Western civilization that had intentionally been undermined by nineteenth- and twentieth-century White scholars who gave ancient Greeks credit for the contributions to civilization established by Africans. Bernal's thesis led to a public debate among classicists like Mary Lefkowitz who denounced his argument. Ronnick responded to the debate by urging scholars to "look beyond the personalized and specific focus of the Martin Bernal–Mary Lefkowitz debate, and turn toward additional types of research in this area of African studies" (5). Ronnick proposed that other topics for consideration might include unearthing the works of eighteenth- and nineteenth-century African Americans who mastered classical languages, or investigating the role of classics in the curricula of eighteenth- and nineteenth-century historically Black colleges and universities.[3]

The third area of *Classica Africana* concentrates on how African American authors have adapted myths. While there have been a number of articles exploring the connection between the classics and African American literature (see Michele Ronnick, Christa Buschendorf, Shelley Haley, Jane Campbell, Elizabeth T. Hayes, Madonne Miner, Jacqueline de Weever, and Therese Steffen), full-length scholarship on Blacks and their adaptations of the classics is scant. There is a longstanding tradition of Black women writers incorporating literary themes, archetypes, and literary figures from Western classical antiquity into their own narratives, and yet only a handful of scholars have written about the major influence of Greco-Roman antiquity on African American women's literature. Jacqueline de Weever's *Mythmaking and Metaphor in Black Women's Fiction* (1991) is the most comprehensive analysis of Black women's appropriation of myth (ancient Greek, African American, and African). In comparison to my own study, which takes into account the political and social implications of the women's classical revisions, de Weever's analysis of Black women and myth primarily focuses on the creative uses of myth. To date there is only one full-length text that interrogates how and why a collective body of African American writers appropriate Western classics. Patrice Rankine's *Ulysses in Black: Ralph Ellison, Classicism, and African American Literature* (2006) is the first text to focus exclusively on African American writers and their reworking of Western classical myth. Rankine explores the Ulysses theme in the works of Ralph Ellison and Toni Morrison. Similar to my own study, Rankine investigates how and why writers like Ellison, Countee Cullen, and Toni Morrison have adopted classical narratives. My book departs from Rankine's, however, because in addition to discussing the establishment of a tradition of African American women's classical revision that dates back to the eighteen century, I focus exclusively on Black *women* writers and their adaptations of myths centering on motherhood. Also, I show how the contemporary renditions of the ancient texts engage in a social commentary about issues relative to urban blight, female victimization, and racial oppression, which contribute to the public discourse of the day.

The lack of scholarship on the connection between Greco-Roman mythology and African American women's literature exists because in large measure, as Ronnick points out, classicists do not give adequate attention to the classical revisions of African Americans. Furthermore, those scholars who investigate the use of myth in Black writing usually focus primarily on how Black writers appropriate African and African American mythology. Lastly, because some African Americanists dismiss the Western classics as Eurocentric and antithetical to a Black literary tradition—or Black aesthetic—those texts reflecting a classical influence are not granted the same critical analysis reserved for non-classically inspired works.

African American Classicism in the Eighteenth, Nineteenth, and Twentieth Centuries

The eighteenth-century African American poet Phillis Wheatley was the first to establish the poetic and political function of mythopoesis that would draw future Black women to it—each for her own reasons that were often shaped by social realities of the times in which these women lived. Wheatley was drawn to the classics because she recognized that those who wrote within the classical tradition garnered respect and acclaim from their literary peers. Seeking to gain recognition and validity as a poet, Wheatley reworked classical Greek myths and mythical heroes into her poetry.

In "Niobe in Distress for her Children Slain by Apollo, From Ovid's *Metamorphoses*, Book VI and from a View of the Painting of Mr. Richard Wilson," Wheatley employs the classics as a political aesthetic, demonstrating that myth could be used metaphorically to discuss social realities, such as slavery and female oppression. The classics held significance for Wheatley because she identified with the accomplishments of the African Roman playwright Terence. In the poem "To Macenas" she makes note of Terence's African ancestry. By referencing Terence's African heritage Wheatley claims the classics as part of an African tradition and at the same time informs readers that the highly revered Western classics included an African presence. It is important to note that during the eighteenth century White males promoted the notion that the Western classics were established by Whites and were accessible only to erudite White males. Wheatley's bold reminder that Terence was Black and her use of neoclassical verse undermines the attempt to marginalize Blacks and women from mastering the codes of elite literary culture. Ultimately for Wheatley, appropriating classical mythology was about artistic legitimization as well as human equality. Wheatley's neoclassical poetry complicated arguments that justified slavery on the basis that Blacks were intellectually and racially inferior. Wheatley's poetry made her an important figure in the abolitionist debate. Those who supported slavery attempted to disregard the relevancy of her poetic contribution. Thomas Jefferson, for example, scoffed at Wheatley's poetic genius, claiming that her classical paraphrases were poorly written and suggesting that her knowledge of classical mythology was elementary. Wheatley was not the only poet discredited by Whites. In 1774 when Francis Williams published his poem "An Ode" in Latin, pro-slavery advocate Edward Long published the poem in English to show that Williams's poem was not written well and that his Latin was flawed. So while proponents of slavery sought to downplay accomplishments of poets like Wheatley and Williams, anti-slavery advocates used their undertakings as an example of the unrealized potential inherent in all of America's enslaved Black people. Wheatley's knowledge of Latin, however elementary, and her classical paraphrases proved her right to equal membership within the human community.[4]

In the nineteenth century Blacks continued to believe that appropriating classical myth would validate not only their poetry but also, more importantly, their humanity. While some focused on classical paraphrase, others devoted their attention to mastering classical languages. The racist beliefs of the pro-slavery movement continued through the Victorian era even after slavery was abolished. Many Whites found it inconceivable that the former slave population was capable of comprehending classically inspired literature or translating Greek and Latin. For example, South Carolinian Senator, John Calhoun, charged "[t]hat if he could find a Negro who knew the Greek syntax, he would then believe that the Negro was a human being and should be treated as a man" (Gates 21). Evidently, Calhoun did not expect the Black community to take up his challenge. According to Henry Louis Gates, Jr., after hearing Calhoun's proposition, Alexander Crummel reacted by "jumping on a boat, sailing to England, and matriculating at Queen's College, Cambridge University, where he mastered, of all things, the intricacies of Greek syntax as part of the broader field of study in theology" (22). Crummel was not the only scholar to meet Calhoun's challenge. W. E. B. Du Bois became a serious classical scholar and served as chair of the Classics Department at Wilberforce University. And as noted previously, William Scarborough's publication of *First Lessons in Greek* (1881) became one of the most important contributions to classical scholarship authored by an African American. Robert Fikes's historical study of Blacks and the classics reveals that during the nineteenth century there were a number of African Americans teaching the classics. Richard T. Greener taught Latin and Greek at the University of South Carolina, Daniel Williams taught Greek and Latin at Virginia State University, Anna Julia Cooper taught Greek and Latin at Saint Augustine College in North Carolina, and George Lightfoot taught Latin at Howard University (Fikes 120–21).

Calhoun's declaration that Blacks could prove themselves by mastering classics might have been the most notorious, but other well-known nineteenth-century public figures made remarks equally as offensive. Mary Church Terrell, for example, recounts that when the poet Matthew Arnold paid a visit to Oberlin and heard her recite Greek he was astounded because "he thought the tongue of the African was so thick he could not be taught to pronounce the Greek correctly" (41). Arnold's remark proved once again that in order to gain admittance into the human family, and to be regarded as equals, Black people would have to not only master the master's language, but master the codes of elite literary discourse, which assumed knowledge of the classical tradition. Ironically, the remarks made by Calhoun and Arnold in the nineteenth century continued to be echoed in the twentieth century. In recollecting her early experience as a student of classical education at the University of Michigan, Shelley Haley recalls experiencing blatant racism in many forms: "One professor at a social function pointedly told other faculty members within my hearing that Black students were 'lousy at Latin' and just not smart enough to take classics. The chair asked me why Blacks were afraid of intellectual disciplines and always went into sociology or education. Another announced during a public lecture that there was no such thing as a 'Black Classicist'" (26). Haley's anecdote confirms that even in the twentieth century Black people were still forced to prove their ability to comprehend classical texts and master classical languages. It should be noted that during the nineteenth century not all Blacks agreed with the idea that the classics validated one's humanity. Martin Delany and Booker T. Washington, for example, were virulently opposed to the idea that the classics were a necessary field of study. Ronnick observes, "to Washington the desire for classical training was an empty and pretentious quest for Blacks living in the years after the civil war" (61). Washington made many public statements denouncing the classics. In his view, learning trades rather than mastering classical languages would better serve Black students. Ronnick shares that Washington once noted: "A young colored man who lately graduated at an Agricultural College in Iowa had three positions offered him before he got his diploma. When a college graduate finishes his classical course, he may look for a position—diploma in hand, and look and look—til whiskers grow on the bottoms of his pantaloons" (Ronnick 63). Classicists like Du Bois and Crummel rejected Washington's anti-classics crusade and encouraged Blacks to continue their pursuit of classical studies.

During the nineteenth century a number of Black women studied classical languages and recreated classical myths. In "Black Feminist Thought and the Classics: Re-membering, Re-Claiming, Re-empowering," Haley contends that nineteenth-century women writers and educators Anna Julia Cooper, Frances Jackson Coppin, and Mary Church Terrell looked to the classics as a way to empower themselves. "Each believed that education was the key to overthrowing the disadvantages the Black women and men faced and still face. Since a classical education was the yardstick for intellectual capability, Coppin, Cooper and Terrell learned classics, that microcosm of their society where Black women were silenced and thought incapable of intellectual endeavor. That learning in turn had a symbolic value for them." (25–26)

While Haley's observation that Coppin, Cooper, and Terrell realized the classics could liberate both their race and their sex lays the foundation for contemporary to the study of Black women and classicism, because she lays the foundation for contemporary Black feminist readings of Black women and the classics, the relationship between the classics and a gendered and racial discourse was actually recognized much earlier by writers such as Henrietta Cordelia Ray, Pauline Hopkins, and again, noted feminist scholar Anna Julia Cooper. These women use classical myth and figures from antiquity to argue for the empowerment of Black women. For example, in *A Voice From the South* (1892), Cooper writes an essay comparing the marginalized status of nineteenth-century women with the freedom and respect given to ancient female poets and writers. While arguing for the necessity of women's education, Cooper points out that female intellectuals were not new phenomena, for ancient women like Sappho and Aspasia were highly educated:

> Sappho, the bright, sweet singer of Lesbos, "the violet-crowned, pure, sweetly smiling Sappho," as Alcaeus calls her, chanted her lyrics and poured forth her soul nearly six centuries before Christ, in notes as full and free, as passionate and eloquent as did ever Archilochus or Anacreon. Aspasia, that earliest queen of the drawing room, a century later ministered to the intellectual entertainment of Socrates and the leading wits and philosophers of her time. Indeed, to her is attributed, by the best critics, the authorship of one of the most noted speeches ever delivered by Pericles. (63)

Cooper cites Sappho and Aspasia to demonstrate that a tradition of female artists and intellectuals has existed since antiquity and to argue that nineteenth-century women should also be afforded the opportunity to develop their artistic and intellectual talents.

By the twentieth century the classics did not hold the same value they did for eighteenth- and nineteenth-century writers. Fikes reveals that between 1896 and 1940 no African Americans took degrees in the classics. And according to Ronnick by the 1920s in most historically Black colleges and universities classics departments were eradicated. It is possible that interest in the classics waned because Black people no longer believed it was essential to prove their humanity or intellectual equality. By the 1940s and 1950s, while there were a number of African American classicists who taught and studied the classics (Annette Eaton and Frank Snowden), most Black writers abandoned classical myth as a source and referent for narratives, replacing Western Greco-Roman mythology with African myth and African American folktales. As Bernard Bell contends:

> By and large Black novelists of the fifties rejected the ahistorical universality of Greco-Roman myth and ritual for a mixture of Christian and social myths and rituals rooted in the particularity of the Black American experience. For example, the myth of White supremacy and the rituals that reinforce and perpetuate the Manichean Black and White, evil and good, significations of Western mythology with its overtones of an apocalyptic clash are still major sources for themes, symbols, and images in the novels of the fifties. (192)

The social climate of the 1950s also impacted the shift in focus from Greco-Roman myth to religious and social myth. Writers who lent their voices to the developing genre of "protest literature" sought literary models that would more readily speak to the reality of their oppressive social condition. While many turned to other forms of mythology, there were a number of writers who continued to find inspiration in classical myth. Ralph Ellison, for example, employed the mythic structure of *The Aeneid* for his masterpiece *Invisible Man* (1952). With "The Anniad" and "In the Mecca" Gwendolyn Brooks continued the tradition of African American women's classical revision. For Brooks the classics offered a structural framework upon which to create stories transforming heroic characters from Greek mythology into African American heroines. Like Phillis Wheatley, Brooks found the classics offered artistic freedom and poetic validation. Brooks' classical revision allowed her to reach a broader audience and at the same time legitimate her poetry. In her autobiography Brooks admits that she wrote the classically inspired epic "The Anniad" to prove to White readers that she could write well. While Brooks might have succeeded in her quest to demonstrate her artistic ability to the mainstream, she lost the support of her Black audience. As examined in Chapter 3, there were some that believed that her classically inspired poetry did not appeal to a Black readership. The rift between classicism and African American readers and writers became more prominent during the 1960s and 1970s when Black Arts Movement writers were encouraged to reject Western literary standards and conventions and instead embrace African American mythology. Some writers were unwilling to compromise their art in order to subscribe to the tenets of the Black Arts Movement. Writers like Robert Hayden, Leon Forrest, and Toni Morrison adhered to their own Black aesthetic. Rather than divorce themselves totally from classical influence, like the modernists before them, they infused narratives with African, African American, Indian, and Greek mythology. In effect these writers recognized the importance of drawing from all cultures to address common, universal experiences relative to humankind. Moreover, for writers like Morrison it has been important not to defend her use of the classics. In numerous interviews Morrison makes the point that her adoption of Greek mythology should be expected because the classics are ingrained in what Jung defines as our collective unconscious. Therefore, from Morrison's perspective, it is only natural that classical myth would appeal to her in the same way they they would attract any writer. With this approach to the classics, Morrison undermines the notion that classics are consigned to a specific group and she claims the literature as her own. Dove shares Morrison's sentiment. In interviews she has also stated that classical revision allows for a universal approach to writing. From the seventies and onward Black women have continued to try their hand at mythopoesis. Audre Lorde's *The Black Unicorn* (1978), Nikki Giovanni's "The Cyclops in the Ocean," (1983), Lucille Clifton's poems about Atlas and Leda in *Quilting* (1988), Angela Jackson's "Arachnia: Her side of the Story" (1993), and Adrienne Kennedy's "Orestes" and "Electra" (1980) are just a few of the texts that have been shaped by classical mythology. Although this study is concerned with African American women's classical revision we should note that a number of Black men, including W. E. B Du Bois, Countee Cullen, Ralph Ellison, Robert Hayden, and Leon Forest, to name a few, have also recast classical narratives. While in this study I focus on how and why women have appropriated classical myth, I also believe it is imperative that scholars begin considering the various ways Black male authors experiment with classical revision.

The Aesthetic of African American Women's Classical Revision

African American women writers of the twentieth and twenty-first century employ myth so that they can create new versions of myths, which include the Black female subject. African American mythmaking, Jane Campbell explains, "constitutes a radical act" because as Black writers create new mythical tales, they also "subvert the racist mythology that thwarts and defeats Afro-America and replace it with a new mythology rooted in the Black experience" (Campbell x). The use of the alternative frame of reference provided by the worlds of classical myth allow writers like Pauline Hopkins and Rita Dove to create a new definition of Black womanhood that confronts prevailing contemporary cultural myths and stereotypes that promote racist, sexist, and elitist attitudes toward Black women and men. The marriage between the mythic world of ancient Greece and Rome and contemporary society results in a syncretism where the individual myth is deconstructed and becomes unrecognizable as it is recreated into a new narrative.[5] Re-creation is crucial for the women of this study because it is their intention to present new stories and new mythologies about Black life from the perspectives of Black women. These women turn to the classics for the freedom to create narratives that offer both victimized and empowered portrayals of women. With the exception of Pauline Hopkins, all the women in this study have revised myths about motherhood. Three primary figures from Greek mythology, Niobe, Medea, and

Demeter, are transformed into African American mothers who are traumatized by witnessing the murder of and or separation from their children either by infanticide or child abduction. Through their adaptations of classical myths about motherhood, Wheatley, Ray, Brooks, Morrison, and Dove uncover the shared experiences of mythic mothers and their contemporary African American counterparts.

While some African American writers and scholars regard the revision of Western classics as inconsistent with the notion of a Black aesthetic, most of the women in this study reveal that writing within the classical tradition does not mean sacrificing an authentic Black voice. Morrison's *Song of Solomon*, for example, demonstrates clearly that the Western classics can be merged with the African American literary tradition to produce a narrative grounded in the Black experience. Moreover, for writers like Wheatley, who notes the contribution of the ancient roman poet Terence, and Morrison, who references Martin Bernal's study of the African contribution to Western classical civilization, the classics are indeed part of a Black aesthetic. Writers like Dove recognize the shared traits between classical literary conventions and African American literary devices. Dove explains that the call-and-response convention used in the African oral tradition (a lead orator poses a statement that is responded to or affirmed by an audience) operates in much the same way as a Greek chorus who explains and responds to actions in the narrative.

Pulitzer prize-winning authors Brooks, Morrison, and Dove all have employed the myth of Persephone and Demeter in the construction of their most important texts.[6] The vegetation myth of Persephone and Demeter traditionally centers on the rape and abduction of Persephone and the struggle of Demeter, her mother, to cope with the loss of her daughter. Brooks, Morrison, and Dove turn to this particular myth because the story highlights a number of significant feminine tropes found in Black women's writing: women and their struggle to define self, the oppression and sexual violation of women, and the conflicts between mothers and daughters. Because there is no conclusive evidence to prove that any of the writers of this study were familiar with or influenced by other existing versions of the Persephone and Demeter myth written by Black women before them, the claim that the women are signifying on each other's texts cannot be made. What is clear, however, is that each woman signifies on the classical tradition by revising key tropes. To this end, each woman who revises the Persephone and Demeter myth builds upon preexisting versions of the narrative and at the same time offers a unique reworking of the story that contextualizes the narrative within a specific historical and social moment. Brooks' and Morrison's adaptation of the Persephone and Demeter myth, set in the 1940s, highlight issues of Black female sexuality, Black female oppression, and the struggle to define a Black female identity.

Like Brooks and Morrison, Dove also sheds light on the subject of self-identity. Unlike Brooks and Morrison though, instead of focusing on the issues of rape and sexual violation, Dove examines the dynamics of Black motherhood and the relationship between Black mothers and daughters in the 1980s. In their retelling of the myth the women also differ in their presentation of the characters. While Brooks and Dove chronicle the experiences of both Persephone and Demeter, Morrison presents only Persephone's journey. What is similar about Brooks', Morrison's, and Dove's texts is that they invert the mythic structure so that their narratives end not with resolution, but with unresolved conflict. Jacqueline de Weever explains that the "open-endedness" is necessary "because the future unfolds in all its danger and fascination. In devising such open-endedness for the text, Black American women writers achieve a stirring emotional response to the reader through such revision and inversion of canonical myths" (24). In Brooks' "The Anniad," at the end of the narrative, her protagonist is left alone reflecting on the past, unsure of the present. In Morrison's *The Bluest Eye*, Pecola receives her blue eyes but she remains victimized by her community. And in Dove's *Mother Love*, Demeter and Persephone maintain their estrangement.

The Persephone and Demeter myth provides Brooks, Morrison, and Dove with the form and structure upon which to build their own stories. From a sociological and cultural perspective, classical mythology also gives the writers a platform upon which to address issues that pervade Black life. In his study "The Archetypes of Literature," Northrop Frye explains that myth is often used metaphorically: "The 'ideas' the poets use, therefore, are not actual propositions, but thought-forms or conceptual myths, usually dealing with images rather than abstractions, and hence normally unified by metaphor, or image-phrasing, rather than by logic" (90). For Brooks, Morrison, and Dove, the Persephone and Demeter myth serves as a metaphor that allows these writers to uncover hidden truths or mythic beliefs concerning issues of rape, incest, and domestic abuse, subjects often considered taboo in the Black community. Essentially, the myths allow women to break their silence and give voice to those are unable to speak for themselves.

African American Literature and the Classicist Tradition: Black Women Writers from Wheatley to Morrison is divided into five chapters. Chapter 1 offers a brief overview of ancient and contemporary versions of the myths of Persephone and Demeter, Niobe, and Medea. Chapter 2 discusses how eighteenth-century poet Phillis Wheatley used classical revision, first to authenticate herself as a writer, and second to liberate herself and other enslaved Africans from the status of intellectually and racially inferior to equal citizens of humanity. Her poem "Niobe in Distress for her Children Slain by Apollo, from Ovid's *Metamorphoses*, Book VI and from a View of The Painting of Mr. Richard Wilson" illustrates how Wheatley used the "Niobe" story to experiment artistically with classical narratives and at the same time address personal and political thoughts about slavery.

Following Wheatley, I examine the poetry and prose of nineteenth-century writers Henrietta Cordelia Ray and Pauline Hopkins. I show how writers like Wheatley, Ray and Hopkins take a feminist approach to classical revision. For example, "Echo's Complaint," a revision of the Ovidian story of Narcissus published in Ray's collection *Poems* (1910), moves the female character from a marginal to a central position. This story, which typically centers on the male protagonist Narcissus, is rewritten to reflect the experience of the female character Echo. Pauline Hopkins' novel *Contending Forces* (1900) is not a revision of a classical story. Hopkins, however, does allude to the iconic figure from Greek antiquity, Sappho of Lesbos, to discuss female sexuality.

Chapter 3 shifts our focus from the eighteenth and nineteenth centuries to the twentieth century and analyzes Gwendolyn Brooks' epic poems "The Anniad" and "In the Mecca." Most critics read "The Anniad" as a reinterpretation of the *Iliad* or *Aeneid*. An alternate reading of the text reveals that Brooks' "The Anniad" is actually a subtle reworking of the Persephone and Demeter myth. The chapter also uncovers parallels between the Persephone and Demeter story and "In the Mecca."

Chapter 4 investigates Morrison's adaptation of the Persephone and Demeter myth for her novel *The Bluest Eye*. A comparative reading of Morrison's and Brooks' appropriation of the Persephone and Demeter myth illustrates that the two writers are drawn to the myth for different reasons but adapt the myth in similar ways. Although most of the chapter is concerned with exploring how Morrison reworks the Persephone and Demeter myth, the chapter also looks at Morrison's use of the Icarus myth in *Song of Solomon* and her revision of Euripides' Medea in *Beloved*. Chapter 5, the concluding chapter, explores Dove's appropriation of Sophocles' *Oedipus the King*, for *The Darker Face of the Earth*. An analysis of *The Darker Face of the Earth* reveals how Dove merges classical myth with elements of the slave narrative. Finally the analysis of *Mother Love* shows how Dove uses the Persephone and Demeter myth to highlight the tension-filled emotionally-charged relationship between both mothers and daughters and to challenge culturally and socially informed definitions of Black womanhood.

African American Literature and the Classicist Tradition: Black Women Writers from Wheatley to Morrison serves as an introduction to the tradition of African American writers and classical revision, offering readers new ways to read and interrogate the texts not only of Brooks, Morrison, and Dove, but also other African

American writers. While the project makes a valuable contribution to African American literary studies those in classical studies can also benefit from seeing how a group not usually associated with the classics—Black women writers—have sought out and used the ancient Greco-Roman myths for aesthetic and political purposes.

Historical Overview of Ancient and Contemporary Representations of Classical Mythology

Roland Barthes, Fritz Graf, and others remind us that myths are made up of multiple versions of the same story and "each of these works is just a single link in a chain of narrative transmission: on either side of the version that it is authoritative for us, there stands a long line of other versions" (Graf 21). When engaging in a comparative reading of contemporary authors and their revisions of ancient classical narratives it is imperative to take into account that the contemporary authors are drawing from ancient and modern versions of narratives that have been modified. To gain a clear understanding of how the African American women authors in this study have transformed myths, we must first look at the ancient and early modern sources to determine which texts the women might have adapted for the creation of their own narratives. Although all the women in *African American Literature and the Classicist Tradition* recast a number of different myths, the myths of Persephone and Demeter, Niobe, and Medea are the only myths discussed in this chapter because they explore the central theme of motherhood that is reflected in the writing of almost all of the authors in this study.

Persephone and Demeter

The Persephone and Demeter myth is by far one of the most popular myths adopted by Black women writers, therefore it will be the first myth discussed here. During antiquity the Goddesses Demeter and Persephone were featured in Greek and Roman literature, pottery, and art—temples and monuments were also erected to them. Classical scholars cite a number of ancient texts that either record the entire Persephone and Demeter story or include elements of the myth as part of unrelated narratives. Timothy Gantz tells us, for example, that Homer's *The Iliad* and *The Odyssey* both make passing references to Demeter and Persephone's story. Helene Foley's comprehensive study of the Homeric version of the Persephone and Demeter myth cites fourteen ancient texts that record all or parts of the myth. Foley's list includes Hesiod's *Theogony*, Orphic hymns 18, 29, 41, 43, Euripides' *Helen*, the Hellenistic *Hymn to Demeter*, and Apollodoros' *Library (Bibliotheca)* (Foley 30).[1] Robert Graves' dictionary of classical mythology includes Ovid's *Metamorphoses* and *Fasti* as two other narratives that recite portions of the Persephone and Demeter myth.

Like all ancient myths, before a written version of the Persephone and Demeter narrative existed it was told orally. The *Homeric Hymn to Demeter*, recorded approximately 650 BCE, is often cited as the earliest written version of the narrative. Karl Keréyni believes that the *Homeric Hymn* is probably an allusion to the Cretan myth, which predated the Homeric version. Although the *Homeric Hymn to Demeter* references the poet Homer, the narrative itself is not necessarily attributed to Homer; rather the text is related to Homer's style of writing. Foley explains, "the Hymn, composed in dactylic hexameter verse (the same meter that is used in the Homeric epics), follows the tradition of oral epic in its diction, style, and narrative technique" (29). Thus, the actual *author* of the *Homeric Hymn* is unknown. The *Homeric Hymn to Demeter* is one of many Homeric Hymns.[2] The Hymns were sung as prayers to deities and were preludes to other songs. The Hymns served to explain how Olympian gods attained their relevance as well as how they received their power.

The *Homeric Hymn* recounts how and why Demeter and Persephone receive honors and details the goddesses' establishment of the Eleusinian Mysteries. Interestingly, the Eleusinian

Mysteries precede the myth itself: rather than the story creating the ritual, here the ritual creates the myth. The Eleusinian Mysteries were considered one of the most important mystery cults in antiquity. The Eleusinian Mysteries, celebrated in the second millennium BCE, were a secret and sacred cult that was established to honor and worship both Demeter and Persephone. The Mysteries were carried out yearly and the ritual ceremony lasted for approximately one week.[3] In ancient times the Mysteries were celebrated across the Greco-Roman world, and men, women, and slaves were able to participate in the events. Initiates bathed, danced, sang, and engaged in purification rites. According to Graves, the Demeter initiates acted out Demeter's affair with Zeus, sacrificed pigs, and often carried torches to symbolize Demeter's search for Persephone. Because the rituals connected to the Mysteries were part of a secret oral tradition, classicists and archeologists who have relied upon art, temples, and literature for their sources have pieced together much of what we know about the rituals. In art the myth was captured on clay stands, vases, and marble relief. These ancient artifacts feature different elements of the story. Hades' kidnap of Persephone, for example, is presented on an Apulian red-figure hydria (fourth century BCE) (Foley 77). And Persephone's return to earth is captured on an Attic red-figure bell-krater (440 BCE) (Foley 79). Historical written sources tell us that there were a number of festivals and rituals established to worship Mother Earth (Demeter) and recognize her inauguration of the Mysteries and gift of grain and agriculture to humankind.

Of all the versions of the Persephone and Demeter myth, the *Homeric Hymn to Demeter* emphasizes the mother–daughter relationship. Much of the narrative directs the reader's attention to Demeter's traumatic response to Persephone's abduction and her unyielding search and commitment to find her daughter. The Hymn offers little from Persephone's perspective, especially her rape by Hades, which is highlighted in so many of the contemporary narratives. The Hymn reports that Persephone is distracted by the beauty of a narcissus flower while playing with friends Athena and Artemis. Gaia, in collusion with Zeus, (Persephone's father) assisted Hades' abduction of Persephone by growing the narcissus.

As Persephone plucks the flower from the earth, Hades ascends from hell and kidnaps her. Persephone, shocked and afraid, cries out to Zeus to save her. Hecate and Helios hear Persephone's cries but neither intervenes to stop Hades. Demeter is crushed by Persephone's disappearance and roams the earth looking for her. In deep mourning Demeter does not eat or bathe for nine days. On the tenth day Hecate[4] comes to assist Demeter and the two confront Helios who reveals Zeus and Hades' conspiracy. Demeter is outraged by her husband's actions and leaves Olympus and travels to Eleusis where she disguises herself as an old woman named Doso.

In Eleusis, Demeter is met by a group of young women who inquire about her well being. Demeter tells the girls she has recently escaped from an ordeal where pirates kidnapped her. The girls are eager to help Demeter and they offer her the job as wet nurse to their brother Demophoön. After meeting Metaneria, Demophoön's mother, Demeter assumes her duties as nursemaid. Perhaps because she desires to substitute Demophoön with Persephone, Demeter conspires to make Demophoön immortal. Each night Demeter secretly places Demophoön on the hearth's embers. One night Metaneria witnesses Demeter roasting Demophoön and she screams out in fear. Demeter is offended by Metaneria's reaction and in retaliation demands that the Eleusians erect a temple in her honor. For one year Demeter sits in the temple grieving. During this time Demeter rejects her duty to nurture the earth. Her neglect of the land threatens the existence of mankind and, with no sacrifices being made, the Olympians become concerned about their own fate. Zeus appeals to Demeter to restore fertility to the earth but Demeter refuses his request, agreeing to acquiesce only if she is reunited with Persephone. Seeking to appease Demeter and re-establish order to the earth, Zeus sends Hermes to Hades to retrieve Persephone. Hades agrees to return Persephone, however, because he wants Persephone to reside alongside him in the underworld, he persuades Persephone to eat a pomegranate. After eating the fruit, Persephone learns that she is obliged to return to Hades for a third of the year (winter)—spending the remaining months with Demeter in the upper world. Once reunited with Persephone, Demeter brings fertility back to the earth. Demeter also teaches Triptolemus, one of the princes of Eleusis who had erected the temple in her honor, the sacred rites: "mysteries which no one may utter, for deep awe checks the tongue. Blessed is he who has seen them; his lot will be good in the world to come" (Hamilton 53).

Next to the *Homeric Hymn*, Ovid's *Metamorphoses* offers another well-known version of the Persephone and Demeter story. Ovid's rendition of the Persephone and Demeter myth (Latin spellings: Proserpine and Ceres) differs from the *Homeric Hymn* in significant ways. First, in the "Rape of Proserpine," Ovid begins with a description of Ceres' (Demeter's) gift of agriculture: "She first gave corn and crops to bless the land; / She first gave laws; all things are Ceres' gift" (Melville 109). Next, Ovid shows that the gods influence Pluto's (Hades) capture of Proserpine. Venus persuades Cupid to make Pluto fall in love with Proserpine. After being struck with one of Cupid's arrows, Pluto, upon seeing Persephone picking flowers (here not a narcissus flower but lilies and pansies), "saw her, loved her, carried her away" (Melville 111). Proserpine calls out, not for her father as she does in the *Homeric Hymn*, but for her mother and her friends. Whereas in the *Homeric Hymn* Hecate and Helios hear Persephone's cries but do not interfere with Hades' capture of the maiden, in *The Metamorphoses* the water nymph Cyane witnesses the kidnapping and tries to persuade Pluto to release Proserpine. Cyane chides Pluto for taking Proserpine by force: "'Stop, Pluto stop!' She cried, 'You cannot take / This girl to wife against Queen Ceres' / will. She ought to have been wooed, not whirled away'" (Melville 111). Pluto ignores Cyane and takes Proserpine down to hell. Cyane is greatly impacted by the rape and dissolves into a pool of tears.

Meanwhile, Ceres looks for Proserpine. During her search she stops at a house to quench her thirst. At the house, a boy mocks Ceres' hasty consumption of her barley-flavored drink. In anger, Ceres throws the drink at the boy, transforming him into a lizard. Ceres continues hunting for Proserpine. Anxious to help Ceres find Proserpine, Cyane ensures that Ceres sees the sash Proserpine dropped before being taken by Pluto. When Ceres identifies the clothing she realizes that foul play is involved and she begins mourning for her stolen child. Ceres "reproached the whole wide world—ungrateful, [and] not deserving of grain" (113) and she destroys all of the earth's crops. Once again, anxious to assist Ceres, Cyane informs Ceres that Pluto took Proserpine to hell. Ceres appeals to Jove (Zeus) to have Pluto return their daughter. In contrast to the *Homeric Hymn*, Jove tries to encourage Ceres to allow Proserpine to remain with Pluto, reminding Ceres that Pluto loves Proserpine. Ceres is not swayed by Jove's plea to leave their child with Pluto and she demands that Proserpine be returned. Jove concedes, but warns Ceres that if Proserpine has eaten food of the dead she must return to Pluto for part of the year. Unlike the *Homeric Hymn*, which conveys that Pluto engages in trickery to make Proserpine eat the pomegranate, Ovid shows Proserpine secretly eating the pomegranate without Pluto's knowledge. Later Proserpine's crime of eating the pomegranate is exposed when Ascalaphus testifies to witnessing her misdeed. To placate both Pluto and Ceres, Jove decrees that for six months of the year (double what is noted in the *Homeric Hymn*) Proserpine will spend time with Ceres and for the remaining six months she must return to Pluto.

In addition to Ovid's *Metamorphoses*, the Orphic texts also differ from the *Homeric Hymn*. Keréyni believes that the Orphic myths, made up of poems and poem fragments, are based on primitive versions of the narrative. The Orphic texts feature several different stories about farmers who witness Hades' rape and abduction. Keréyni reports that in one Orphic version, Eubouleus, a pig farmer, tells Demeter that his pigs fell into the chasm left by Hades' entry through the earth. Eubouleus says that when he looked down into the chasm he saw Persephone with Hades. After hearing Eubouleus' story Demeter travels to hell and retrieves both the pigs and Persephone. Graves describes a similar Orphic story. Graves notes that the Eleusian prince Triptolemos tells Demeter that while tending to his herd he saw Hades take Persephone and rape her. Demeter rewards Triptolemos by teaching him the Eleusian Mysteries and the tools of agriculture.[5] One of the most significant changes found in the Orphic tales is a narrative recording that Zeus, not Hades, rapes Persephone. The rape results in the birth of Zagreus, also known as Dionysus, god of the vine. Lastly,

Orphic narratives mention that instead of Hecate helping Demeter find Persephone, Athena and Artemis assist Demeter in her search. The Persephone-Demeter myth becomes the prototype for all later Persephone stories. As Elizabeth Hayes notes, "the patterns, imagery, and symbols in this first narrative establish the basis for later recurrences. The myth, therefore, has to a certain extent been conflated with the archetype it animates" (Hayes 5). Modern translations of the Persephone and Demeter myth remain close to the Homeric, Ovidian, and Orphic versions. Edith Hamilton's *Mythology* (1940), for example, seems not to deviate too much from the *Homeric Hymn*. Robert Graves' *The Greek Myths* (1955) and Thomas Bulfinch's *Mythology* (1959), each a marriage of Ovid's *Metamorphoses* and the Orphic texts, make some subtle changes to the story. Bulfinch downplays Cyane's role in trying to dissuade Pluto from taking Proserpine. In fact he narrates that when Cyane sees Ceres searching for Proserpine she is too afraid to anger Pluto and remains silent: "The river nymph would have told the goddess all she had witnessed, but dared not, for fear of Pluto; so she only ventured to take up the girdle which Proserpine had dropped in her flight, and waft it to the feet of the mother" (53).

Also in Bulfinch's interpretation, instead of describing a group of women who invite Ceres to serve as Demophoön's nursemaid, King Celeus offers Ceres the job of nursing his sick son. The child Ceres nurses is not Demophoön, but Triptolemus, who Ceres nurses to health using the medicinal properties of poppies. Graves' interpretation of the Persephone and Demeter myth borrows from the *Homeric Hymn*, Orphic fragments, and Ovid's *Metamorphoses*. A significant change in Graves' narrative is the discussion of Hades' capture of Proserpine. Graves shows that Pluto is not solely interested in raping Proserpine, rather he wants to make her his wife; and before taking Proserpine he asks Jove's permission to marry her. Also, when Metaneria witnesses Ceres' attempt to make Demophoön immortal, Ceres "broke the spell" (90) and Demophoön dies. As consolation, Ceres promises that she will pass on great gifts to Metaneria's sons.[6]

Throughout the ages, writers and poets, from John Milton, Geoffrey Chaucer, and D. H. Lawrence, to Hilda Doolittle, Gwendolyn

Brooks, and Toni Morrison, have recast the Persephone and Demeter myth. A comparative reading of ancient versions alongside the modern adaptations by Brooks, Morrison, and Dove illustrate that the writers make subtle and overt allusions to versions of the *Homeric Hymn to Demeter*, Ovid's *Metamorphoses*, and the Orphic texts. In Brooks' *In the Mecca*, for example, as in the Orphic myth, Ms. Sallie ventures deep into the depths of hell where she discovers Pepita. And in *The Bluest Eye*, similar to an Orphic version, which recounts that Persephone's father (Zeus) rapes her, Pecola's father rapes his daughter. And finally, Dove alludes to Ovid's version of the narrative. In addition to featuring Persephone picking poppies, Dove also presents a scene where a Cyane-like character witnesses Persephone's abduction.

The complexity of the mother–daughter relationship and the discussion of female sexual exploitation and victimization have drawn a number of writers and scholars from various disciplines to the Persephone and Demeter myth. Feminists like Adrienne Rich, and psychoanalysts like Carl Jung, for example, have used the myth to discuss archetypal patterns of behavior between mothers and daughters and the development of female identity.[7] All three of the contemporary writers in this study write about motherhood and the separation of mothers and daughters. But, whereas the ancient writers present an unbreakable mother–daughter bond, contemporary writers like Morrison and Dove portray mothers and daughters who are estranged. In *The Bluest Eye*, Pecola and Pauline are estranged and in *Mother Love*, the Persephone character ensures that she remains apart from her mother. Another difference between the contemporary versions of the myth and the ancient renditions is that writers like Brooks and Morrison reveal that in the real world there is often no reunion between mothers and daughters because the mothers are unable to save their daughters from violent attack and abduction.

Hades' sexual violation of Persephone plays a major role in the feminine revisions presented by Brooks, Morrison, and Dove. In contrast to the ancient versions and modern versions by Bulfinch and Hamilton, who either omit the mention of rape or mention it briefly, the contemporary women writers describe the rape scene in detail. In the case of "The Annaid," for example, Brooks carefully describes Tan Man's sexual violation of Annie; and in Morrison's *Bluest Eye*, readers are given an in-depth account of Cholly's rape of Pecola. Critics like Christine Downing argue that rape in the ancient myth is symbolic of Persephone's initiation into woman-hood, which had to occur in order for Persephone to pass on the Eleusis Mysteries and agriculture. In a similar fashion, twentieth-century women writers use the rape to show not only Persephone's victimization but also her rite of passage from girl-hood to womanhood.

For African American women writers in particular, the Persephone figure serves as an archetype for Black women who by virtue of their race and gender see themselves as double minorities oppressed by patriarchy. Hayes argues, "the subtext of the myth presents rape and abduction of women as perfectly acceptable to the male power structure, with men treating women as objects while reserving subjectivity for themselves alone" (14). Some scholars disagree with the Hayes' interpretation of the text. Vera Bushe, for example, regards Persephone's time in the underworld as a liberating experience that allows her to develop an identity independent from her mother's. Dove's *Mother Love* seems to pick up on this theme too. Dove's narrative reveals that Persephone's experience in the underworld is empowering because after separating from her mother she can begin developing a sense of identity.

The most significant variation between ancient versions of the myth and the revisions by Brooks, Morrison, and Dove is that the women rewrite the narrative so that Persephone's perspective is presented. The Homeric, Ovidian, and Orphic versions of the nar-rative highlight Demeter's traumatic response to Persephone's absence, her search to find her, and her fight to be reunited with Persephone. Brooks, Morrison, and Dove bring to life Persephone's story. These writers imagine Persephone's experience with puberty and Hades' sexual violation of her, Persephone's journey to hell, and Persephone's experience being separated from her mother. As Hayes observes, African American women who write about Persephone give her voice: "An African American Persephone must forge for herself, in the heat of hell, an identity and a voice powerful enough to overcome the forces of White domination and male domination arrayed against her" (193). Through their reenactments of the Persephone and Demeter story, writers like Brooks and especially Dove allow their Persephone characters to speak out against patriarchal oppression. While the African American women write from Persephone's point of view, they also privilege Demeter's voice too. Brooks' "In the Mecca" and Dove's *Mother Love* focus on the experiences of African American mothers who fight to be reunited with their lost daughters.

Niobe

The Niobe story is the ultimate tale of maternal loss. Like Demeter and Medea, Niobe suffers the fate of being separated from her children. In contrast to these other mythic women though, the fate that befalls Niobe and her children is the result of Niobe's arrogance and defiance of the gods. Niobe's story was captured in ancient Greek and Roman art and literature. Book twenty-four of Homer's *Iliad* first introduces audiences to Niobe's story. Gantz tells us that Achilles uses Niobe's story to show Priam that even though Priam is distraught by the death of his son Hector, he should follow Niobe's example of persevering through adversity. Achilles records that Niobe's children, six sons and six daughters, had been killed because Niobe had insulted the goddess Leto, mocking Leto for having birthed only two children. Apollo and Artemis, Leto's children, defend their mother's pride and kill all of Niobe's children. For nine days Niobe's children lie dead until the gods bury them. Achilles says that, despite her traumatic state, "Niobe remembered she had to eat" (Lombardo 486). Achilles maintains that Niobe mourns and weeps and finally turns into stone, brooding "on the sorrows the gods gave her" (486). Paralleling Niobe's plight with Priam's, Achilles advises Priam to focus on his task at hand (fighting the Trojans) and to defer mourning for his dead son. Gantz contends that there are discrepancies within Homer's version of Niobe's tale.

First he contests the idea that Niobe, after witnessing her children die, would not consider food a priority and then casually go on with life. Gantz points out that Niobe's actions seem in conflict "with her subsequent metamorphosis, which we presume is in some way caused by her grief" (537). Gantz believes that Homer's story was modified to underscore Achilles' analogy. He also argues that it is unlikely that the gods would bury Niobe's children, and he claims there are inconsistencies about the number of children that were killed. While Homer mentions that twelve children were killed, other sources say Niobe had more children. Gantz maintains that Hesiod records ten of each, Mimnermus lists twenty in total, Sappho nine of each, and Aischylos, Sophocles, and Euripides list seven boys and seven girls (537). Most post-Homeric texts such as Ovid's *Metamorphoses* show that Niobe had seven children. While the Niobe story was recorded in epic poems, dramatists such as Sophocles and Aischylos wrote *Niobe* plays.[8] Some versions of the Niobe story seek to absolve Niobe from her participation in the massacre of her family. Aischylos' play, for example, "entertain[s] a questioning of the gods' actions" (538) suggesting that Niobe and her children are unjustly persecuted. Aischylos also concludes his Niobe play without transforming Niobe into stone. Ancient writers have treated Niobe's demise in different ways.

In Homer, Niobe turns into a mourning rock, but Pherekydes shows that after the killings, Niobe returns home to Lydia where she sees that her kingdom is destroyed by the gods (all the residents have been turned to stone) and prays to be turned into stone. In some narratives Niobe goes to Mount Sipylus where it is reported that a figure resembling Niobe was carved into stone and when it rains the rock looks as if it is weeping. Sophocles, Telesilla, and Ovid also modified the story. Sophocles only features the murder of Niobe's daughters and Telesilla narrates that two of Niobe's children, Amyklas and Meliboia, are saved and the gods slay Niobe's husband Amphion. Ovid plays up Niobe's insolence. He shows that Niobe is given the opportunity to keep her seven daughters alive, but Niobe reminds Latona (Leto) that even after killing her sons she still has more children than Latona: "After so many deaths I triumph still" (130). Phoebus (Apollo) and Phoebe

(Artemis) immediately silence Niobe's bragging and kill the remaining children. Immediately after, Niobe changes into a rock that is later uprooted in a "whirlwind [and carried] to Lydia to take its accustomed place as a local landmark" (539). Graves observes that Parthenius' *Love Stories* offers a completely different Niobe story.[9] In Parthenius' narrative, Leto plans for Niobe's father Tantalus to fall in love with Niobe. When Niobe rejects Tantalus' advances, he burns "her children to death" (260) and ensures that her husband is "mangled by a wild boar" (261). Niobe commits suicide by throwing herself off a rock.

While there were a number of written Niobe stories recorded in the Archaic period, in Archaic art there are few artistic renditions of the Niobe story. According to Gantz, a Tyrrhenian amphora (560 BCE) depicts Apollo and Artemis' pursuit of three of Niobe's children. Graves notes that the Niobid painter revisits this image in 450 BCE. In other works, a sarcophagus in 160 CE features the gods slaying all of Niobe's children and a sculpture from 4 CE depicts Niobe and one of her daughters. Paintings of Niobe became especially popular during the seventeenth and eighteenth centuries. In 1772 Anicet-Charles-Gabriel Lemonnier painted a scene portraying the two gods slaying Niobe's children and in 1760 Richard Wilson produced a series of Niobe paintings, some of which inspired Wheatley to create her own Niobe story. In addition to being influenced by Wilson's Niobe paintings, Wheatley's account of the Niobe narrative, as she tells us, is also influenced by Ovid. It is likely that for her Niobe poem Wheatley refers to the popular translations of Ovid's *Metamorphoses* by George Sandys (1632) or John Dryden (1717). Wheatley's narrative differs from Ovid's version. In addition to offering a detailed description of Niobe's deep affection for her children Wheatley, like Aischylos, shows that the gods treat Niobe and her children mercilessly. Finally, similar to Aischylos, Wheatley's Niobe does not metamorphose into stone.[10] Nineteenth-century African American writer Henrietta Cordelia Ray was also inspired by the Niobe story. Ray's brief paraphrase of the Niobe story reads as an allusion to Wheatley's Niobe poem. Similar to Wheatley, Ray is empathetic toward Niobe and heightens the portrayal of Niobe as the victimized mother.

Medea

Next to the Persephone and Demeter myth, the story of Medea is arguably one of the most popular myths reenacted by contemporary authors. Like the Persephone and Demeter myth numerous ancient versions of the Medea story were recorded in art and literature. Medea's story is attached to the Jason and the Argonauts myth. In Jason and the Argonauts, Jason embarks on a quest to steal the Golden Fleece from the kingdom of Colchis. Upon arrival to Colchis, described as a barbarian land, King Aeétes promises Jason that if he succeeds in completing a number of tasks he will be rewarded with the Fleece. The king has no intention of giving Jason the fleece, but sends him on a series of challenges hoping to kill him. The king says Jason must first plough the earth with fire-breathing bulls and then sow the earth with dragon's teeth, which turn into armed guards. Medea, who in some versions is shot by Cupid's love potion, is immediately enamored with Jason. Medea is willing to do anything to protect the handsome warrior, and she betrays her kingdom. Drawing on her knowledge of witchcraft, Medea helps Jason defeat her father. She gives Jason magic potions that save him from being killed by the wild bulls and she helps him defeat soldiers who are transformed from the dragon's teeth into men. Medea also drugs the serpent that guards the fleece, allowing Jason to retrieve it. Once King Colchis learns that Jason has stolen the fleece, he sets out to kill him. In her ultimate act of disloyalty, Medea dismembers her brother's body and throws his limbs overboard from their vessel with the hopes that her father will stop his pursuit of Jason to gather his son's remains.

Next, Medea and Jason sail to Iolcus and upon arrival Jason learns his uncle Pelias has killed Jason's father. Once again drawing on her powers, Medea tricks Pelias' daughters into dismembering their father. Jason and Medea leave Iolcus and travel to Corinth. In most accounts, once in Corinth, Jason—either persuaded or by his own volition—leaves Medea for Glauce, King Creon's daughter.

Medea is heartbroken and humiliated by Jason's rejection. She speaks out publicly against Jason's selfishness and his abandonment of herself and their children and she condemns Glauce and Creon. Medea also talks about her foreign identity and she expresses her feeling of alienation from the Corinthian community, ultimately claiming that Jason abandoned her because of her ethnic difference. Seeking revenge on both Jason and his new bride, Medea sends a poisonous robe and crown to Glauce as a wedding gift. When Glauce puts on the garment her skin begins to burn (some stories describe the robe engulfing Glauce in flames) and Creon dies trying to save his daughter. Glauce's death does not satisfy Medea and she looks for a more direct way to punish Jason. Certain that Jason will be crushed by the death of his children she slays their sons and leaves Corinth in a serpent-drawn chariot loaned to her by her grandfather Helios.

Ancient writers treat Medea's murder of her children in various ways. Gantz says that pre-Euripides stories from the Archaic period offer two versions of Medea's story, "one in which Medeia inadvertently kills her children, the other in which the Korinthians do it deliberately. To these Euripides would then add as a third possibility the slaying of them by their mother for revenge on Iason" (369–70). The scholia to Euripides, according to Gantz, maintains that the Corinthians kill Medea's children because they resent the fact that she is a foreign queen and they distrust her knowledge of witchcraft. Graves says later that the Corinthians wanted to be absolved from the murder so they bribe Euripides to change the ending and charge Medea with killing two of her children. The number of children Medea kills varies according to how many children the authors assign to her. Didimos' account of Medea's story notes that instead of killing her children Medea leaves them in Corinth with Jason. In retaliation for Glauce and Creon's deaths, the Corinthians kill the children.

Gantz maintains that it is not until Euripides produces his play *Medea* (approximately 431 BCE) that audiences are given a motive for Medea's infanticide. Euripides' play begins with Medea lamenting Jason's abandonment of her and their sons. Euripides shows Medea is also frustrated by the fact that as a Colchian she feels out of place in the Corinthian society. Medea bemoans her inability to return home and regrets betraying her family for Jason. Medea remains in her home inconsolable until at the urging of the Corinthian women she comes out and addresses them. During her speech, Medea denounces Jason's callous behavior and his impending nuptials. She also talks about the subordinate status of women in ancient society. Medea maintains that because of her sex Jason can freely abuse her without punishment: "Of all the creatures that can feel and think, we women are the worst-treated things alive. To begin with, we bid the highest price in dowries just to buy some man to be dictator of our bodies. . . . When a man gets bored with wife and home, he simply roams abroad, relieves the tedium of his spirit: turns to a friend or finds his cronies. We women, on the other hand, turn only to a single man" (Roche 40–41).

After her speech, Medea appeals to the women to not judge her for the actions she will take to punish Jason. Jason arrives and tries to placate Medea, suggesting that the marriage is a selfless act to afford a better life for himself as well as for Medea and their children. He claims, "first, it was an act of common sense, secondly, unselfish, and finally, a mark of my devotion, to you and all my family. . . . My intention was . . . to help the ones I have, through those I hope to have" (50–51). Medea is unconvinced by Jason's story and tells him that her age and race caused Jason to replace her with a new wife.

Euripides shows that Medea gains the sympathy of the Colchian women who regard Jason's actions as deplorable. Medea creates a plan to leave Corinth and move to Athens with Aegeus who promises to shelter her. Medea confides in the Corinthian women that before leaving she will punish Jason, Glauce, and Creon, and she will kill her children. The women remind Medea that she must "uphold the laws of life" (58) and find another way to repay Jason for his unfaithfulness. But Medea is determined to make Jason suffer the agony she has experienced and she tells the women she *must* kill her sons because it will be "the supreme way to hurt my husband" (58). Although Euripides emphasizes Medea's determination to kill her sons, he does not depict Medea as a merciless, unloving mother. At times Medea is actually conflicted about her decision. At one point, for example, she contemplates taking her sons away with her: "Why damage them in trying to hurt their father, and only hurt myself twice over? No. I cannot. Goodbye to my decision" (65). Unfortunately, at the next moment pride takes over and Medea refuses to allow her enemies to defeat or ridicule her. Medea acknowledges that her actions are immoral, but she convinces herself that she cannot control her anger: "The evil that I do, I understand full well, but a passion drives me greater than my will. Passion is the curse of man: It wreaks the greatest ill" (66). At the end of the narrative Medea bludgeons both boys. When Jason confronts Medea about the murders she absolves herself of blame, maintaining the position that Jason provoked the murders. Ultimately, Euripides' play suggests that Medea is blinded by an impassioned rage that leads to irrational behavior.

Euripides' play helped popularize Medea's story, both in literature and art. One of the most famous visual representations of Medea's story is found on "an Apulian volute krater in Munich (3296), [where] we find Kreon's daughter called 'Kreonteia'" (Gantz 371).[11] While Euripides highlights Medea's trauma and her acts of retaliation, Ovid's *Metamorphoses* centers more on Medea's knowledge of witchcraft and her many ruthless acts of murder. In several passages Ovid goes into detail about Medea's secret charms and spells. Ovid's characterization of Medea as a witch is essential to his narrative because, as Carole Newland points out, Medea's witchlike characteristics show she has experienced a metamorphosis. Whereas Euripides' play highlights Medea's struggle to determine the fate of her children, Ovid's narrative says nothing about Medea's ambivalence toward killing her children. Moreover, the infanticide itself is barely noted. At the end of the narrative Ovid remarks that after killing Glauce, Medea's "wicked sword was drenched in her son's blood; and thus winning a mother's vile revenge" (Melville 156).

Unlike Euripides, Ovid does not explain why Medea commits infanticide and readers are left with the impression that Medea is a ruthless killer who uses her powers to kill her enemies. But Ovid's depiction of Medea in the *Metamorphoses* contrasts sharply with his portrayal of Medea in the *Heroides*. In the *Heroides*, Ovid takes Euripides' approach and focuses less on Medea's deeds and more on her inconsolable grief. Harold Isbell notes that in the *Metamorphoses* Ovid's narrative effectively observes the objective state of the character, but fails to adequately portray the subjective belief of the character. In the *Heroides* Medea's letter to Jason humanizes Medea and gives her the opportunity to defend herself and fully express her torment. Harold Isbell asserts, "as she outlines the intensity of her love for Jason and the grief for her family she has betrayed, we see a woman of somewhat greater depth than the monster we find in more traditional accounts" (104). Isbell points out though, that although Ovid allows Medea to present her argument, Ovid ensures that "her criminality is never denied" (104). Moreover, "even as she pleads mitigating circumstances her argument is so flawed that finally she cannot be pitied" (105). In the *Heroides* Medea berates Jason for his ungratefulness and she reminds him of her sacrifices, which estranged her from her family and made her a foreigner in Corinth. And in an even more important contrast to the *Metamorphoses*, Medea suggests that she has to kill the children because she fears for their safety. She writes, "no stepmother would treat them with kindness" (112). With the *Heroides* Ovid allows Medea to tell the story from her own perspective, thus offering an explanation for her deeds.

Along with Ovid's *Heroides*, Seneca's play, *Medea*, also gives Medea a platform to defend her actions. Nussbaum says Seneca removes the emphasis of treachery and shows "that none of us, if we love, can stop ourselves from the wish to kill" (222). Seneca's play stresses that although Medea's murderous act is unjust, Medea has been driven to commit her crime. Nussbaum observes that Medea is no different from other Senecan heroines who "are not criminals to begin with; they are made criminals by love" (224). Like Euripides, Seneca features Medea wrestling with her decision to kill the children. Medea appears conflicted: "One minute they appear to her as inexpressibly dear and wonderful— as innocent, as special, as hers. The next minute they strike her as pieces of their father and tools to wound him with" (227). Seneca's *Medea* highlights Medea's emotional anguish and demonstrates that she has difficulty carrying out the crime against her children.

Like the ancient writers, the modern writers also differ in regard to their depiction of infanticide. Bulfinch glosses over the infanticide and, like Ovid, focuses more on Medea's witchcraft and her foreign status. In Graves' version, despite her hurt and anger, Medea does not kill her children. Graves contends that at the end of the story, Medea has killed Glauce and Creon, but she makes no plan to kill her boys. Zeus is impressed with Medea's "spirit" and falls in love with her, but Medea does not reciprocate his affection. Hera is grateful to Medea for rejecting Zeus and as a reward makes Medea's children immortal. In contrast to Bulfinch and Graves, Hamilton creates a very compassionate rendition of Medea's tale. Hamilton indicates that after Cupid pierced Medea's heart with love potion, Medea's love for Jason is so strong it overwhelms her. Medea is tormented by both her love for Jason and her allegiance to her country. Hamilton rewrites Ovid's narrative by showing that Medea was so overwrought that she considers killing herself: "She sat alone in her room, weeping and telling herself she was shamed forever because she cared so much for a stranger that she wanted to yield to a mad passion and go against her father. 'Far better to die,' she said. She took in her hand a casket which held herbs for killing, but as she sat there with it, she thought of life" (124). Another major difference between Hamilton's text and others is that Hamilton underscores the fact that Medea's motive for killing her sons is not about revenge but rather about protecting her children. Hamilton recounts that after devising to kill Glauce Medea automatically thinks about the fate of her children. Medea realizes that she has no choice but to kill her sons because they would not be safe in Corinth. Hamilton deduces, "there was no protection for her children, no help for them anywhere. A slave's life might be theirs, nothing more. 'I will not let them live for strangers to ill-use, she thought'" (129). Hamilton's reworking of Medea's story probably served as the inspiration for Morrison's *Beloved*. Similar to Harrison's narrative, Morrison emphasizes the point that Sethe's infanticide is also motivated by her need to protect her children from a life of enslavement and brutality.

Throughout the ages the Medea story remained popular with artists who have composed operas and written plays, novels, and poetry about her. In 1797, Luigi Cherubini wrote the Italian opera, *Medee*, in 1998 Christa Wolf wrote the novel *Medea*, and in 1999 Michael Jean LaChiusa produced the Broadway musical "Marie Christine." LaChiusa's play featured African American opera singer Audra McDonald as Medea. LaChiusa's portrayal of Medea as a Black woman was not the first. Countee Cullen's translation of Euripides' *Medea* for *The Medea and Some Poems* (1935), presented an African American Medea. Rankine notes, Cullen uses the play to present "the issue of race in America—blackness—as a parallel to the Greek-barbarian dichotomy" (97). Rankine also observes that for his play *Medea*, Cullen "had a black actress, Rose McClendon, in mind to play the role of Medea" (97). In addition to Cullen's *Medea*, Yusef Komunyakaa's "Modern Medea," and Toni Morrison's *Beloved* also feature African American Medeas. African American writers easily imagine Medea as a Black woman because, as Haley notes, Medea was one of the "'Children of the Sun,' an epithet people of African descent have used in pre-literate and literate texts to describe themselves. For example the ancient Ethiopians, beloved by and favorites of the Olympian gods, frequently referred to themselves as 'children of the sun'" (Haley 183). While some African American writers might be attracted to Medea's story because they identify with her Ethiopian heritage, others like Morrison relate to Medea's narrative because she depicts the predicament of so many Black mothers who during slavery felt pressured to commit infanticide.

The discussion at hand has shown that the stories of Persephone and Demeter, Niobe, and Medea have captured the imagination of ancient and modern writers in different ways. The forthcoming chapters explore how African American women writers bring their own perspectives to the myths and create new contemporary tales that make the myths relevant for our time.

2

Classical Discourse as Political Agency:
African American Revisionist Mythmaking by Phillis Wheatley, Henrietta Cordelia Ray, and| Pauline Hopkins

Phillis Wheatley

In 1773 Phillis Wheatley established the tradition of Black women's classical revision when she published a number of classically-inspired poems in her first and only collection, *Poems on Various Subjects, Religious and Moral*. Wheatley's affinity for the classics came as a result of her informal education under the tutelage of her slave owner's daughter Susannah Wheatley. Susannah Wheatley introduced Phillis to Greco-Roman writers including Virgil, Ovid, and Terence, and neoclassical writer Alexander Pope (Caretta xiv). It was Pope's neoclassical verse that greatly influenced Wheatley's own classical renderings, most notably his translation of Homer (Mason 16). According to Henry Louis Gates, Jr., "imitating Pope in rhythm and meter Phillis wrote in decasyllabic lines of closed heroic couplets. There is much use of invocation, hyperbole, inflated ornamentation, and an overemphasis of personification all of which characterize neoclassical poetry" (228). Pope's neoclassical influence is evident in poems such as "To Macenas," "Niobe in Distress," and "Ode to Neptune." In these poems Wheatley employs classical elements such as invoking the muse and adapting the Homerian epic modes of writing.[1]

Wheatley's version of the "Niobe" story demonstrates her ability to translate classical tales using her own distinct voice, from her own unique Black feminine perspective.

Although Pope greatly influenced Wheatley to write her own classically inspired poetry, we should also recognize that writing within the classical mode appealed to Wheatley because mythical stories gave her an opportunity to explore themes of female oppression. More importantly, she believed that appropriating the classics would grant her credibility as a poet and prove her humanity at a time when pro-slavery advocates questioned the Africans' ability to do more than menial labor.

For Wheatley, classical revision was about artistic license as well as poetic validation. Wheatley's aim was not only to write poetry well, but to achieve the public recognition enjoyed by ancient and contemporary authors whom she regarded as the quintessential artists: Homer, Horace, Terence, Milton, and Pope.[2] Wheatley, like earlier seventeenth-century writers Edmund Spenser, Ben Jonson, and John Milton, desired to assume public status as the premiere writer of the day. According to Richard Helgerson, Spenser, Jonson, and Milton desired "not only to write great poems but also to fill the role of the great poet. [This idea] shaped everything these men wrote in the remainder of their active and productive literary lives . . . they were always presenting themselves" (Helgerson 2). Eventually Spenser, Jonson, and Milton all became the voices of their generation and earned the coveted title of *poet laureate* that Wheatley desired. Wheatley's intent to gain public recognition and laureate status is clearly identifiable in the poem "To Macenas" where she expresses her ambitions to write as well as Virgil: "O could I rival thine and Virgil's page" (50). She also threatens to snatch the laurels from Macenas' head: "While blooming wreaths around they temples spread, / I'll snatch a laurel from thine honour'd head, / While you indulgent smile upon my deed" (50). In this same poem, Wheatley admits her envy of the African playwright Terence, who in her view received the public validation she longs for: "The happier Terence all the choir inspir'd, / His soul replenish'd, and his bosom fir'd; / But say, ye Muses, why this partial grace, / To one alone of Afric's sable race; / From age to age transmitting thus his name / With the first glory in the rolls of fame?" (50).

Wheatley's reference to Terence is highly significant because she uses Terence to emphasize the point that an African writer belongs to the classical tradition: the revered epitome of White civilization. To ensure that readers acknowledge Terence's ethnicity, Wheatley places an asterisk by his name and includes a notation citing that Terence was "African by birth." As touched upon briefly in the introduction, in *Black Athena: The Afroasiatic Roots of Classical Civilization* (1987), Martin Bernal writes about the African influence on Western civilization. According to Bernal, in order to maintain the idea that civilization was created in the Western hemisphere, Europeans disregarded the profound ways that Egyptians influenced the Greeks and dismissed the fact that Africa was the true "cradle of civilization" (30). Ultimately, by highlighting Terence's ancestry Wheatley undermines the notion that the classics are a White Western phenomenon and reclaims the classics as part of an African heritage that she rightfully inherits. While Terence's contributions to the classics inspire Wheatley, she might have also been motivated by Terence's experience. Although he was a slave, Terence was given writing privileges that later led to his emancipation.[3] Wheatley believed that, just as Terence's plays had liberated him, her poetry, especially her neoclassical verse, would emancipate her and other African slaves from their inferior position in society.

In comparison to other poems by Wheatley that include classical elements, "Niobe in Distress for her Children Slain by Apollo From Ovid's *Metamorphoses*, Book VI and from a View of the Painting of Mr. Richard Wilson" best exemplifies Wheatley's attempt to use the classics to establish credibility as a poet. "Niobe" is Wheatley's longest (224 lines) poem. It is written as a short epic, complete with a ten-line invocation to the muse, esoteric language, scenes of gods doling out punishment, and passages describing brutal bloodshed—although here the bloodshed does not take place on the battlefield but rather in the domestic sphere. Ovid's story portrays Niobe as a proud queen whose hubris is her tragic flaw. Niobe's excessive pride causes the deaths of her fourteen children, which she is forced to witness.[4] Much like contemporary writers of her time, Wheatley's version of the story is more in the form of paraphrase in that the original story is loosely reinterpreted. Since Wheatley had learned Latin, and she does note that she is inspired by Ovid's Metamorphoses; she probably draws directly from Ovid's rendition of the Niobe story. However, others suggest Wheatley's version of the Niobe story probably came from from Samuel Croxall's rendition of the Niobe story published in Dryden's *Ovid's Metamorphoses in Fifteen Books* (1717). Wheatley presents a feminine recreation of the story that differs considerably from other existing adaptations.

A comparison of Wheatley's version of this story with popular seventeenth- and eighteenth-century translations by Samuel Croxall and George Sandys demonstrates Wheatley's alternative approach to the story. First, unlike the two other renditions, the title of Wheatley's poem underscores the poem's main subject: "Niobe's distress after witnessing the massacre of her children." Wheatley's poem also explicitly draws from a visual representation of the Niobe story. As her title indicates, Richard Wilson's series of Niobe paintings have been invoked to heighten the reader's image of Niobe as the fallen victim. The influence of Wilson's Niobe paintings is most visible toward the end of Wheatley's poem. Wheatley features the gods descending from Heaven to shoot Niobe's son: "With clouds incompass'd glorious Phoebus stands; / feather'd vengeance quiv'ring in his hands" (101). With this statement, Wheatley verbalizes an image present in Wilson's painting.

Another variation is the manner in which Wheatley portrays Niobe. Whereas Sandys and Croxall both characterize Niobe as insolent and audacious—and therefore much more deserving of punishment—Wheatley downplays Niobe's arrogant, haughty tone. For example, when discussing Niobe's reaction to the order that all must humble themselves before Latona, Sandys presents Niobe this way:

> A Phrygian mantle weav'd with gold she wears.
> Her face, as much as rage would suffer, fair
> She stops, and shaking her dishevell'd hair.

The Godly troup with haughty eyes surveys.
What madness is it unseen God (she says)
Before the Celestials to prefer.
Or, while I Altars want, to worship her? (110)

Sandys' Niobe is hysterical with rage. Her face is contorted, and her hair "dishevell'd."

Although Croxall's characterization of Niobe is less indicting than Sandys', he also emphasizes Niobe's impertinence:

The royal Niobe in state appear'd;
Attr'd in Robes embroiderd o'er with Gold,
And mad with Rage, yet lovely to behold.
Her comely tresses, trembling as she stood,
Down her fine Neck with easy Motion flow'd;
Then, darting round a proud disdainful Look,
In hauty Tone her hasty Passion broke,
And Thus began; What Madness to this Court
A Goddess founded merely on Report? (183)

Once again Niobe is portrayed as arrogant and defiant. Conversely, Wheatley's Niobe lacks the pretentious attitude that Sandys' and Croxall's Niobes possess.

Wheatley focuses less on Niobe's emotions and more on her physical appearance, thereby deflecting our attention from Niobe's obstinate demeanor:

Niobe comes with all her royal race,
With charms unnumbere'd, and superior grace:
Her Phrygian garments of delightful hue,
Inwove with gold, refulgent to the view,
Beyond description beautiful she moves
Like heav'nly Venus, 'midst her smiles and loves:
She views around the supplicating train,
And shakes her graceful head with stern distain,
Proudly she turns around her lofty eyes,
And thus reviles celestial deities. (99–100)

In contrast with the other versions, Wheatley's Niobe is not represented as a trembling, angry woman who in hasty passion expresses her rage against the gods. Rather, she smiles calmly, enters the court, and regally addresses the Theban women. Wheatley's Niobe *is* offended by Latona's directive, but she is not as enraged as the character depicted in the male versions.

A third contrast between Wheatley's Niobe poem and others', shows that Wheatley emphasizes Niobe's victimization. Again, while Croxall and Sandys create a story about a haughty, belligerent instigator who deserves the punishment imposed upon her, Wheatley describes the experiences of a woman who engaged in wrongdoing and receives a punishment greater than her crime. One of the most striking distinctions between Wheatley's story and Sandys' and Croxall's is Wheatley's emphasis on Niobe's maternal connection with her children. Unlike other versions of the story, Wheatley includes a passage describing Niobe as the adoring mother who watches her children as they sleep: "Seven sprightly sons the royal bed adorn, / Seven daughters beauteous as the op'ning morn, / As when Aurora fills the ravish'd sight, / And decks the orient realms with rosy light / From their bright eyes the living splendors play, / Nor can beholders bear the flashing ray" (99). This description of Niobe's sleeping children is, as John Shields notes, a strategic move on Wheatley's part: "[While] acquainting the listener with Niobe's beautiful children and with her excessive pride in them, Wheatley at the same time solicits pity for the children and prepares the listener for the imminent doom" (109). Niobe's intense love for her children is presented again when Wheatley writes:

> Wherever Niobe, thou turn'st thine eyes,
> New Beauties kindle, and new joys arise!
> But thou had'st far the happier mother prov'd,
> If this fair offspring had been less belov'd
> What if their charms exceed Aurora's teint,
> No words could tell them, and no pencil paint,
> Thy love too vehement hastens to destroy
> Each blooming maid, and each celestial boy. (99)

Adding these sentimental images of Niobe and her children to the opening of the poem shifts our attention from Niobe's insolence to Niobe's maternal love. Where other renditions of the narrative introduce Niobe as a reckless woman whose actions bring harm to her children, Wheatley introduces us to a proud mother who oversteps her boundaries.

A final difference between Wheatley's version of the narrative and Sandys' and Croxall's is the manner in which the male authors treat the conclusion of the story. Like Ovid, Sandys and Croxall describe Niobe's transformation into a stone figure "[h]arden'd with Woes a statue of Despair" (Croxall 189). Although the conclusion of Wheatley's poem also features Niobe transformed into stone, as the editor of her collected poems notes, the last stanza was "the Work of another hand."

> The queen of all her family bereft,
> Without [sic] or husband, son, or daughter, left,
> Grew stupid at the shock. The passing air
> Made no impression on her stiff'ning hair.
> The blood forsook her face: admist the flood
> Pour'd from her cheeks, quite fix'd her eye-balls stood.
> Her tongue, her palate both obdurate grew,
> Her curdled veins no long motion knew;
> The use of neck, and arms, and feet was gone,
> And ev'n her bowels hard'ned into stone:
> A marble statue now the queen appears,
> But from the marble seal the silent tears. (104)

Whoever added this last stanza obviously presumed Wheatley's poem was incomplete and included the description of Niobe's metamorphosis. But when considering that Wheatley's Niobe poem had been modified in numerous ways, it is likely that Wheatley intentionally ends her poem without Niobe's metamorphosis. Similar to the ancient play by Aischylos, which does not describe Niobe's transformation into stone, Wheatley allows Niobe to remain as a woman of flesh and blood because in her immortal state Niobe is a symbolic image of all grieving mothers who lose their children.

Much has been written about Wheatley's failure to address her experience as a slave or to provide an indictment of slavery. Given her position as a slave and the period in which she was writing, Wheatley had to be cautious about how she approached a politically charged topic like slavery.[5] Wheatley disguises her political beliefs in a kind of double-voiced narrative, using poetry, in this case the Niobe poem, as a metaphor to discuss the powerlessness of slaves who, like Niobe, either witnessed the murder of their children or watched their children being sold into slavery.[6] Wheatley observed first-hand the anguish of her own parents who, similar to Niobe, could do nothing to save their child from being taken from them. Evidence of Wheatley's own feelings of being separated from her family are recorded in the poem, "To the Right Honorable William, Earl of Dartmouth, His Majesty's Principal Secretary of State for North America, &c." This poem, addressed to the Earl of Dartmouth, is written in support of America's fight for liberation from England. Midway through the poem Wheatley explains how she was personally forced apart from her parents, and she reflects on how her father reacted when she was abducted:

I, young in life, by seeming cruel fate
Was snatch'd from Afric's fancy'd happy seat:
What pangs excruciating must molest,
What sorrows labour in my parent's breast?
Steel'd was that soul and by no misery mov'd
That from a father seiz'd his babe belov'd. (83)

Wheatley's description of the "excruciating" pains in her "parent's breast," most specifically her father's, is reminiscent of the description of Niobe's husband Amphion who commits suicide: "Amphion too, with grief oppress'd, / Had plung'd the deadly dagger in his breast" (103). In what might be dismissed as eighteenth-century sentimentalism, Amphion—like Wheatley's own father—clutches his breast in pain. Rather than regarding this image as a mere convention, we might consider that Wheatley relates Amphion's pain to her fathers.

In addition to identifying with Niobe's traumatic experience as she watched the gods slay her children, Wheatley also identified with Niobe's bold persona. Just as Niobe challenged the gods, as a Black female poet, Wheatley defied the rules and the code of conduct for slaves of the day. In addition to working within the classical tradition, a practice reserved only for the most elite White males of the day, Wheatley presented herself as a member of Boston's learned class and rejected her slave status.

Rewriting Niobe's story was an amazing feat for this Black female slave. Wheatley proved that if given the opportunity, Black people could not only write poetry but could write it well. Acquiring knowledge of the classics allowed Wheatley to challenge the racist belief of her time that Black people were racially and intellectually inferior. Wheatley threatens the institution of slavery because she represents the potential ability of all slaves to become educated and establish their humanity. A reviewer for the British publication *Critical Review* argues this point: "Negroes of Africa are generally treated as a dull, ignorant, and ignoble race of men, fit only to be slaves, and incapable of any considerable attainments in the liberal arts and sciences. A poet or a poetess amongst them, of any tolerable genius, would be a prodigy in literature. Phillis Wheatley, the author of these poems, is this literary phenomenon" (145).

Through her poetry, Wheatley validates her own and the humanity of other slaves.

Wheatley's published collection of poetry prompted abolitionists to use Wheatley's accomplishments as proof that slaves were not intellectually inferior and that with guidance they could be trained to do more than pick cotton. Alternatively, proponents of slavery sought to discredit Wheatley's achievement and discounted the abolitionists' claims that Wheatley was a poetic genius. In *Notes on the State of Virginia* (1785), for example, Thomas Jefferson argued that Wheatley's poetry was mediocre: "Misery is often the parent of the most affecting touches in poetry. Among the Blacks is misery enough, God knows, but no poetry. Love is the particular oestrum of the poet. Their love is ardent, but it kindles the senses only, not the imagination. Religion, indeed, has produced a Phillis Whately [*sic*]; but it could not produce a poet. The compositions published under her name are below the dignity of criticism. The heroes of the Dunciad are to her, as Hercules to the author of that poem" (quoted in Caretta xxxvii).

Jefferson's scathing critique of Wheatley's poetry undermines the relevance of Wheatley's poetic contribution. It is likely that Jefferson refused to recognize Wheatley as a poet because to do so would be to acknowledge her humanity.

Although pro-slavery Americans disregarded Wheatley's poetic talent, the British were more receptive of her brilliance and regarded her as a prominent literary figure. According to Mukhtar Ali Isani, at least nine British periodicals reviewed and reprinted Wheatley's poetry. Some reviewers were less impressed with the quality of Wheatley's poetry and more impressed with what she had accomplished. For example, a reviewer for the *London Magazine* observed that "[Wheatley's] poems display no astonishing power of genius; but when we consider them as the productions of young untutored African, who wrote them after six months casual study of the English language and of writing, we cannot suppress our admiration of talents so vigorous and lively. We are the more surprised too, as we find her verses interspersed with the poetical names of the ancients, which she has in every instance used with strict propriety" (147).

British women writers also took note of Wheatley's poetry. In 1774, Mary Scott included Wheatley in her collection *The Female Advocate*, an anthology dedicated to recognizing the achievements of women writers from the sixteenth century through to the late eighteenth century. According to Moira Ferguson, "Among her contemporaries she cites . . . Phillis Wheatley. . . . Scott identifies the African poet specifically as one of the 'Female Authors of late [who] have appeared with honor'" (128). The eighteenth-century poet Mary Deverell was also in awe of Wheatley. In her collection *Miscellanies* (1781), Deverell includes a panegyric to Wheatley:

> Though no high birth nor titles grace her line,
> Yet humble Phillis boasts a race divine;
> Like marble that in quaries lies concealed,
> Till all its veins, by polish, stand reveal'd;
> From whence such groups of images arise,
> We praise the artist, and the sculptured prize. (131)

Wheatley's acknowledgment by these eighteenth-century female writers underscores her significance not only as a Black poet, but also as a female writer.

In addition to British reviews, Wheatley's poetry garnered attention from other Europeans such as French writer and philosopher Voltaire, who praised Wheatley for her "very good English verse." A number of Black poets and writers also applauded Wheatley's achievements. Vincent Caretta notes that both fellow-American slave Jupiter Hammon and the free Black British writer Ignatius Sancho acknowledged Wheatley's accomplishments. In a letter addressed to a friend, Sancho wrote: "Phyllis's poems do credit to nature—and put art—merely as art—to the blush. It reflects nothing either to the glory or generosity of her master—if she is still his slave—except he glories in the low vanity of having his wanton power a mind animated by Heaven—a genius superior to himself" (Sancho xxiii).

In the poem "To Macenas," Wheatley shared her laureate ambitions. Although during her lifetime Wheatley did not earn the official laureateship title, later many (especially those in the Black community) came to regard her as a poet genius and poet laureate. An article on Wheatley written at the turn of the twentieth century and published in the *Colored American Magazine* illustrates Wheatley's significance for American Americans: "Phillis Wheatley merits the judgment of being the only Negro who, during slavery, through culture coupled with her own native wit, rose to a status on a plane with those of the other race. And today, we can find no truer poet, Black or White, than this little African singer . . . the poet of our race, the poet of her race's history, the master of another race's civilization" (440–42).

Contemporary African Americans continue to view Wheatley as the "Black poet laureate" and foremother of African American literature. As Helen Burke writes: "Given her aim to acquire a political and literary identity, it could be said that her strategy worked. Phillis Wheatley made, and is still making, a name for herself. In her own lifetime, her writing won her the notice of the governing elite of her day, both in this country and in Europe. . . . As a literary subject, her claim to an equal place within the tradition was . . . successful. Since her death, her small volume of poetry has been reprinted more than two dozen times" (200).

Wheatley has had a major impact on literature and today she is by far one of the most celebrated figures of early American and African American literature. Sadly, Wheatley's appropriation of classical myth has not always been appreciated by scholars who have viewed her adoption of European literary conventions as one of her weaknesses. But when one understands that Wheatley's employment of European literary models is motivated by the need to authenticate her poetry and establish her humanity, it becomes clear that classical revision is one of the strengths of her poetry. Fortunately, the political and aesthetic relevance of classical myth-making was realized by the next generation of African American women writers who were inspired to continue the tradition of classical revision put forth by Wheatley.

Henrietta Cordelia Ray

In the nineteenth century the classics appealed to Black writers for the same reason that they attracted Wheatley: a competent knowledge of the classics would liberate the Black man and woman from their inferior societal status. In contrast to Wheatley though, nineteenth-century writers emphasized the significance of both learning classical languages and revising classical myths. A passage from Anna Julia Cooper's *A Voice from the South* illustrates the value of mastering classical languages:

> [T]he Negro's ability to work had never been called in question, while his ability to learn Latin and construe Greek syntax needed to be proved to sneering critics. "Scale the heights!" was the cry. "Go to college, study Latin, preach, teach, orate, wear spectacles and a beaver!" Stung by such imputations as that of Calhoun that if a Negro could prove his ability to master the Greek subjunctive he might vindicate his title to manhood, the newly liberated race first shot forward along this line with an energy and success which astonished its most sanguine friends. (260)

In an effort to prove to Whites that they were mentally and socially equal, Blacks scrambled not just to learn but to *master* Greek and

Latin. Black scholars like William S. Scarborough, W. E. B. Du Bois, and Ann Julia Cooper were all credited for their mastery of classical languages. Cooper was fortunate to have the opportunity to learn classical languages because during the nineteenth century serious academic classical study was limited mostly to men. While a number of nineteenth-century universities such as Oberlin, Fisk, Wilberforce, and Ann Arbor, were liberal in their admissions policies for women, female students were relegated to taking Ladies' courses. The Ladies' courses consisted of literature, music, and art; classes in Hebrew, Latin, and Greek were not offered to female students.

Because knowledge of classical languages and classical narratives represented cultural capital, Black writers like Eloise Thompson, George McCellan, Timothy Fortune, Ann Plato, Henrietta Cordelia Ray, and Pauline Hopkins heighten their essays, speeches, prose, and poetry with classical allusions. While some writers sought out classical figures and myths for creative inspiration, others were drawn to the classics for reasons that transcended aesthetics. Women writers Henrietta Cordelia Ray and Pauline Hopkins, for example, found that, like Wheatley, they could use the classics as a liberating space to engage readers in a feminist critique of the misrepresentation, silencing, and subjugation of Black women both in literature and society.

Although today few are familiar with the work of Henrietta Cordelia Ray, during the mid-nineteenth century, she was a prominent figure in the African American literary community. Before publishing a complete collection of poetry, individual works appeared in the *AME Review*. She became established as a poet in 1876 when she wrote the poem "Lincoln," which was written for the unveiling of the Washington, D.C. Freedmen's Monument. In 1887, Ray collaborated with her sister Florence to publish her father's biography *Sketch in the Life of Rev. Charles B. Ray*. After the biography, she published two collections of poetry, *Sonnets* (1893) and *Poems* (1910). While most of Ray's poetry is reflective of nineteenth-century romanticism and centers on themes of religion, nature, and philosophy, poems such as "Venus de Milo," "Antigone and Oedipus," "The Quest of the Ideal," "Listening

Nydia," "Niobe," and "Echo's Complaint" reflect an obvious classical influence.

"Niobe" and "Echo's Complaint" serve as examples of how Ray uses the classics to redefine the image of women in literature and highlight the voiceless and oppressed status of Black women in literature and society. In both poems, Ray reverses traditional representations of women: Niobe transforms from the aggressor to the victim, while Echo's passive nature is traded for an aggressive demeanor. Ray's reenactments of the Echo and Niobe stories also explore the theme of silence. Patricia Laurence says "silence in women has been viewed as the place of oppression, the mark of women's exclusion from the public spheres of life and from representation as speakers in a text" (Laurence 156). In "Echo" and "Niobe," Ray examines the relationship between silence and oppression, revealing that since antiquity, women have been restricted from freely expressing themselves politically and sexually. In "Niobe," Niobe's imposed silence is a result of speaking out, but in "Echo," Ray's protagonist breaks her silence and covertly verbalizes the sensual desires of nineteenth-century Black women.

Ray's approach to the Niobe story is similar to Wheatley's and considering Wheatley's lasting popularity in the nineteenth century it is possible that Ray is rewriting Wheatley's version of the Niobe story. In his study of intertextuality in African American literature, Gates suggests that Black women writers pay homage to writers who came before them by Signifyin(g) on their texts:

> This [Signifyin(g)] can be accomplished by the revision of tropes. This sort of Signifyin(g) revision serves, if successful, to create a space for the revising text. . . . The revising text is written in the language of the tradition, employing its tropes, its rhetorical strategies, and its ostensible subject matter, the so-called Black Experience. This mode of revision, of Signifyin(g), is the most striking aspect of Afro-American literary history. If Black writers read each other, they also revise each other's texts. Thereby they become fluent in the language of tradition. (124)

Reading Ray's Niobe poem as an intertextual revision of Wheatley's Niobe poem emphasizes the point that certain mythical figures appeal to Black female writers, because these characters experience oppressive circumstances relative to the Black female experience. Where Wheatley constructs a lengthy epic, Ray captures the essence of the Niobe story in a fourteen-line sonnet. Similar to Wheatley, Ray focuses on Niobe's distress and the gods' undue persecution of Niobe's children. Incidentally, Ray gives no evidence to explain what provoked the gods to brutally murder Niobe's children. Either Ray assumes readers are familiar with the story and do not need the background detail, or she is not concerned with Niobe's provocation of the gods.[7] In either case she launches into the narrative and details Niobe's experience of watching defensively as her children die: "Oh Mother heart! When fast the arrows flew, / Like blinding lightning, smiting as they fell, / One after one, one after one, what knell / Could fitly voice thy anguish!" (76). Niobe is optimistic that the gods will spare just one of her children, but as each child dies she realizes that even "Thy youngest, too must go" (76). Eventually, after all the children have been slain, Niobe has no recourse but to be imprisoned by her grief; the murder of her children is too great a burden to bear:

> The flinty stone, O image of despair,
> Sad Niobe, thy maddened grief did flow
> In bitt'rest tears, when all thy wailing prayer
> Was so denied. Alas! what weight of woe
> Is prisoned in thy melancholy eyes!
> What mother-love beneath the stoic lies! (77)

Ray ends her poem with Niobe's metamorphosis into stone, her "mother-love" "prisoned" in her eyes. Ray's sympathetic characterization of Niobe indicates that she might have been drawn to this myth because, like Wheatley, she regards Niobe as a victim. Ray's omission of a crucial component of the story, Niobe's verbal assault, indicates that Ray also wants her readers to focus solely on the idea that Niobe is a woman who is unfairly castigated and silenced by authority.

As a nineteenth-century Black woman in a society where women had few opportunities to speak freely, Ray could identify with Niobe. In suffragette and abolitionist movements, White women's voices were privileged over Black women's voices. And in the literary arena, one of the few places where Black women could express themselves, Black women's ideas were often censored as they could write only about subjects suitable for women. In *A Voice from the South* Anna Julia Cooper spoke against the silencing of women. Cooper suggested that a Black woman's voice is like a "muffled chord" a "voiceless note" that "has not yet been heard from" (i-ii). Those women (Black and White) who tried to assert their voices they often faced consequences for their actions. In *Women Race and Class*, for example, Angela Davis notes that during the nineteenth century when the activists Angelina and Sarah Grimké spoke out on behalf of women's rights, they were castigated by a number of men in the community:

> The most devastating attack came from religious quarters: on July 28, 1837, the Council of Congregationalist Ministers of Massachusetts issued a pastoral letter severely chastising them for engaging in activities which subverted women's divinely ordained role: "The power of woman is her dependence, flowing from the consciousness of that weakness which God has given her for her protection." . . . According to the ministers, the Grimkés' actions had created "dangers which at present threaten the female character with wide-spread and permanent injury. . . . The echoes of this assault did not begin to fade until the Grimkés finally decided to terminate their lecturing career. (Davis 41)

Davis' example illustrates that the Grimké sisters were "silenced" by the men of their community who were obviously threatened by their opinions in regards to women's rights.

In an example of Black women's silencing, the radical and extremely vocal African American educator and journalist Ida B. Wells was punished for speaking out against racism and social injustice. In 1892, when three of Wells' friends were lynched for refusing to close their grocery store that was in competition with White businesses, Wells used her newspaper, *The Free Speech and Headlight*, to launch an anti-lynching campaign. Wells' campaign resulted in the destruction of her office and threats against her life

(Logan 76–77). So while women like the Grimkés and Wells dared to speak out, for doing so, they faced the repercussions.

While Ray uses the mythical Niobe story to expose the silencing of women, in "Echo's Complaint" she uses a mythical narrative to highlight women's voices. "Echo's Complaint" is a paraphrase of Ovid's "The Story of Echo and Narcissus" found in Book III of *Metamorphoses*. In Frank Miller's Loeb Library translation of Ovid's story, Echo is a young nymph who falls in love with Narcissus. Echo professes her love to Narcissus, but he rejects her because his pride and self-love consume his thoughts. After he rejects Ameinius, one of his many admirers, Artemis, the goddess of the hunt, curses Narcissus with the misfortune of falling in love with his own image. Upon finally seeing himself in a pool of water, Narcissus is anxious to embrace the person he sees before him. But when he finds the image in the water does not respond to his advances, he is overwhelmed by feelings of rejection and intense love. Narcissus is unable to cope with his heartbreak and forgoes his will to live. When Narcissus dies, Echo is heartbroken. Ray takes Ovid's story and in verse form re-imagines it through the eyes of the female character Echo.

Ray empowers Echo not only by allowing her to speak but also by giving her the opportunity to express her emotions. Ray's rendition of the Narcissus poem transforms Echo from a secondary to a primary character. In most versions of the Narcissus tale, Narcissus and Echo are dependent upon each other in order to speak: As Anne-Emmanuelle Berger notes, "Ovid has given speech not only to Echo, but to Narcissus as well: he gives it to Echo in Narcissus and to Narcissus in the forest of Echo. And what makes them both speak is desire" (Berger 633). However, we should note, Echo's voice is audible only when Narcissus speaks. As her name implies, Echo *echoes* or speaks only by repeating what another has said. In Ray's narrative, Echo does not rely upon Narcissus to speak. She asserts her authority by speaking first and by choosing her own words. Echo's voice is privileged throughout the entire narrative and it is Narcissus who is mute. Ultimately, Ray alters the traditional portrayal of Echo from silent and passive to aggressive and vocal.

Ray's experimentation with breaking Echo's silence operates in several ways. Not only does Ray allow Echo to gain and establish her own voice, but Ray, along with her protagonist, engages in an open discussion of feminine desire and sexuality that was culturally unacceptable for women of the day. In her study of the codes of decorum for nineteenth-century African American women, Claudia Tate argues that female writers were supposed to "follow stringent literary and social codes. These codes demanded, in particular, that they delete all references to 'coarse language, coarse manners, and coarse ideals,' which included not only allusions to sexual passions but anger as well (Bruce, p. 19)" (Tate 63). Tate also notes that

> [W]hile subscribing to the rigid standards of Victorian ladyhood . . . these [Black women] writers enlarged its criteria, thereby granting access to Victorian ladyhood that served to counter the racist stereotype of black female wanton sexuality. Unfortunately, these writers found themselves locked not only within color codes but within Victorian codes of literary gentility as well. (63)

Although Ray was no doubt aware of the literary code of womanhood that discouraged women from writing poems referencing women's sexual passions, she also recognized the importance of allowing women to speak freely and honestly about their sexual desires. The protagonist of "Echo's Complaint" gives Ray the platform for this discussion of feminine desire.

Echo behaves in a manner antithetical to the code of nineteenth-century Black womanhood. Echo is not submissive and coy and her pursuit of Narcissus is relentless. Similar to the female protagonists of Ovid's *Heroides*, Ray's protagonist conveys neither shame nor intimidation as she continuously expresses her feelings:

> O rare Narcissus! Sunny-haired!
> O mild eye youth of godlike mien!
> O thou that sittest by fair streams,
> And in their trembling, silv'ry sheen
> Thy lovely countenance dost view,
> Turn but once more thy magic gaze
> On one who will love thee many days? (109)

Instead of portraying Echo as the sexual object of desire waiting for her male suitor to make his advance, Ray's Echo assumes the role of the passionate lover and initiates the mating ritual. In doing so, Ray inverts the conventions of the male poetic tradition, which typically grants male characters the opportunity to express their love for their woman of choice.

Echo takes charge and expresses her feelings for Narcissus. She tells him: "come . . . and let me kiss thy sunny hair / Thy marble brow; aye, let me kiss / Thy dewy lips, thy peerless eyes. / One clasp from thee / One long-love clasp / Will change to joy-notes all my sighs" (110). Despite her appeals, Ray's Narcissus never recipro-cates Echo's affections. She begs him "not to leave me not unloved and alone" (109). At the dénouement when Echo realizes Narcissus will not return her affection, she leaves dejected: "Sweet Echo, thus in love sore tried, / Was seen no more; but on the breeze / Her voice was heard, her voice alone / was left,—an answering cadence there / Love thrilling still lingering tone" (111). Ray's Echo is no more successful than Ovid's in her attempt to capture Narcissus' affection. However, while Ovid describes a woman who is a mere echo—or one who repeats what others have to say—here in Ray's version, Echo is a woman with her own voice and her own story to tell.

For her time, Ray's poetic approach to women's sexuality was quite radical. Martha Cutter explains that during the nineteenth century "[c]ontrol of language [was] also linked to control of female sexuality: to speak out [was] to be immodest, sexual, unruly" (7). By articulating the feelings most women could not openly express but surely must have felt, Ray demonstrates her own apparent unruliness. Ray also liberates Echo (and other women) from her sexual silence. The few writers who have ana-lyzed Ray's poetry have overlooked the significance of the Echo poem. For example, in her biographical sketch of Ray, Joan Sherman writes: "Like so many nineteenth-century poets, H. Cordelia Ray versified only socially acceptable sentiments and a picture-book world. She suppressed natural feelings and thought-ful scrutiny of human relationships, actions, and ideas to serve a Muse for whom poetry was more a skill than an art, more a penmanship exercise than a new, complex creation of heart and mind" (134).

Clearly, Sherman did not recognize that poems like "Echo," and perhaps others, do address "natural feelings" of heart and mind.

While Ray uses the Echo poem to break the silence of feminine desire imposed on women by the cult of womanhood, other nineteenth-century Black women writers like Francis Ellen Watkins Harper and Pauline Hopkins used their novels to advocate for Black women's sexual morality.

Pauline Hopkins

Pauline Hopkins is another nineteenth-century writer who appropriates antiquity to explore how Black women have been silenced into sexual oppression. In contrast to Ray however, Hopkins adopts an alternative approach to revising myth. Instead of rewriting an existing mythic story, she defers to Greek antiquity by giving the protagonist of her novel, *Contending Forces* (1900), the same name and socially-constructed mythical sexual identity as the ancient Greek poet Sappho of Lesbos. Hopkins features Sappho of Lesbos as the heroine of her novel because Sappho represented both sexuality and female empowerment.

In *Contending Forces* Hopkins transports Sappho into the nineteenth century and imagines her life from the perspective of a sexually traumatized Black woman. Hopkins' nineteenth-century Sappho, renamed Sappho Clark, is transformed from a sexually liberated woman into a sexually oppressed woman who fights to assume an asexual identity. Due to her past history of sexual assault, Clark is unable to completely divorce herself from the stigmatized image of the sexually deviant Black woman. At fourteen, Clark is raped by her White uncle, sold into prostitution, and bears an illegitimate child. Despite the fact that she is forced to compromise her chastity, Clark assumes responsibility for her sexual impropriety and lives her life silenced into shame, afraid her secret will be revealed. Hopkins uses Clark's experience to a) demonstrate that Black women sought to uphold moral standards of sexuality and b) expose the exploitative and oppressive

White patriarchal practices that fostered negative representations of Black womanhood.

Those familiar with Sappho of Lesbos' legacy will readily detect a number of parallels between Hopkins' protagonist and the ancient poet. One of most significant similarities between the two women is the fact that they both had dual identities as two different women; each identified as either a respectable member of her community or a sexual deviant. During antiquity, Sappho's double identity was created after rumors about her lesbianism tarnished her reputation. According to Margaret Williamson, a "revival of cultural nationalism among the Greeks of the second to fourth centuries led to a desire to rehabilitate Sappho, dissociating her from the disrepute in which Roman writers in particular had brought her" (33). In an attempt to preserve a respectable image of Sappho, during the third century a myth developed suggesting that charges of lesbianism against Sappho of Lesbos' resulted from "a case of mistaken identity." There were two Sapphos, from two different towns in Lesbos, one, a poet and respectable, the other neither" (Williamson 32). Williamson observes that this notion of "two Sapphos" continued long after antiquity. She notes: "Nineteenth-century scholars had their own version of the 'two Sapphos' theory, with one school seizing disapprovingly on assertions about her love of women and the other leaping chivalrously to her defense" (91). We cannot be certain that Hopkins was aware of nineteenth-century debates concerning Sappho of Lesbos' dual identity. But, as Hazel Carby notes, Hopkins' narrative strategy reveals that her "political intention was at its clearest in the construction of the two identities of Sappho Clark" (Carby 142).

Hopkins' Sappho is also represented as two distinct entities: Sappho Clark and Mabelle Beaubean. The Sappho Clark to whom we are introduced is a woman of integrity and moral virtue. Clark is depicted as an upstanding member of her community. She holds a respectable job as a stenographer and is well mannered, well spoken, and educated. In essence, judging by her appearance and deportment, Clark betrays no indication of a soiled past. Clark's reputation is antithetical to her former identity as Mabelle Beaubean, a beautiful young girl who was raped, sold into prostitution, and who bore an illegitimate child. In order to, as Hopkins says, "destroy her identity," a story is devised reporting that after delivering a son Mabelle died. Considering the mores of the day, Mabelle's fate should have resulted in what Tate calls a "social death." However, "Mabelle does not die, rather she grants herself social rebirth by changing her name to 'Sappho Clark'" (Tate 175) and reenters society as the personification of Black female virtue. If Mabelle's intention was to disassociate herself from an image of sexual immorality, why would she name herself after Sappho of Lesbos, a woman equated with a dark sexual history? Clark's adoption of Sappho's name is ironic. While the alias, Sappho, gives Clark the freedom to live as a moral woman, the name is actually synonymous with sexual immorality. Essentially the name Sappho reflects Clark's paradoxical double identity as a liberated, but sexually repressed, woman who remains enslaved by her past.

In addition to their dual identities, Sappho of Lesbos and Sappho Clark both share intimate relationships with women. Many have regarded Sappho of Lesbos' feminine friendships as lesbian relationships. Sappho's coterie of women and her homoerotic poetry have both been used as evidence to support her lesbian activity. Scholars have viewed Sappho's coterie as both an educational as well as social circle. For example, Claude Calame observes "[f]rom a pedagogical point of view, Sappho's circle looks like a sort of school for femininity destined to make young pupils into accomplished women: through the performance of song, music, and cult act, they had lessons in comportment and elegance" (118). He continues, "The education of Sappho in her group prepared young girls to be adult, married women by teaching feminine charm and beauty" (119). Calame also notes, however, that while Sappho's circle emphasized "companionship" and educational instruction, "homophilia" is also "found among the basic elements that make up Sappho's group" (121). Calame argues that, while it is false to assume that all the girls in the group were involved romantically, "we must presume . . . some girls had a homoerotic relationship with the poet" (121). Others have suggested that Sappho's poetry, especially her love poems composed to women, present evidence of her lesbianism. Page duBois asserts, for example, "it is clear from the language she uses that she writes as a woman narrator in a feminine voice, desiring other women. . . . Sappho sings again and again of her love and desire for women" (18). Margaret Williamson says that scholars have focused much interest "on a scrap of papyrus" (99), that may or may not be by Sappho, on which one badly damaged word can be construed to read "receivers of the dildo" (91). Williamson maintains though that this kind of evidence holds little credibility.

Despite contemporary charges that Sappho was lesbian, a number of scholars point out that reports concerning Sappho's lesbianism would not have been considered immoral during the seventh- to early sixth-century BCE when Sappho was writing. As duBois contends, "we must conclude that her expressions of love for women were completely acceptable to her readers in ancient Greece, since they excite no comment, neither praise nor blame" (21).[8] Sappho's lesbianism or heterosexuality continues to incite scholarly discussion, but the reality is, considering the fact that there is little concrete biographical information about her, and therefore not much to base a legitimate argument concerning her sexuality, it is difficult to argue for or against lesbian accusations. What is clear, however, is the idea that Sappho was a lesbian has been transmitted through the ages and remains a part of her mythology.

Sappho of Lesbos' intimate female friendships clearly influenced Hopkins' creation of Clark's close friendship with the character Dora Smith.[9] Sappho's close bond with Dora Smith is established from their first meeting. The narrator maintains that Dora is instantly attracted to Sappho: "Sappho Clark seemed to fill a long-felt want in her life, and she had from the first a perfect trust in the girl" (98). While Sappho and Dora's relationship is regarded by most as "sisterly," some have suggested that the friendship is homoerotic. For example, in her discussion of the two women together in Sappho's room, Amy Wolf observes, "the room becomes the site of homoerotic tension between the two women. After a 'scramble' for pie, 'mingled with peals of merry laughter,' Sappho emerges 'from the fray' all rosy and sparkling"(2). Wolf's interpretation of this scene insinuates that the two women are engaged in sexual flirtation that moves beyond the platonic realm. Furthermore, Wolf suggests that the bond between Dora and Sappho is so strong that "when Dora later marries, she names her daughter Sappho"(2). Moreover, Laura Doyle suggests "that Sappho the younger serves as a continuing sign of the homoeroticism between Dora and Sappho"(180) (qtd. in Wolf 2). Wolf and Doyle present a titillating reading of the two women's friendship, but considering Sappho's endeavor to disassociate herself from her sexuality, it is unlikely that Sappho would engage in a relationship that was considered even more sinful than working as a prostitute and having an illegitimate child.

In addition to establishing the significance of Sappho of Lesbos' relationships with women, Hopkins also takes on Sappho of Lesbos' preoccupation with feminine desire. Written from the perspective of male and female narrators, Sappho of Lesbos' poetry centers on erotic themes. In some poems she takes the position of the jilted lover lamenting her abandonment by male/female lovers. The poem *Parting* (fragment 94), for example, presents Sappho's anguish as she laments her lovers' departure:

> frankly I wish I were dead:
> she was weeping as she took her leave from me
>
> and many times she told [me] this,
> "Oh what sadness we have s[uffe]red,
> Sappho, for I'm leaving you against my will." (Hallet 143)

Sappho's sentimental account of the tormented lover is duplicated in Hopkins' novel. Despite her attempts to resist romantic urges, Sappho Clark falls in love with Will Smith. Like the ancient Sappho and the mythological Echo, Sappho is overwhelmed by the idea of loving someone whom she could not possess. In one scene, Hopkins features Sappho's anguish as she is forced to conceal her feelings for the man she loves:

> Under the cover of the friendly darkness she gave up the long struggle for self-control, and indulged in the grief she knew was hers for all eternity. Oh, for death, the solitude of the grave and self-forgetfulness. "What have I done, what have I done to suffer thus?

To give up all my joys, and have only misery for all my life. I love this man; I know it now! I want his love, his care, his protection. I want him through life and beyond the grave, we two as one—my husband." (182)

The melodramatic language and the heartfelt statements are easily reminiscent of any number of Sappho of Lesbos' ancient poems professing unrequited love. The passage also puts us in the mind of Ray's Echo poem where Echo expressed her undying love for Narcissus. But whereas Echo is free to reveal her desires, Sappho is restricted from exposing her feelings.

While Hopkins' novel is not a revision of a classical myth, the novel does seek to revise social myth. Hopkins uses her text to correct the mythological image of the sexually perverse Black woman. The idea that Black women were lascivious was a myth that developed during slavery. Slave women earned their sexually deviant reputation from White slave owners who forced Black men to routinely engage in forced sexual relationships with female slaves to allow for the economic growth of slavery. Additionally, in an attempt to justify their own sexual urges and their rape of Black women, White men led the charge that a White slave holder was "merely prey to the rampant sexuality of his female slaves" (Carby 27). Black slaves became stereotyped as "jezebels," sexually aggressive women who were willing participants in their sexual degradation. Thus "[r]ape became the specified act of sexual violence forced on Black women, with the myth of the Black prostitute as its ideological justification" (Collins 147).

Even after slavery, Black women continued to wrestle with negative representations of themselves. Hopkins' novel "[r]enounc[es] racist myths that erode self-respect, myths posited on the alleged wantonness of Black Americans, Hopkins challenges her readers to contextualize those myths in order to understand the historical origins of them" (Campbell 33). In fact, in the preface to *Contending Forces*, Hopkins writes that the purpose of the book is to "erase the stigma of degradation from my race" (13). Black women like Hopkins found that the best way to destroy the myth of Black women's hypersexuality was to align themselves with White women. Black women began emulating White female standards of womanhood known as the "cult of true womanhood." The cult of true womanhood upheld the notion that "the attributes of True Womanhood, by which a woman judged herself and was judged by her husband, her neighbors and society, could be divided into four cardinal virtues—piety, purity, submissiveness, and domesticity. . . . With them she was promised happiness and power" (Carby 23). In one section of her narrative, Hopkins addresses the significance of the expected moral standards for Black women of the day.

In the chapter, "The Sewing-Circle," a group of women assemble to discuss "the place which the virtuous woman occupies in upbuilding a race." The group leader, Mrs. Willis, a prototype of the upstanding moral Black woman, tells the women present that they have a responsibility to "refute the charges brought against us as to our moral irresponsibility, and the low moral standard maintained by us in comparison with other races" (148). Mrs. Willis' statement serves to address the reader directly about the false image of Black women as willingly lascivious, showing that Black women, like White women, wish to uphold standards of the cult.

Sappho raises the question, is "the Negro woman in her native state truly a virtuous woman?" (149). Mrs. Willis replies, "the native African woman is impregnable in her virtue. . . . But let us not forget the definition of virtue—'Strength to do the right thing under all temptations.' Our ideas of virtue are too narrow. We confine them to that conduct which is ruled by our animal passions alone. It goes deeper than that—general excellence in every duty of life is what we may call virtue" (149). What Mrs. Willis proposes is that Black women cannot be judged solely by their chastity. Her comment clears Sappho from her belief that she is not virtuous. Yet Sappho does not accept Ms. Willis' statement and she poses the question, "Do you think, then, that Negro women will be held responsible for all the lack of virtue that is being laid to their charge today? I mean, do you think that God will hold us responsible for the *illegitimacy* with which our race has been obliged, as it were, to flood the world?" (149). Sappho's comment illustrates that she is less concerned with how the community will judge her and is more concerned with how God will judge women like her.

While Hopkins uses her text to correct the myth of the sexually deviant Black woman, through Mrs. Willis' comments she also challenges the cult of true womanhood and shows its ineffectiveness for judging standards of Black womanhood. As Carby states, through their heroines, Hopkins as well as Jacobs, in her novel *Incidents In the Life of a Slave Girl,* show how Black women needed to form "unconventional definitions of womanhood," which stood "outside the parameters of the conventional [White] heroine" (Carby 59). However, Sappho does not recognize that she is free from conventional definitions of womanhood in some regard. Sappho is a liberating figure who presents a new image of womanhood. As Tate suggests, "the novel presents a heroine whose virtue is not simply the product of sexual innocence. She qualifies herself as a virtuous person through the strength of her character" (161).

In *Contending Forces* Hopkins' treatment of Black women's sexuality is antithetical to Henrietta Cordelia Ray's previous discussion of Black women's sexual liberation. Whereas in the poem "Echo," Ray illumines that expressing one's sexual desires can be empowering, Hopkins demonstrates that, for the protagonist of her novel, silence is empowering. Sappho's silence about her past sexual indiscretion allows her to blend into society and be treated as an equal among her peers. She fears that breaking the silence will cost her respectability and result in rejection by those she loves. Interestingly, whereas Hopkins' heroine tries to bury her sexual misconduct, the protagonist of Jacobs' *Incidents In the Life of a Slave Girl,* knows that speaking out about past injustices against her is an empowering act both for herself and other women. In the essay "Silences in Harriet 'Linda Brent' Jacobs's *Incidents In the Life of a Slave Girl,"* Joanne Braxton contends, "While the cost of breaking these silences is great, the human cost of remaining silent is even greater. It is the thought of these abuses continuing unexposed that inspires Jacobs to take the risk" (Braxton 147). While Sappho's silence protects her, it also restricts her from forming romantic relationships. In effect, her sexuality is "silenced" when she tries to avoid Will Smith's male companionship. It is only at the end of the novel when Sappho is forced to break her silence that she becomes free of her shame and is finally able to embrace her sexuality. What Hopkins achieves then is a discussion about Black female sexuality that uncovers the myth of Black women's sexual deviance, proving that most Black women attempt to adhere to respectable standards of womanhood. She also notes though that a new discourse of womanhood is necessary to define Black womanhood.

Hopkins' *Contending Forces* presents an intriguing parallel between her heroine's experiences and those of the ancient poet Sappho. Surprisingly, despite the overwhelming interest in this novel, few scholars have focused on the significance of Sappho of Lesbos in the construction of this narrative. Recognizing the similarities between both the fictional Sappho and the ancient poet offers a new way to interpret and appreciate Hopkins' text. Although she does not revise a classical myth, Hopkins, like Wheatley and Ray, looks back to antiquity to create another narrative focusing on the oppression and silencing of women. Relating Hopkins' text with Wheatley's and Ray's illustrates that the ancient world appeals to all three writers because they can use the experiences of mythical female characters, or real-life women from antiquity, to talk about the marginalization of women in their own societies. As the women defer to antiquity they find a liberating space where women are free to express their desires, challenge authority, and define their own identities.

3

Gwendolyn Brooks' Racialization of the Persephone and Demeter Myth in "The Anniad" and "In the Mecca"

After the Harlem Renaissance most Black writers of the 1940s and 1950s traded the fantasy of the mythical world for realism and naturalism.[1] Despite this move away from Greco-Roman mythology, however, writers like Ralph Ellison, Robert Hayden, Leon Forrest, and Gwendolyn Brooks continued looking to the classics for literary inspiration, often marrying Western classical myth with contemporary cultural mythology. "The Anniad" (1949) and "In the Mecca" (1968), are two examples of how Brooks experiments with the classics. In these poems she rewrites the traditional archetypal epic to reflect the experiences of two Black female protagonists who, like the protagonists of Greek myth, suffer trauma and victimization at the hands of men and the larger society. In addition to appropriating classical myth she also tackles cultural myths concerning romanticized notions of love, European standards of beauty, and utopian ideals of the American dream.

Brooks' awareness of the classics came as a result of her own informal training as a poet. In her autobiography, *Report from Part Two*, Brooks says her parents' bookshelf gave her access to *The Harvard Classics*, a selection of major classical texts. Brooks says: "I shall never forget . . . over and over selecting this and that dark green, gold-lettered volume for spellbound study. Oh those miracles. *Nine Greek Dramas* . . . White [W]hite [W]hite. I inherited these White treasures" (12). Brooks first tried her hand at classical revision while she was in high school. Michele Ronnick observes that in 1934 Brooks "made a rhymed and a prose translation of the *Aeneid*, Book III, lines 1–444 [Aeneas in Crete, meets the Harpies and is told about the Sibyl who entrusts signs and symbols to leaves], a prose and lyric translation of lines 472–77 [Anchises sets sail]" (3). Ronnick also notes that Brooks wrote a mock lament entitled "To Publius Vergilius Maro"(3). Brooks' interest in reworking classical narratives probably began after James Weldon Johnson encouraged her to read the poetry of modernist authors T. S. Eliot, Ezra Pound, and E. E. Cummings. Brooks was mainly inspired by the modernists' technique of deconstructing pre-existing narratives, infusing several classical works into a single text, and combining the classical world with modern reality. The chaotic era of World War I had presented modernist writers with an attitude of uncertainty. Modernists looked to the classics for a sense of order and structure. In a review of James Joyce's *Ulysses*, for example, T. S. Eliot said myth was "a way of controlling, of ordering, of giving a shape and significance to the immense panorama of futility and anarchy which is contemporary history" (62). During World War II, Brooks also found that the classics provided a solid structural framework for writing about her perception of a chaotic world. The two poems "The Anniad" and "In the Mecca" illustrate how Brooks effectively fuses the classical world with the frenzy of modern urban America.

"The Anniad"

"The Anniad" is a complex forty-three-stanza epic that constitutes the second section of the three-part narrative *Annie Allen*. The narrative is a poetic *bildungsroman* chronicling the experiences of Annie Allen from childhood to womanhood. In the first section, "Notes from the Childhood and the Girlhood," Brooks places emphasis on imagery and symbolism. The poems in this section— mostly sonnets and ballads—describe Annie's entrance into the world, her perception of her parents, images of Sunday dinners, portraits of deceased relatives, memories of afternoons at vaudeville shows, and a blossoming romance. In the third section, "The

Womanhood," tone and subject matter are placed in the foreground. Here the poems relay Annie's mature thoughts as she reflects on issues of motherhood, racism, and aging. Stylistically, "The Anniad" stands apart from the first and last sections of the poem. In contrast to "Notes from the Childhood and the Girlhood" and "The Womanhood," "The Anniad" is extremely challenging to read. Not only does Brooks' employment of *ottava rima* and *rhyme royal* force readers to focus on the technicality of the verse, but the antiquated, esoteric vocabulary—consisting of words such as *paladin* and *thaumaturgic*—obstruct the reader's ability to interpret the stanzas.[2] While it is apparent that with "The Anniad," Brooks takes the opportunity to display her mastery of prosody, in one interview she states proudly that she "labored over the poem," the complicated nature of the verse fittingly reflects the poetic theme: the complex, Persephone-like epic journey from puberty to adulthood.

"The Anniad" has intrigued and baffled scholars and readers who take a variety of approaches in their analysis of the poem. Structuralists examine the language and technique while others devote themselves to establishing the poem's genre. Critics who have preoccupied themselves with attempting to determine the poem's genre often focus on whether the poem should be read as an epic or mock epic. For example, on one hand Claudia Tate recognizes the poem's epic qualities, such as the universality of the epic theme of "the deteriorating relationship between men and women" (146) and the "consequences of the intervention of fate, in the form of world war, on these relationships" (146). But she also argues that "The Anniad" is a "mock-heroic satire, in that commonplace characters and events have been elevated in a ceremonious manner by using lofty diction and complicated techniques" (149). Others, like R. Baxter Miller, contend that while Brooks attempted to write an epic, her effort resulted in a mock epic because "the style was too lofty for the theme" (160) and she failed stylistically to hold to epic conventions.

While some adamantly argue for "The Anniad" as a mock epic, the poem can just as easily be recognized as an epic.[3] In addition to following epic formulas such as opening with the epic theme, starting in *medias res*, cataloguing the principal characters, and using esoteric language, one of the most obvious parallels between "The Anniad" and the epic is the -ad suffix in the poem's title. The -ad suffix prompted a number of critics to conclude that Brooks' title invokes well-known epics such as the *Aeneid* and the *Iliad*. Brooks admits that when writing the poem she "thought of 'The *Iliad*' and said, I'll call this 'The Anniad.' At first, interesting enough, I called her 'Hester Allen,' and I wanted then to say 'The Hesteriad,' but I forgot why I changed it to Annie. . . . I was fascinated by what words might do there in the poem" (158). Since Brooks' epic emphasizes the Black female experience, I propose that, rather than interpret "The Anniad" as a reworking of the *Iliad* or the *Aeneid*—male centered narratives—we might read "The Anniad" as a reworking of the feminine epic, *The Homeric Hymn to Demeter*, a text that, according to Mary Louise Lord, thematically takes on conventions of the epic. Lord maintains that the *Hymn to Demeter* follows a "narrative pattern" that parallels six thematic episodes or "mythic themes" that appear in traditional epics such as the *Odyssey* or the *Iliad*: "(1) the withdrawal of the hero (or heroine), which sometimes takes the form of a long absence—this element is often closely linked with a quarrel and the loss of someone beloved; (2) disguise during the absence or upon the return of the hero . . . ; (3) the theme of hospitality to the wandering hero; (4) the recognition of the hero . . . ; (5) disaster during or occasioned by the absence; (6) the reconciliation of the hero and the return" (182).

At least three of these mythic themes are also detected in "The Anniad" (numbers one, fives, and six previously listed), but in Brooks' narrative the experiences of the protagonist are often exchanged with the antagonist and the journey motif becomes emotional rather than physical. Another significant change in Brooks' epic is that she transforms her protagonist from the archetypal White male hero into a Black woman and makes her the central figure in the text. In *The Female Hero in American and British Literature*, Carol Pearson and Katherine Pope's discussion about the archetypal hero illustrates the necessity for women authors to revise the image of heroic characters. Pearson and Pope point out that the typical hero "is always assumed to be white and upper class" and "racial minorities, the poor, and women—are seen as secondary characters important obstacles, aids, or rewards in his journey" (4). Acknowledging that Black women do not fit the mold of the traditional hero, Brooks presents an epic that is not merely a reversal of the traditional European male epic genre, but instead, a counter-narrative about the experiences of a contemporary African American Persephone. Thus, in "The Anniad" Brooks' protagonist does not embark on a grueling physical voyage to the underworld, nor does she engage in bloody, tragic fights on the battlefield. Annie is an ordinary Black woman who possesses heroic qualities. Like Persephone, her heroism is evidenced by her ability to survive through the chaotic process of puberty and all that it entails: the loss of virginity, blossoming sexuality, thwarted love and rejection, and the death and rebirth of the self.

With "The Anniad," Brooks followed in the tradition of female poets such as Hilda Doolittle and Elizabeth Barrett Browning who, according to Jeremy Downes, constructed epics that "deliberately opposed epics that have gone before. The key difference in these epics by women, however, is that this opposition is explicitly phrased in terms of gender, usually against male inscriptions of the female self" (212). Brooks' "The Anniad" is also a female-centered epic that seeks to challenge male inscribed projections of the feminine self. Brooks' epic differs from other feminine epics though because in addition to transforming the traditional epic from masculine to feminine, she also adds a racialized discourse to the epic form. The racialization of Brooks' feminine epic is overlooked by most critics who focus on the high-modernist technicality of the poem rather than the Black aesthetic conventions of signification operating throughout the work. Yemisi Jimoh's examination of "The Anniad" though, insightfully points to Brooks' employment of signifying as an example of the African American poetics present in the narrative. According to Jimoh, in stanza five Brooks' description of Annie looking in the mirror at her "[B]lack and boisterous hair / Taming all that anger down" (100) can be read as a signification of a line from Countee Cullen's poem "Heritage" (1925), which describes Jesus as "Crowned with dark rebellious hair" (247). Jimoh also suggests that "The Anniad" evidences "veiled allusions" to Langston Hughes' 1947 poem "Trumpet Player." In this poem, much like Annie, the character "Has his head of vibrant hair / Tamed down" (Jimoh 168).[4]

Brooks' racialized version of the Persephone-Demeter myth is loosely modeled on the Homeric "Hymn to Demeter." In brief, the Homeric version of the vegetation myth recounts how Persephone is abducted and raped by Hades, god of the underworld. When Demeter learns that her daughter has been abducted she mourns and retaliates against Hades by creating a famine. Persephone is eventually reunited to Demeter with the stipulation that for a third of the year she must return to Hades. The protagonist of Brooks' "The Anniad" assumes the role of the young naïve Persephone caught up in a system of male dominance that threatens to destroy her spiritual, sexual, and emotional being. While her encounter is hurtful, Annie, just like Persephone, must experience this rite of passage in order to be initiated into womanhood. Following in the tradition of other twentieth-century writers who adapt the narrative to fit the framework of contemporary experience (Toni Morrison's *Bluest Eye*, Alice Walker's *The Color Purple*, Rita Dove's *Mother Love*, Barbara Kingsolver's *Pigs in Heaven*, and Maggie Gee's *Lost Children*), Brooks casts her narrative in the twentieth century. Also similar to other contemporary writers, Brooks writes from Persephone's perspective rather than Demeter's. In "The Anniad," Persephone is a young Black girl who loses her virginity during a unfulfilling sexual encounter, descends into an emotional underworld, endures loss and separation from her husband, and in accordance with the seasonal changes goes through a metamorphosis of death and rebirth that transforms her from child to woman.

The opening of "The Anniad" remains consistent with the Greek myth, which begins with an image of young Persephone, the image of fertility and naïveté, mindlessly picking flowers. Annie is also depicted as virginal, fertile, and innocent. Mirroring the actions of her mythical counterpart, Persephone is also lost in reverie. Instead of picking flowers, as Persephone does, Annie is: "Fancying on the featherbed," imagining sweet scenarios about

"What was never and is not" (99). What was "never and is not" is Annie's childish, deluded reality that Tan Man loves her as much as she adores him. What is factual is the reality that Tan Man is one whom "no woman ever had" (99). In the concluding poem from "Notes," "Notes of my own sweet good," Annie admits that she knows Tan Man is unfaithful and therefore finds it difficult to commit to her: "You kiss all the great-lipped girls that you can. / If only they knew that it's little today / And nothing tomorrow to take or to pay" (95). But Annie, like the other girls, settles for any attention Tan Man shows her. Annie is certainly not the first woman to choose a man whose reputation for womanizing is legendary. Knowing that Tan Man will never settle down to become the monogamous suitor she dreams of, she chooses to create an image of him as the ideal man. Like most adolescent girls, Annie is blinded by a cultural mythology of "ideal love" that results in the creation of a false image of Tan Man. In *Puberty, Sexuality, and the Self: Boys and Girls at Adolescence*, Karin Martin explains that teenage girls "construct narratives about their boyfriends that cast them in the light of ideal love. Stories of ideal love are not stories of passion and sexuality but are stories of romance. . . . In these 'narratives of ideal love girls often describe boys as heroes. They are "heroes" of the high school'—athletes, military men, reggae singers and so on" (62). In "The Anniad," Annie's perception of Tan Man is consistent with Martin's assessments.

Tan Man is not described as an ordinary man, instead, he is as strong and powerful as Hades. In Annie's mind, Tan Man is a *paladin*, a soldier she deifies.[5] As already noted, romanticizing love is commonplace for most young girls. However, for Black girls like Annie, this kind of thinking is detrimental for it forces Annie to subscribe to an ideal Eurocentric notion of love.[6] By attempting to subscribe to a White American aesthetic of beauty, to which she can never belong, Annie sets herself up for emotional trauma.[7] If we consider Annie's perception of her own parents' marriage, we can begin to understand why she creates an idealized version of love. In "Notes" the poem entitled "the parents: people like our marriage Maxie and Andrew" presents Annie's parents' marriage as one that has abandoned notions of romance. She notes that in the marriage "[t]here are no swans and swallows any more" (86). Annie wants to imagine the possibility of an everlasting romance that is counter to what she learns from her own parents' marriage. While Annie's daydreams may be unrealistic, her fantasies are significant because they are empowering. When we examine how Annie is portrayed throughout the poem, we realize that it is while Annie imagines a perfect life with Tan Man that she displays the most agency. Ultimately, daydreaming gives Annie the freedom to make Tan Man into an image of anything she wants him to be, and more importantly, she can participate in the fantasy according to how she defines herself, rather than according to how he defines her. As Annie mentally prepares to take on the experience of a lover, her body physically prepares for its sexual awakening, or in this case, harvesting. In the *Homeric Hymn* and in Ovid's *Metamorphoses*, Hades' abduction of Persephone occurs during the spring, which coincides with the fecundity of the earth. Foley describes Persephone "plucking flowers in the lush meadow—roses, crocuses, and lovely violets, irises and hyacinth and the narcissus, which Earth grew as a snare for the flower-faced maiden" (2). Annie's fertility is highlighted by stanzas three and four, which describe her metaphorically as ripened crop ready for cutting. Annie's "untried" sexual "ornaments," which align her with Persephone's virginal state, are the seasonal crop ready for Tan Man's harvest. Her breasts are described as "Buxom berries beyond rot" and her whole body is "ripe and rompabout, / all her harvest buttoned in, / All her ornaments untried" (99). Annie's "ripeness" also signals the beginning of her menstrual cycle and her pubescent state.

The Persephone and Demeter myth presents Persephone's first sexual encounter as an act of violation. After plucking the narcissus flower, a trap devised by Zeus, the earth opens up and Persephone plummets to the underworld where Hades rapes her. In contrast to the mythic tale, Annie is not raped. In "The Anniad," Annie and Tan Man engage in consensual sex. In stanza four, Annie is described as actually "Waiting for the *Paladin*" to take her virginity or "rub her secrets out" and "behold the hinted bride." Christine Downing suggests that Hades' rape of Persephone is essential, for it allows Persephone to develop her sexual self (227). Brooks' Persephone figure also relies upon Tan Man to help her experience her sexual awakening. It is important to note that although consenting, Annie's sexual encounter is described quite brutally. Tan Man "Eats the green by easy stages, / Nibbles at the root beneath / With intimidating teeth. / But no ravishment enrages. / No dominion is defied" (100). One could argue that, in a sense, Annie is raped. Rape, as defined by Richard Gelles is "less a sexual act and more an act of power in the relations between men and women" (342). In the sexual encounter between Tan Man and Annie, Tan Man establishes his dominance with his "intimidating teeth." Annie, like other rape victims, is forced to assume a role of sexual subservience.

Brooks' description of Tan Man's rough lovemaking is reminiscent of a passage from Eliot's "The Wasteland." In "The Fire Sermon," Eliot describes a sexual encounter between a typist and her lover. Like Annie, the typist plays a passive role in the sex act:

> The time is now propitious, as he guesses
> The meal is ended, she is bored and tired,
> Endeavors to engage her in caresses
> Which still are unreproved, if undesired.
> Flushed and decided, he assaults at once;
> Exploring hands encounter no defence;
> His vanity requires no response,
> And makes a welcome of indifference. (44)

The words "assault," "indifference," and "patronizing" demonstrate that the clerk is as selfish in his lovemaking as Tan Man is.

Tan Man's domination of Annie is further exemplified by his control of the sexual encounter. He is able to control Annie sexually, first because he is clearly more experienced than she is, and second because she dare not challenge his dominion. Ultimately, allowing Tan Man to satisfy his sexual urge results in the suppression of her own sexual desires. By presenting Annie as sexually subordinate to Tan Man, Brooks highlights a central component of the Persephone and Demeter myth—Annie, like Persephone, is powerless. Moreover, just as the ancient writers give us no impression of Persephone's verbal response to Hades' attack, Brooks also illumines Persephone's silenced state.

While it is possible that Annie's virginal innocence explains her silence, or inability to express her own sexual desires, others offer a different reading of her silence. Claudia Tate's commentary on social myths concerning Black women's sexuality suggests that Annie's silence is calculated. Tate maintains that Annie has bought into a specific moral code of conduct dictating that women are to be sexually passive, coy, and silent. Annie's "will has been rendered inactive by conventional codes of decorum [. . . .] flattening and silencing her displeasure are the ways in which she responds to the circumstances of her life" (148). Rather than express her real sexual desires, she pretends to be overwhelmed by Tan Man's virility. Like Sappho Clark of Pauline Hopkins' *Contending Forces* discussed in Chapter 2, Annie is silenced because she also falls prey to adopting a White Western hegemonic discourse of Black female sexuality. This contrasts the ancient Persephone who is muzzled by the classical writers who omit her perspective. In "The Anniad" Annie is silenced by virtue of her sexual immaturity and cultural standards of decorum. Annie is emblematic of the triple-silenced Black woman: her race, class, and gender account for her lack of voice and subordination.

Annie's silence not only reflects her marginal position in the society, but her silence also impacts on her own development in regards to the establishment of her sexual identity and self-empowerment. According to Martin, the pubescent teen's first sexual encounter can "have profound effects on feelings of agency and sexual subjectivity" (11).

In "The Anniad," after the sexual encounter, Annie is indeed different from the young girl presented before the sex act. This change in personality is significant because it connects Annie with Persephone. If we agree with Jaffar-Agha's contention that in the Persephone and Demeter myth rape "must be read as a metaphor for violent penetration of the psyche, a breaking of the psychological hymen that precipitates a transformation in consciousness" (146), we can regard Annie's sexual encounter as an emotional rape that transforms her from sexually immature virgin to demure matron.

In the archetypal myth, Persephone's epic descent into the underworld marks a journey of self-discovery. After Persephone physically descends into the underworld she undergoes an experience that is both traumatic and empowering. Separation from Demeter is painful at first, but the experience allows Persephone to mature and develop a new identity independent from her mother. In Helene Foley's translation of the *Homeric Hymn*, Hades tells Persephone that he has given her powers: "Do not be so sad and angry beyond the rest; in no way among immortals will I be an unsuitable spouse, myself a brother of Zeus. And when you are there, you will have power over all that lives and moves, and you will possess the greatest honors among the gods. . . . Thus he spoke and thoughtful Persephone rejoiced" (20).

Thus, the rape, or sexual initiation, that occurs while Persephone is in Hades marks a death and rebirth whereby Persephone is transformed from maiden, Kore, to Persephone [powerful] wife of Hades (Jaffar-Agha 49). In contrast to the myth, Annie does not physically plunge into the depths of hell, but she does embark on an emotional journey that is both traumatic and transforming.

Annie's figurative descent into the underworld begins while Tan Man is on the battlefield. In Tan Man's absence, Annie grieves and prays. She passively waits for his return in a "lowly room. / Which she makes a chapel of. / Where she genuflects to love. / All the prayerbooks in her eyes / Open soft as sacrifice / Or the dolour of a dove" (101). Here Annie's response to Tan Man's absence reveals her emotional dependency. To be fair, Annie is a new bride who is left alone while her husband fights in the war. But as Brooks observes in a 1951 editorial "Why Negro Women Leave Home," some women found war granted them freedom and independence:

> Many a woman who had never worked before went to work during the last war. She will never forget the good taste of financial independence. For the first time, perhaps, she was able to buy a pair of stockings without anticipating her husband's curses. If she went on working after the war she required her husband to treat her as a fellow laborer, deserving of his respect and tact. If she stopped working, she herself had a new respect for work she was doing at home,

and she still expected her husband to think of her as a cooperating human being. (28)

Unfortunately, Annie does not find the empowerment and independence of which Brooks writes in her essay. Instead, she passively waits in her lowly room worshipping the image of Tan Man.

While Annie is experiencing her emotional descent in her own inner hell in the underworld, Tan Man undergoes a hellish experience of his own as a solider fighting in World War II. Unlike the Persephone and Demeter myth, which centers primarily on female experiences of oppression, Brooks' text offers a social critique of how Black men are also victims of patriarchy. In her feminine epic, Brooks returns to conventions of the archetypal epic and incorporates the epic battlefield into the narrative. As in Homer, Brooks describes Tan Man's physical war—or voyage in battle—in epic proportions.

> Yet there was a drama, drought
> Scarleted about the brim
> Not with blood alone for him,
> Flood, with blossom in between
> Retch and wheeling the cold shout,
> Suffocation, with a green
> Moist sweet breath for mezzanine. (Stanza 17)

In contrast to earlier stanzas Tan Man on the battlefield is not the all-powerful paladin imagined by Annie. Instead he is as powerless as Annie is: "Tan man twitches: for long / Life was little as a sand / Little as an inch of song, / Little as the aching hand" (102). Feeling like a pawn in "this white and greater chess" (103), Tan Man realizes that as a Black man in White America, his life is insignificant. When Tan Man is relieved of his duty, he relinquishes what he realizes is a false sense of power: "With his helmet's final doff / Soldier lifts his power off" (103). Without the armor Tan Man feels "bare and chilly" and wishes to regain his power while he "shudders for his impotence." In aligning Tan Man's oppression with Annie's, Brooks presents a womanist discussion of patriarchal dominance.[8]

Tan Man tries to combat his feelings of inferiority and insignif-
icance by rejecting Annie for another woman. Tan Man's rejection
of Annie points to his own rejection of self. Similar to the character
Cholly, of Toni Morrison's *Bluest Eye*, who allows his insecurities to
lead to the victimization of his daughter, Tan Man finds that Annie's
offensive weakness reminds him of his own vulnerability. Tan Man
decides that Annie is not the kind of "socially constructed" virtuous woman he wants to be with: thinking of returning to Annie,
he remarks, "not that woman! (Not that room!) / Not that dusted
demi-gloom!) / Nothing limpid, nothing meek. / But a gorgeous
and gold shriek / With her tongue tucked in her cheek"(Brooks
104). Tan Man's rebuff leaves Annie emotionally distraught. She is
hurt by his rejection, not only because she faithfully awaited his
return, but also because he leaves her for a "maple banshee"—a
woman of a lighter complexion. Here the reference to the mistress's "maple" complexion adds a racial dimension to Brooks'
retelling of the Persephone and Demeter myth.[9]
     The issue of skin complexion and identity has long plagued the
black community. The intraracial politics concerning skin complexion developed during slavery when hierarchies based on skin
tone were first established. White skin denoted the highest form of
beauty that was unattainable to Blacks. In order to create divisions
between slaves, those who were lighter or biracial were afforded
privileges like working inside the plantation house; those who were
darker were relegated to the fields. Bi-racial slaves (descendents of
the slave master) were often educated and emancipated before
other slaves. They "maintained their elite position in the black
community for fifty years following emancipation by passing their
advantages on to their children and avoiding intermarriage with
darker blacks" (Keith and Herring 763–67). Darker Blacks resented
light-skinned Blacks. Those with darker complexions also bought
into the notion that their dark skin made them inferior and unat-
tractive. When Brooks published her poem in 1949, she proved that
the same hostility between dark- and light-skinned Blacks and the
rejection of dark skin continued in the twentieth century.
     Brooks' poem describes Annie as "sweet and chocolate." The
word "chocolate" refers to Annie's dark brown skin, which she

believes makes her less desirable than people with lighter complexions. Like other dark skin women of the African American community, Annie has been reared to accept the social and cultural myth that European standards of beauty (light skin and straight hair) are more favorable than dark skin and curly hair. In her autobiography, Brooks brings first-hand knowledge of Annie's insecurities about her skin complexion. Brooks records: "when I was a child, it did not occur to me even once, that the Black in which I was encased . . . would be considered, one day beautiful. . . . [T]o be socially successful, a little girl must be Bright (of skin). It was better if your hair was curly too . . . but Bright you marvelously *needed* to be" (qtd. in Collins 37). Annie's discontent with her features is recorded in stanza five when she angrily looks in the mirror at herself, "[a]t the unembroidered brown; / Printing bastard roses there; / Then emotionally aware / Of the Black and boisterous hair, / Taming all that anger down" (Brooks 100).[10] Annie rejects her "unembroidered brown" skin and unruly "Black and boisterous hair." Her preference for lighter skin is intimated in her attraction to Tan Man's "Tan" or light skin. Annie's chocolate skin tone leaves her insecure and threatened by the possibility that Tan Man might abandon her for a woman with a lighter complexion, which he does.

Critics like Betsy Erikkla have also noted the significance of skin complexion and beauty in the poem. She writes: "Annie's tamed down anger registers Brooks' own rage against an impossible ideal of white female beauty that is enforced by Black and white men alike" (203). Similar to the protagonist of Brooks' novella *Maud Martha*, who also grapples with internalized racism, Tan Man's rejection of Annie has implications for Annie's self-esteem and perception of self. In the essay "A Belief in Self Far Greater than Anyone's Disbelief," Tracy Robinson and Janie Ward note: "For the African American adolescent female, the ability to move beyond the internalization of racial denigration to an internalization of racial pride involves a process of confronting and rejecting oppressive negating evaluations of Blackness and femaleness, adopting instead a sense of self that is self-affirming and self-valuing" (91).

As Annie transitions from child to woman she fails initially to gain a sense of self that is redeeming. Constantly reliant on Tan Man for feelings of self-worth, she resumes her emotional spiral decent. Once again, the Demeter-Persephone myth comes closely into view as Annie experiences a death and rebirth that corresponds with the vegetative cycle of the earth. In the myth, each seasonal change is marked by Persephone's reunion with Demeter. In the springtime, when mother and daughter unite, the earth is fruitful. In the winter, when Persephone must return to Hades, the earth becomes barren. Annie's transformation begins in the winter. She "seeks for solaces in snow / In the crusted wintertime" (105), but she is unsuccessful. She searches for happiness in the spring and by the summer "Runs to summer gourmet fare / . . . Wanting richly not to care / That summer hoots at solitaire" (105). Autumn shows promise for Annie. She aligns herself with nature and "Runs to parks." As she sits in the park, she "Glances grayly and perceives / This November her true town: All's a falling falling down" (105). The pessimistic tone of this stanza is replaced by the optimism of the next passage, which shows Annie's transitional rebirth. Annie substitutes her grief and solitude for felicity and friendship. When Annie reunites with her friends, for the first time, we hear her voice when she cries, "I am bedecked with love!" (106). Finally Annie realizes the importance of self-love. Annie comes alive as she taps into creative pursuits that lie dormant in Tan Man's wake. Like the women described in Alice Walker's well-cited essay "In Search of Our Mother's Gardens," Annie finds creativity in the every day. She:

Twists to Plato, Aeschylus,
Seneca and Mimnermus,
Pliny Dionysius. . . .
Who remove from remarkable hosts
Of agonized and friendly ghosts. (106)
Tests forbidden taffeta.
Meteors encircle her.
Little lady who lost her twill,
Little lady who lost her fur
Shivers in her think hurrah,

Pirouettes to pleasant shrill
Appoggiatura with a skill. (106)

One should not overlook Brooks's deliberate inclusion of ancient classical scholars and artists as part of Annie's intellectual development and personal liberation. In some ways, Brooks' character Annie is reminiscent of Wheatley and Ray, and perhaps Brooks herself. Just as the classics allow women writers to create a space where they can imagine a reality different from the one in which they live, Annie can read the classics and escape to a world that is different from the oppressive one in which she lives.

By summer she has blossomed, and in the fall—like leaves on a tree—she has discarded the negative, old ways of thinking. Unfortunately, in the same way that Persephone's return to Demeter is temporary, Annie's transformation is short-lived. When Tan Man returns he interrupts Annie's self-development. Just as Demeter returns to her sullen state once Persephone leaves (thus signaling the death of vegetation and the return of winter), Tan Man's presence marks the end of Annie's newfound sense of self. She stops dancing until "no music plays at all" (107), the "Perfumes fly before the gust, / Colors shrivel in the dust, / and the petal velvet shies" (107).

Tan Man returns sick and begging for Annie's sympathy. Annie is outraged but, as the dutiful wife, takes him back. Here Annie becomes more like Demeter than Persephone, and similar to how Demeter plays nursemaid to Demophoön, Annie assumes the role of nurturer and nurses Tan Man back to health. Before long, Tan Man, like the inevitability of spring, returns to his old ways and, despite Annie's devotion, for the last time leaves her for a "caramel doll." Here we have an inversion of the traditional myth that features Persephone leaving Hades rather than Hades abandoning Persephone. Tan Man's betrayal is hurtful, but Annie is mature enough to know that heartache will not destroy her. The last stanza reflects that Annie has transformed from maiden to woman. Annie is now "tweaked and twenty-four." In contrast to the beginning of the poem where Annie was described "in the springtime of her pride," by the end "All [is] hay-colored that was green" (109). Just as Persephone experiences a cyclical death and rebirth, Annie also undergoes a symbolic death and rebirth. Annie's transition from a "green" naïve girl to an experienced "hay colored" woman, illustrates that she has survived the turmoil of puberty and she is a woman who is no longer lost in foolish, childish daydreams of romantic idealism.

> Think of almost thoroughly
> Derelict and dim and done.
> Stroking swallows from sweat.
> Fingering faint violet.
> Hugging old and Sunday sun.
> Kissing in her kitchenette
> The minuets of memory. (109)

The esoteric language and fantastic imagery of earlier stanzas is replaced with simplified language and an image of Annie reflecting on the past, a past grounded in reality.[11]

Stephen Behrendt argues that myth can be used as an effective means of addressing

> present issues, present crises, by removing them momentarily from the immediacy of what is current, by distancing them somewhat from the temporal reality of the audience's own personal, social, or political reference system. Thus insulated from the threatening "now-ness" of immediately topical discussion, individuals may publicly articulate feelings and fears that might otherwise be expressed only awkwardly and objectively, if at all. (23)

With "The Anniad," Brooks takes an abstract approach to discussing social issues relative to racial and sexual politics. The tumultuous relationship between Tan Man and Annie is more than just a revisionist myth about thwarted love. The poem raises questions about the power dynamics in Black male–female relationships and the disempowerment of Black women both sexually and verbally. Brooks's narrative also serves as a commentary on the social myth of marriage and romantic idealism. In the 1950s, women were expected to get married and assume the roles of wife and mother. Women like Annie learned to depend on men for economic and sexual well being. As Tate remarks, "Although marriage, in and of itself, is not described as a destructive force in the poem, it can become the site on which the fullness of a woman's evolving character and ambitions are sacrificed. In this manner, maturity and ambitions are often exchanged for 'domestic bliss'" (150). Ultimately, in "The Anniad," Brooks calls for women to recognize the danger of being co-opted by false notions of marriage and romance. She suggests that instead of investing emotionally in male partners women should first learn to love themselves.

Comparing Brooks' revision of the Persephone and Demeter myth to Wheatley's and Ray's appropriation of the Niobe story reveals that Brooks, like her predecessors, is attracted to feminine-centered myth because the mythic themes of patriarchal dominance and female silencing are universal and therefore adaptable to the African American woman's experience. In addition to being attracted to the universality of the Persephone and Demeter myth, Brooks is drawn to this myth in particular because she wanted a feminine archetypal story to serve as the framework for her recreation of the typical masculine epic. The Persephone and Demeter myth helps Brooks create a feminine epic showing how the journey through puberty is as heroic as the archetypal epic male's quest to find self.

Like Wheatley, Brooks has artistic as well as political motivations for classical revision. In an interview with Gloria Hull, Brooks admits that "when writing 'The Anniad,' she didn't have the best intentions and that she wrote the poem because 'I wanted to prove I could write well'" (qtd. in Hull 201). Although Brooks claims that she had something to prove, her mythic adaptation also related to her attempt to reach a broad audience. Brooks was rewarded for her effort. In 1949, she became the first African American to be awarded the Pulitzer Prize. In 1968 and 1985 respectively, Brooks was awarded the highest honor bestowed on any poet. First she was named Illinois's official poet laureate and later became the twenty-ninth and final appointment as Consultant in Poetry to the Library of Congress. As America's first African American laureate, Brooks held a powerful position in the society. She was the voice of the American people both Black and White. As noted in the previous chapter, in the eighteenth century the laureate was the most important literary authority in society. Similarly, in the twentieth century the laureateship is given to the person who most exemplifies this spokesperson. Critic William Stanford recognized Brooks' role as the nation's spokesperson: "Coming to Gwendolyn Brooks, we find a writer avowedly a spokesman, and in this sense a writer who 'looks in' to a group more than any of the earlier writers. Indulging a fancy to make a point, one could say that Gwendolyn Brooks writes in the confidence and momentum of a tradition that intends to be established" (26). As laureate, Brooks bridged the gap of racial discordance that plagued American society. Her laureateship proved that Blacks were legitimate intellectuals and artists. Although Brooks was the voice of the American people, some felt she spoke for Whites only. Houston Baker, for example, felt that the "tense, complex, rhythmic verse" of Brooks' poetry was more appealing to White readers than to Black readers:

> The world of white arts and letters has pointed to her with pride; it has bestowed kudos and a Pulitzer Prize. The world of Black arts and letters had looked on with mixed emotion, and pride has been only one part of the mixture. There have been troubling questions about the poetry's essential "Blackness," her dedication to the melioration of the Black American's social conditions. . . . [W]hen one listens to the voice of today's Black-revolutionary consciousness, one often hears that Brooks's early poetry fits the white, middle-class patterns that Imamu Baraka has seen as characteristic of "Negro Literature." (22)

Haki Madhubuti agreed with Baker:

> *Annie Allen* (1949), important? Yes. Read by Blacks? No. *Annie Allen* more so than *A Street in Bronzeville* seems to have been written for Whites. For instance, 'The Anniad' requires unusual concentrated study. . . . *Annie Allen* is an important book. Gwendolyn Brooks's ability to use their language while using their ground rules explicitly shows that she far surpasses the best European-Americans had to offer. There is no doubt here. But in doing so,

she suffers by not communicating with the masses of Black people." (85–86)

Madhubuti makes a revealing statement when he suggests that, by mastering the master's language, Brooks sacrifices her ability to communicate with the Black reading audience. Unlike writers of the nineteenth century who would have been praised for their classical revisions, Brooks' classical renderings received a lukewarm reception. By the 1960s, the classics were considered outdated and counter to a black aesthetic.

Artists of the Black Arts Movement began focusing on art that divorced itself from European models and embraced an Afrocentric aesthetic. Larry Neal, for example, proposed that Black artists should "reject white ideas, and white ways of looking at the world" and create "a separate symbolism, mythology, critique and iconology" (183–86). Unfortunately, writers like Neal forget that the classics were part of an African aesthetic, from its origins in Terence. Margaret Walker was one writer who recognized that Blacks were part of a literary tradition that began before the literature of Greece and Rome. In her essay "Humanities with a Black Focus" (1972) Walker argues that "world literature begins with the ancient *Egyptian Book of the Dead*, which predates all epics of Homer and Virgil (100).[12] Walker, Brooks' contemporary, applauded Brooks for the artistic experimentation of poems in *Annie Allen*: "[C]oming after a long hue and cry of white writers that Negroes as poets lack form and intellectual acumen, Miss Brooks' careful craftsmanship and sensitive understanding reflected in *Annie Allen* are not only personal triumphs but a racial vindication" (130).While classical revisions like "The Anniad" prove that Brooks was heavily inspired by Eurocentric literary traditions, her poetry, as Joyce Anne Joyce argues, "emerges as African-centered in its persistent placement of Blacks as subjects rather than as objects, in its emphasis on communal human values and the integrity of forms (117). Brooks' engagement of "communal human values" universalizes the experiences presented in her poetry, therefore making her narratives appealing to readers both Black and White. In "Self-Criticism: The Third

Dimension in Culture," Alain Locke proposed that Black artists should commit to writing from a universal perspective because "in universalized particularity there has always resided the world's greatest and most enduring art" (59). With "The Anniad," and the next poem, "In the Mecca," Brooks creates the "enduring art" Locke speaks of.

The Mecca

The title poem of Brooks' 1968 "*In the Mecca*" returns to the epic genre and the mythic tale of Demeter and Persephone. As in "The Anniad," in "In the Mecca" the Demeter and Persephone myth is recast into the twentieth century, highlighting the African American female experience.[13] Once again Brooks feminizes the traditional epic. Here though, instead of focusing on the female heroine's emotional journey to find self, the narrative details a mother's physical sojourn to find her daughter. In this poem the archetypal story of Demeter's separation from Persephone and her journey to find her plays out as a dual narrative. The plot follows Sallie Smith's desperate search to find her daughter, Pepita, in the dark, forbidding halls of the Mecca, an impoverished South Side Chicago housing complex. As Sallie solicits help from her Meccan neighbors to aid in the search for Pepita, a second allegorized narrative is revealed: the Black community's search for escape and survival in the hells of urban America.

The protagonist of the narrative, Sallie Smith, assumes the role of Demeter. Whereas Demeter's duty is to nurture the earth, Sallie, mother of nine, takes on the role, not of cultivating the earth, but nurturing her brood. While Sallie and Demeter are similar in their nurturing and unyielding motherhood, social circumstances alter their commonality. Demeter is the all-powerful Goddess of Grain, the daughter of Cronus and Rhea. After Persephone has been abducted, she threatens to destroy the earth and avenge the gods for their role in her daughter's kidnapping. Conversely, Sallie, by virtue of her race, class, and gender, is powerless. Myth departs from reality as Brooks shows that in the real world a lower-class Black woman like Sallie can do nothing to retaliate against the abduction of her child. Where Demeter can risk the earth's destruction, Sallie can only hope for the protection of her remaining eight children. Like the narrator in the concluding section of *Annie Allen's* "children of the poor" who asks, "What shall I give my children? Who are poor, / Who are adjudged leastwise of the land, Who are my sweetest lepers, who demand / No velvet and no velvety velour" (116), Sallie realizes that prayer and faith are the only available armor to combat her defenselessness. While Demeter and Sallie are diametrically opposed, their commonality resides not in their fighting abilities, but in their shared circumstance. Despite her ability to punish the earth for the gods' crime against her and her daughter, Demeter is as vulnerable as any other woman. Ultimately, Demeter can do nothing to protect Persephone from abduction and rape any more than Sallie can protect Pepita.

"In the Mecca" begins with a description of Sallie returning home from work, tired from her job as a domestic but once more ready to play her role of mother and homemaker. Upon entering her apartment, she goes straight to work helping her daughter prepare the meager meal of "hock of ham," yams, "and cornbread made with water" (410). The meal of ham hocks emphasizes the family's poverty and at the same time alludes to the Persephone and Demeter myth. According to Foley, pigs were often sacrificed as part of the Eleusinian Mysteries. As Sallie sits at her kitchen table her eyes survey the dingy kitchen and she thinks, "I want to decorate!" But what is that? A / pomade atop a sewage. An offense. / First comes correctness, *then* embellishment!" (410). Sallie wants more for her life but she knows that decorating a kitchen in a dilapidated slum is neither going to camouflage its dinginess nor expunge the frustration she experiences as a struggling, working-class mother of nine. In contrast to Annie, who is initially lost in hyperbolic daydreams of romance, Sallie faces reality.

In the Demeter and Persephone myth Demeter's prime responsibility is to create and sustain life on earth. Brooks' protagonist is also armed with the task of providing a nurturing environment, but unlike Demeter, Sallie fails to produce a healthy crop. With the exception of Pepita, all of her children—Yvonne, Cap, Casey, Melodie Mary, Thomas Earl, Tennessee, Emmett, and Briggs—are broken spirits who have adopted a pessimistic, jaded outlook on life. These children harbor a deep-rooted contempt for their impoverished and inopportune lives leading to the projection of their hatred toward those who enjoy basic comforts. They hate: "sewn suburbs; / hate everything combed and strong; hate people who have balls, dolls, mittens and dimity frocks and trains / and boxing gloves, picture books, bonnets for Easter. Lace handkerchief owners are enemies of Smithkind" (412). As we read on, we learn it is not only the children who resent those more fortunate than themselves, Sallie also finds herself envious of the White middle-class family for whom she works:

> Mrs. Sallie
> evokes and loves and loathes a pink-lit image
> of the toy child. Her Lady's.
> Her Lady's pink convulsion, toy-child dances
> in stiff wide pink through Mrs. Sallie. Stiff pink is
> on toy-child's poverty of cream
> under a shiny tended warp of gold.
> What shiny tended gold is an aubade
> for toy-child's head! Has ribbons too!
> Ribbons. Not Woolworth cotton comedy,
> not rubber band, not string. . . .
> "And that would be my baby be my baby. . . .
> And I would be my lady I my lady." (415)

It is while considering the privileges of her young ward and the simple luxuries afforded her (such as satin ribbons as hair ties as opposed to the rubber bands or string that she must use for her own daughters' hair), that Sallie sets aside her thoughts and "SUDDENLY, COUNTING NOSES . . . SEES NO PEPITA" (412). In one of the few times we hear Sallie's voice, loudly she exclaims: "WHERE PEPITA BE?" This question, responded to swiftly by her eight children "Ain seen er I ain seen er I ain seen er / Ain seen er I ain seen er I an seen er" (516), precipitates Sallie's search for Pepita through the Mecca building. In the Greco-Roman myth, Demeter's response to Persephone's abduction is frantic. Upon learning that Persephone is missing she descends into an emotional hell:

"[S]harp grief seized the mother's heart; she tore the headdress upon her ambrosial hair and threw her dark veil down from both her shoulders, and like a bird she darted over land and sea, searching" (Rice 27). For nine days she cries, does not bathe, and will not eat. She searches the earth looking for Persephone until it is revealed that Hades has taken her. Similar to Demeter, Sallie is equally distressed by Pepita's disappearance. But Brooks handles Sallie's response to the crisis less frantically. In contrast to Demeter, Sallie's initial response to Pepita's disappearance is panicked but not hysterical. Rather than focus on Sallie's emotional response to Pepita's abduction, Brooks concentrates on detailing the epic physical journey Sallie undertakes to find Pepita. Moreover, whereas the Demeter myth focuses on what the search for Persephone uncovers about Demeter herself, here in the Mecca, Sallie's search for Pepita reveals truths about her community and the society at large.

Sallie, along with her eight children, embark on their quest to find Pepita: "In twos! In threes! Knock knocking down the halls of the martyred halls" of the Mecca building. Karl Keréyni contends that in one Orphic text Demeter travels to hell to retrieve Persephone. Sallie and her children also descend into hell to look for Pepita, their journey invoking Dante's *Divine Comedy*. Sallie must navigate her way through the depths of hell and encounter a number of grotesque characters. Sallie's neighbors (deranged men and women, murderers, pimps, and hustlers) all become potential suspects in Pepita's abduction. We are introduced to Great-Uncle Beer who was a "joker gambler killer too" (428); Wezlyn, "the wandering woman, the woman who wanders the halls of the Mecca at night, in search of Lawrence and Love" (428); Insane Sophie who screams in the hallways; Mr. Kelly "who begs subtly from door to door, Gas Cady, the man who robbed J. Harrison's grave of mums and left the peony bush only because it was too big (said Mama)"; and many others (429). Like Sallie's children, the neighbors "aint seen" Pepita either, and as the narrator notes, few care about her disappearance. The neighbors have not seen Pepita because they are preoccupied with their own losses and hurts. While they have not seen Pepita, they *have* witnessed heartache, penitentiary walls, world wars, poverty, and haunting horrors. In some sense Brooks' description of these emotionally bankrupt people brings to mind the soulless state of the characters portrayed in T. S. Eliot's "The Wasteland."[14]

Eliot's "The Wasteland" is a commentary on the fall of Europe, specifically London, after World War I. Eliot describes post-WWI London as an "unreal city" inhabited by men and women who had been "undone" by death. The Londoners described in his wasteland are lost souls trying to survive in a city bereft of hope and life. Brooks recasts the European wasteland into a 1950s Chicago tenement building detailing the despair of the inhabitants. Before addressing the soulless state of the inhabitants of the Mecca, it is first important to describe the historical significance of the Mecca in post-Depression era Chicago. The Mecca was not a place born out of Brooks' imagination for she had first-hand knowledge of the building. In her autobiography, she reports working in the building as a clerk. At the turn of the century, the Mecca was a significant luxury apartment complex that, like Europe before the war, symbolized wealth and luxury. As the prelude of Brooks' poem details, the building was "constructed as an apartment building in 1891, a splendid palace, a showplace of Chicago" (404). The Mecca building represented the promise of the development of North America. It gave those who were wealthy the opportunity to participate in the mythology of an American dream. But when the nation was temporarily derailed by the Depression, the building deteriorated along with the dream.

After the Depression, the building was abandoned and taken over by poor Blacks. Within fifty years the Mecca transformed from idyllic haven to blighted squalor. Urban decay and poverty contributed to the corrosion of the building and its subsequent razing in 1952. In a 1950 article, "The Strangest Place in Chicago," John Bartlow Martin described the Mecca as "a great gray hulk of brick, four stories high, topped by an ungainly smokestack, ancient and enormous, filling half the block north of Thirty-fourth Street between State and Dearborn. . . . The Mecca Building is U-shaped. The dirt courtyard is littered with newspapers and tin cans, milk cartons and broken glass" (404). While Martin chronicles the rise and fall of the Mecca, his description could relate to any other slum tenement in America. As Arthur P. Davis maintains, the Mecca is really "a microcosm of the ghettos of all the Northern cities. Its blight, never stated, but implied, is the blight that comes from being Black and poor" (101).

In 1968 when Brooks published "In the Mecca," her poem became part of a larger emerging discourse about poverty in the United States. Byron Lander notes that it was not until 1964, when president Lydon Baines Johnson delivered his State of the Union address, that poverty became an issue discussed in the political arena: "Previous to [the speech] most Americans believed the New Deal and World War II had ended the problem of poverty as a major national problem" (514). Four years after Johnson's speech, as Brooks' poem illumines, poverty remained a national problem that actually grew worse in the Black community. High crime rates, increasing unemployment, the Vietnam War, and racial violence paralyzed the Black community.

The historical details about the Mecca building's fall from glory helps further connect Brooks' poem to the Demeter and Persephone myth. When Demeter neglects her duty as nurturer of the soil, the earth becomes barren and the crops do not yield—subsequently threatening mankind's existence. The same is true in Brooks' poem; society neglects those who inhabit places like the Mecca and as a result these communities foster death and destruction. Also, taking into account Martin's description of the Mecca as a place of "concrete streets, brick building walls, Black steel viaducts" (404), we are reminded that in the urban landscape vegetation competes to stay alive amidst the machinery of industrialization. In the poem, this death of vegetation is illustrated when Sallie and her children knock on doors behind which "many flowers start, choke, reach up, want help, get it, do not get it, rally, bloom, or die on the wasting vine" (417). The flowers in these homes cannot flourish in an environment that is not life-affirming for plants and human life.

A land bereft of vitality cannot nurture the souls of its inhabitants. Thus in "The Mecca," the characters personify the living dead. The sixtyish sisters, for example, are "the twins with the floured faces, / who dress in long stiff blackness, / who exit stiffly together and enter together stiffly" (430), mourning either the passing of their loved ones or preparing for preeminent deaths. These women, although they are alive, are ready to pass into the next world. Portraying characters that are both living and dead once again relates Brooks' narrative to the Persephone and Demeter myth. In the spring, when Persephone emerges from hell, she is alive, but in the fall, when she descends into hell, she dies. Ultimately, her existence is a perpetual cycle of life and death.

In the archetypal myth, Demeter's search for Persephone is an individual quest. Conversely, in Brooks' poem, Sallie's search for Persephone is a symbolic communal search for self.[15] As Sallie searches her tenement building the text reveals a second narrative: the Black community's loss and search for communal values. When Sallie questions her neighbors about Pepita's disappearance, she learns that her neighbors have lost things too and like her they are searching to find them. When Sallie poses the question "Where is Pepita?" almost all of her neighbors respond with the same reply, "ain't seen her." Gayle Jones suggests that when Sallie's neighbors claim they have not seen Pepita they are really "answering the question of where they themselves are in reference to their world past and present (and anticipated)" (200). These neighbors do not know where Pepita is neither do they know their own standing in the world, they are as lost as Pepita. Although the neighbors cannot tell Sallie how to find Pepita, they can tell Sallie what they have seen and experienced in their own lives. Gram, for example, has not seen Pepita, but she does remember the horrors of slavery:

I ain seen no Pepita. But
I remember our cabin. The floor was dirt.
And something crawled in it. That is the thought
Stays in my mind. . . .
Pern and me and all,
We had no beds. Some slaves had beds of hay
Or straw, with cover-cloth. We six-uns curled
In corners of dirt, and closed our eyes,
And went to sleep. (417)

Gram's account is coupled with Loam Norton's remembrance of the Jews who were forsaken by God during the Holocaust: "Although he has not seen Pepita, Loam Norton considers 'Belsen and Dachau, / regrets all unkindness and harms. / . . . Anointings were of lice. Blood was the spillage of cups. / Goodness and mercy should follow them / all the days of their death'" (417–18).

Like many other characters in the poem, Gram and Loam are locked into memory of an oppressive past that impedes on their ability to move forward into a present life devoid of despair. While Gram and Loam are preoccupied with the past, others are focused on escaping from the bleakness of their present lives. However, the historical legacy of political and economic oppression and disempowerment makes it difficult for those in the Mecca to alter and escape their present circumstance and secure the most basic virtues in life. For those who are unable to physically escape from their present, others find refuge in books, religion, or even daydreams. The character Dakara escapes into the pages of *Vogue* magazine, St. Julia Jones keeps her eyes on the Lord, and Alfred loses himself in books and African politics. The Prophet Williams offers the Meccan inhabitants their best chance of escaping from their present. Williams' potions and readings give temporary relief from the bleakness of life. He "will give you trading stamps and kisses, / or a cigar. / One visit will convince you. / Lucky days / and Lucky Hands. Lifts you / From Sorrow and Shadows. Heals the body" (426). Williams' remedies and promises of redemption are, of course, only temporary.

The police finally aid Sallie's search for Pepita. The officers, though, are no more helpful than the neighbors. In fact, they treat Sallie as a potential suspect: "The Law arrives—and does not quickly go / to fetch a Female of the Negro Race. A lariat of questions" (420–21). The police officers' slow response to the news that "a female of the Negro race" has been abducted suggests that Pepita's race and gender make her insignificant to the police officers. Until this point in the poem Sallie has been relatively calm. Soon the realization of Pepita's abduction sets in and she becomes more like the mythic Demeter who "tore her ruffled hair and beat her breast" (Melville 113). Sallie "screams and wants her baby,

Wants her baby, / and wants her baby wants her baby" (421). Any hope of Pepita's return is abandoned when Aunt Dill details the recent rape and abduction of another young girl:

"Little gal got
raped and choked to death last week. Her gingham
was tied around her neck and it was red
but had been green before with pearls and dots
of rhinestone on the collar, and her tongue
was hanging out (a little to the side);
her eye was all a-pop, one was; was one
all gone. Part of her little nose was gone
(bit off, the Officer said). The Officer said
that something not quite right been done that girl." (421)

Aunt Dill's gruesome account foreshadows Pepita's death and underscores the fact that Pepita is one of many young girls who has been subjected to rape and murder. In both the *Homeric Hymn* and the *Metamorphoses* Persephone and Demeter myth, the reunion between mother and daughter is crucial. Once Demeter reunites with Persephone, order in the universe is restored. Demeter gives humankind the gift of grain and passes on her sacred rites. Here, as the opening stanza foreshadowed, there is no happy ending, "the fair fables fall" (407). When Sallie finally finds Pepita she is dead under Jamaican Edwards' bed: "Beneath his cot / a little woman lies in dust with roaches" (433). Brooks' reworking of the Persephone and Demeter myth contrasts with Ovid's classical version to show life as it truly is: each day children are raped and abducted and the mothers who search for their children do not find them alive.

At the end of the poem, though we do not see mother and daughter reunited, we are given the opportunity finally to see Pepita. Despite her social circumstance Pepita lived with optimism and imagination. "I touch"—she said once—"petals of a rose. / A silky feeling through me goes!" (433). Pepita's recollection of touching the rose relates to Persephone's thrill of seeing and touching the narcissus flower. Her admiration for the rose petal also shows that in contrast to her siblings or her neighbors, even in the midst of her dull life, she knew how to appreciate life's small gifts. Finally, Brooks draws upon the mythic archetype to show that, like Persephone, Pepita's character is symbolic of death and rebirth. In the Demeter and Persephone myth Persephone's life is sacrificed for mankind. In "In the Mecca" Pepita's life is also sacrificed, here for the community rather than mankind. Pepita's death is a reminder to the Black community that despite their circumstances they must return to communal values that uphold the notion that it takes a village to raise a child. What we see in the poem is that Jamaican Edwards rapes and murders Pepita because either the neighbors are unaware that he abducts Pepita or they are so numbed by their own losses that they assume an attitude of indifference. Brooks suggests that this kind of communal neglect must be replaced with communal responsibility. The concluding stanza reveals that Pepita's death actually symbolizes renewed hope for the community:

> She whose little stomach fought the world had
> wriggled, like a robin!
> Odd were the little wrigglings
> and the chopped chirpings oddly rising. (433)

Like the robin, which is synonymous with the beginning of spring, Pepita, whose name means seed, also represents new life. Through her struggle to remain alive, Pepita showed the community that even though racial and social circumstances accounted for their hellish, death-like existence, they could not give up on life. Pepita's spirit of optimism was consistent with the attitude of hope expressed by many in the Black community during the 1960s. Political and social movements such as the Black power movement pointed to the possibility that the Black community could be resurrected.

Almost twenty years after the publication of "The Anniad," Brooks once again rewrites the Persephone and Demeter myth as a Black feminine epic. In her second rewriting of the myth, Brooks expands her previous discussion about sexist oppression into a new debate concerning the intersecting oppressions of Black women's race, gender, and class. Through her characterization of Demeter's heroic quest to find her daughter, Brooks reveals that in the 1960s Black women continued to face the same hardships Brooks wrote about in "The Anniad." And in contrast to "The Anniad," which focused on the individual heroic feat of puberty and idealized romance, in "In the Mecca" Brooks fuses classical myth with urban reality to spotlight the collective failures of the Black community and American society. Brooks suggests that the breakdown of the Black community is a direct result of racial and social inequality. Situating her narrative in a building that was once a mythological utopia, Brooks highlights the futility of American dream.

The Destruction and Reconstruction of Classical and Cultural Myth in Toni Morrison's *Song of Solomon, Beloved,* and *The Bluest Eye*

African American women writers are constantly drawn to the Persephone and Demeter myth because the mythic themes of patriarchal dominance and female sexual oppression remain central to the Black female experience. In *The Bluest Eye* Toni Morrison's recreation of the mythic narrative also highlights the theme of Black female victimization. But rather than focusing on the physical abuse of the Persephone character, Morrison, like Brooks, underscores the significance of examining the psychological trauma experienced by young Black girls. In "The Anniad" Annie's insecurities about her skin tone contribute to her emotional crises and Tan Man's domination. Morrison's intertextual revision of "The Anniad" extends Brooks' discussion of internalized racism and reveals that young girls who reject their Blackness have been psychologically raped and abused by White society's promotion of an unattainable white aesthetic.

Through the story of Pecola Breedlove, Morrison not only uncovers how the white aesthetic is perpetuated but also explores the psychological impact of this Eurocentric value. In the narrative Pecola's psychological trauma occurs as a result of familial- and communal-bred internalized racism. Constant emotional and physical abuse from family and members of the community, who project their own frustrations with poverty and self-hatred on to Pecola, lead Pecola to believe that if she had blue eyes she would be accepted and loved by her family and society at large. As Morrison chronicles each emotional and physical assault heaped upon Pecola, she encourages us not only to identify with Pecola's victimization, and also recognize our role in the destruction of the Pecolas of the world.

During the 1960s and 1970s a number of women (Ann Sexton, Audre Lorde, Alice Walker) began revising Western classical myths. Alicia Ostriker contends that women's revisionist mythmaking in the 1960s were corrective revisions "of representations of what women find divine and demonic in themselves; they are retrieved images of what women have collectively and historically suffered; in some cases they are instructions for survival" (318). In this vein, for Morrison, revising myths is about stripping myths down to find new ways of interrogating them. While the main focus of this chapter is on Morrison's reworking of the Persephone and Demeter myth in the *Bluest Eye*, this chapter also explores Morrison's use of myth in other novels such as *Song of Solomon* (1977), which borrows from the Daedalus and Icarus myth, and the celebrated neo-slave narrative *Beloved* (1987), which evokes Euripides' *Medea*. Morrison's repeated allusion to mythic characters and employment of mythic themes evidences her obvious intrigue with classical mythology and strong interest in African and African American mythos. Morrison's frequent appropriation of Western, African, and African American mythology grows out of her belief that all of these mythologies reflect the universality of human experience.

Morrison's interest in mythology developed when she was a young child growing up in Lorain, Ohio. In an interview with Kathy Neustadt, Morrison recounted hearing elders in the community share folktales. Folklore for Morrison became part of an informal education that offered an alternate "way of looking at the world that was not only different than what we learned about in school, it was coming through another sense" (*Neustadt* 90). The idea of using myth to view the world from an "alternate" reality inspired Morrison to use stories from the mythic world to explain events in modern day reality. For Morrison myth is an invaluable part of our cultural heritage. She laments that contemporary society no longer regards mythology as culturally relevant: "Words like 'lore' and 'mythology' and 'folktale' have very little currency in most contemporary literature. People scorn it as discredited information held by discredited people. There's supposed to be some kind of knowledge that is more viable, more objective, and more scientific. I don't want to disregard that mythology because it does not meet the credentials of this particular decade or century. I want to take it head on and look at it" (*Neustadt* 113).

With revisions of mythical stories like Persephone and Demeter or Medea, for example, Morrison proves that myth and folklore remain pertinent because even in our post-modern technological world, stories about rape, incest, and infanticide resonate with our reality. The 1996 murder of child pageant performer Jon Benet Ramsey, as well as Andrea Yates' 2001 murder of her five children, are contemporary versions of the mythical stories of infanticide and child abduction and murder recorded in classical mythology. Like the Greco-Roman storytellers and African Griots before her, Morrison forces us to confront the horrors of life, not in the realm of the fantastic, but in the discomfort of our reality. Essentially, for Morrison myth is what Marilyn Mobley describes as a "usable past" from which to create contemporary narratives based on perennial themes addressed by the ancients.[1]

In the early sixties, when Morrison began crafting *The Bluest Eye*, and as demonstrated in the previous chapter, most Black artists, especially those of the Black Arts Movement, regarded the classics as antithetical to a Black aesthetic ideology. In the introduction to *19 Necromancers From Now* (1970), Ishmael Reed expresses the sentiment of Black Arts Movement writers who scorned Western European literary constructs: "The history of Afro-American literature is abundant with examples of writers using other people's literary machinery and mythology in their work. W. E. B. Du Bois, in some of his writing, is almost embarrassing in his use of White classical references. . . . Black writers . . . have been neo-classicists,

Marxists, existentialists, and infected by every Western disease available" (qtd. in Buschendorf 73).

While Reed regards the appropriation of classical narratives as a compromise to Black art, Morrison proves that she can write novels that draw from classical narratives and still produce texts grounded in a Black aesthetic. In fact, as noted in the introduction, Morrison, like Wheatley before her, claims ownership of the classics as her rightful heritage. In "Unspeakable Things Unspoken" Morrison references the research of scholars like Ivan Van Sertima and Martin Bernal who expose the African contribution to Western civilization. Drawing from Sertima's and Bernal's research, Morrison maintains that it took "seventy years to eliminate Egypt as the cradle of civilization and its model and replace it with Greece. The triumph of that process was Greece lost its own origins and became itself original" (373). For Morrison, the classical tradition is entrenched in a Black aesthetic. Morrison also contends that when looking closely at Greek myth one can find parallels between the mythical world of the Greeks and the African American experience. Morrison views the exchange between the Greek chorus and the audience, for example, as tantamount to the call-and-response convention conveyed in the Black church and in jazz music. She expounds: "A large part of the satisfaction I have always received from reading Greek tragedy, for example, is in its similarity to Afro-American communal structures (the function of song and chorus, the heroic struggle between the claims of community and individual hubris) and African religion and philosophy. In other words, that is part of the reason it has quality for me—I feel intellectually at home there" (369).

Ultimately by establishing structural and thematic analogies between Greek myth and the African American vernacular tradition, Morrison illumines the universality of classical myth. Furthermore, as Rankine argues, "[r]ather than rejecting what has been perceived as a male hegemony (classical mythology), Morrison constructs her characters—male and female—out of inherited material" (108) that is accessible to Black readers.

African American and Greco-Roman mythology in *Song of Solomon*

Morrison is often ambivalent about her use of Greco-Roman myth. On one hand she makes blatant mythical allusions that are easily detectable. At the same time, though, she downplays the Western classical mythic elements in her narratives. Morrison occasionally undermines the significance of appropriating Western mythology because she wants to be clear that although structurally or thematically her narratives might be comparable with Greek myth, her texts are consciously rooted in an African American aesthetic. When reflecting upon the flying motif in *Song of Solomon* she clarifies her use of myth: "If it means Icarus to some readers, fine; I want to take credit for that. But my meaning is specific: it is about Black people who could fly (*Neustadt* 122). Even though Morrison explains that the flying motif in *Song of Solomon* is drawn from African and African American folklore, most readers of *Song of Solomon*, especially those who have received a traditional Western education, immediately relate Morrison's invocation of the flying/freedom motif with the Greek story of *Daedalus and Icarus*—and perhaps even Phaeton.[2] Ovid's account of the Greco-Roman myth reports that King Minos of Crete had imprisoned Daedalus and Icarus. Daedalus devises a plan for escape by fashioning wings from thread, feathers, and wax. Before the escape, Daedalus cautions Icarus: "To fly a middle course, lest if you sink / Too low the waves may weight on your feathers; if too high, the heat may burn them. Fly half-way between the two" (Ovid 177).

Once Icarus takes flight he becomes intoxicated with the feeling of freedom. Ignoring Daedalus' warning, Icarus flies too close to the sun and melts the wax on his wings resulting in his descent from the air into the water below where he dies. While many readers of *Song of Solomon* might associate the flying motif as an allusion to Daedalus and Icarus, Morrison demonstrates that the flying/freedom trope is as much African and African American as it is Greek.[3] Rankine argues, "if African American folklore is privileged in the novel, this is the case because Morrison is a Black

author; her personal experiences and cultural memory take prece-
dent over any notion of a western heritage. Yet similar to classical
authors like Euripides and Seneca, she works with received motifs
and symbols" (110). *Song of Solomon* recounts the African
American mythic belief that Africans could fly. Morrison records
that as a child she grew up hearing folkloric tales about Black people who could fly: "That was always part of my life; flying was one
of our gifts . . . people used to talk about it, it's in the spirituals and
gospels. Perhaps it was wishful thinking—escape, death and all
that. But suppose it wasn't. What might it mean?" (*Neustadt* 122).
In *Song of Solomon* Morrison explores the possibility of transforming the myth into reality. *Song of Solomon* chronicles the
experiences of Milkman (Macon Dead III). Milkman is depicted
as the archetypal epic hero. Consistent with the definition of
the epic hero as defined in Joseph Campbell's *The Hero with a
Thousand Faces* (1949), Milkman experiences separation, initiation, and return. Like Oedipus, Ulysses, and other great heroes,
Milkman embarks on a physical journey away from home that
tests his mental and physical strength.

Flying is the central metaphor in *Song of Solomon*. The book
begins and concludes with characters that take flight. The first to
soar into the air is the insurance agent Robert Smith. Smith leaves
a brief suicide letter to his loved ones explaining, "At 3:00 p.m. on
Wednesday the 18th of February, 1931, I will take off from Mercy
and fly away on my own wings. Please forgive me. I loved you all"
(3). Here blue sheets replace Icarus' wings. As Smith prepares for
his departure from the roof of Mercy Hospital, the resident wine-
maker, Pilate (a pun on pilot), sings "O Sugarman done fly / O
Sugarman done gone" (6), a folksong about flying that Morrison
reworked for the narrative.[4] Smith's flight is a symbolic psychological ascent to freedom. Although Smith falls to the ground—blue
sheets are clearly an ineffective apparatus for flying—his leap signifies his freedom from his oppressive position as a Black man in a
racist society.

Milkman is the next to take flight. Like Icarus, as a child he is
intrigued with the notion of physically flying in the air, but learns
soon, "that only birds and airplanes could fly" (9). Parallel to

Smith, Milkman is disillusioned with his life. He rejects his father's ruthless capitalistic ambitions, resents his mother and sisters, and feels alienated from his community. Just as Daedalus and Icarus must escape from their confinement, Milkman desires to escape from his domestic life. As an adult Milkman remains fascinated with the idea of flying. Finally, when he travels to the South on family business, he is granted the opportunity to take flight. As he sits in the airplane, Milkman feels as free as Icarus: "In the air, away from real life, he felt free, but on the ground, when he talked to Guitar just before he left, the wings of all those other people's nightmares flapped in his face and constrained him" (220). Similar to Jason and the Argonauts who embark on a journey to capture the Golden Fleece, Milkman travels South to search for the family gold. Shortly after his journey begins, Milkman trades his hunt for gold for a quest to discover his ancestral roots. As Milkman travels southward he transforms into a Ulysses-like character and encounters many strange characters, including Circe from Homer's *Odyssey*. Much like Homer's Circe, the Circe in Morrison's narrative is also surrounded by vicious animals (in this case dogs instead of wolves and tigers). But whereas Homer's Circe is a crone or the witch who transforms Ulysses' men into pigs, Morrison "revises the mythic figure of Circe and the negative stereotype of the crone by transforming them both into a positive depiction of the crone as shaman" (Mobley 120–21). Instead of trying to turn Milkman into a pig, Morrison's Circe, like the wise sage Tiresas, guides Milkman to the truth.

As Milkman connects the pieces of his past he learns of the myth of his great grandfather Solomon who flew back to Africa. At first Milkman thinks the folktale is used as a metaphor for escaping from slavery but the character Susan Byrd (note that Byrd's last name is symbolic of flying) corrects him: "Oh, it's just foolishness, you know, but according to the story he wasn't running away. He was flying. He flew. You know, like a bird. Just stood up in the fields one day, ran up some hill, spun around a couple of times, and was lifted up in the air. Went right on back to wherever it was he came from" (322–23). Once again alluding to the Icarus-Daedalus myth,

Milkman's great grandfather, like Daedalus, makes his escape from imprisonment (slavery) by physically taking flight with his son. At the novel's conclusion, Milkman makes his return home. Congruous to Smith and his great grandfather, Milkman attempts to fly. In comparison with these men though, Milkman's leap is about understanding fully the significance of being free—free from the past, free from hurt, and free from fear. In the final pages of the novel Milkman has an altercation with his friend Guitar who mistakenly believes that Milkman betrayed him by hoarding the gold. As Milkman stands on Solomon's leap, the same place where his great grandfather made his departure, he knows his death is inevitable: if he remains on the rock Guitar will shoot him and if he jumps he will fall to his death. Milkman leaps into the air "without bending his knees. . . . For now he knew what Shalimar knew: If you surrendered to the air, you could *ride* it" (337). Similar to Icarus and the flying African, Milkman learns that he too can be spiritually liberated, even if only temporarily. *Song of Solomon* reads as a conflation of Greek myth and African American folklore. Morrison's use of myth in this novel reinforces the point that, "Western myth works in tandem with African and African American folklore to form the writer's broader imagination. That is, classicism enriches—and is enriched—by these correlatives" (Rankine xviii).

Morrison's Modern Medea

Along with *Song of Solomon*, the Pulitzer Prize winning novel *Beloved* is another work by Morrison readily associated with Greek myth. Morrison's novel about infanticide and maternal heroism has drawn parallels with Euripides' *Medea*. As with *Song of Solomon*, Morrison indicates that her narrative is inspired by African American mythology rather than by Western classical myth. *Beloved* is inspired in part by Margaret Garner, a slave woman who committed infanticide. Garner escaped Archibald Gaines' Kentucky plantation with her husband, in-laws, and four children. From Kentucky the fugitives traveled to the free state of Cincinnati, Ohio. The Garners' freedom was short-lived. Several hours after they arrived in Cincinnati their former owners captured them. Steven Weisenburger's historical account of Garner's life reveals that when Garner learned the slaveholders were coming to re-enslave her children she attempted infanticide. Garner managed partially to slit the throat and partially decapitate her two-year-old daughter and she injured both sons, "the one having received two gashes in its throat, the other a cut upon the head" (Weisenburger 73). Before Garner could execute her plan to kill the two remaining children, the other slaves stopped her. Garner's infanticide became a highly publicized and politicized subject for national debate. Pro-slavery advocates argued that Garner's brutal act of murder was evidence that slaves were unfit to govern themselves. Anti-slavery proponents on the other hand used Garner's case to appeal for the end of slavery. They reasoned that inhumane treatment drove the slaves to commit brutal acts like infanticide. Considering that infanticide was a common practice during slavery the public interest in Garner's infanticide was ironic.

Garner's infanticide became subject to national attention because in this case her slave owners witnessed the infanticide. Garner was eventually imprisoned and placed on trial. Garner was not charged for murder, but instead, according to Morrison, charged for the "*real* crime" (Neustadt 251) of escaping from slavery. Weisenburger records that tragically Garner was returned to her owner and was later sold and separated from her children. In *Beloved* Morrison sets out to re-imagine what precipitates Garner's decision to commit infanticide. Morrison poses relevant questions raised by Garner's case: how did slaves define motherhood, why does Garner commit infanticide, and what moral truths does Garner's tale provide?

For some during the nineteenth century, Garner became an anti-hero and rose to the status of a mythical figure. Weisenburger reports that Thomas Noble painted Garner "as a heroic, defiant mother confronting slave catchers over the outstretched bodies of her children, and the renowned Matthew Brady produced a lithograph of Niobe's infanticidal tableau" (8) entitled "The Modern Medea." Brady's "Modern Medea" established the connection between Garner and the mythic Medea.

As noted in Chapter 1, most Greco-Roman writers like Euripides and Ovid portray Medea as the jealous lover whose act of infanticide is motivated by her husband's betrayal and her pride. But Shelley Haley contends that in other versions of the narrative known to the Athenians and Corinthians, "Medea is not a furiously scorned woman who kills her children, but rather a queen priestess of divine ancestry with ambitions of immortality for her children by Jason (*Self Definition*179). Scholars like Haley and Lillian Corti regard Medea's actions as heroic. Corti, for example, points out that Medea had to kill her children because otherwise they would be in danger: "The survival of a Greek child was so much dependent on the willingness of a man to provide support that marriage was regarded as a 'yoke' to be born by the father" (65). Paul Roche's translation of Euripides' narrative supports Corti's assertion. When Medea plots to kill her sons she remarks that she has no intention of leaving her sons "in a hostile place for those who hate me to maltreat" (57). In this case, similar to Garner, Medea was trying to protect her sons. Since Jason had abandoned her, she was sure he would not protect their children.[5]

Haley contends that some readers do not identify with Medea as heroic because writers like Euripides portray her as the stereotypically scorned woman, thus skewing the reader's view. "Medea's characterizations and motivations belong to the traditionally male sphere. Given the patriarchal essence of the cultural norm, in Euripides' hands, Medea becomes an exemplum of the masculine ideal of the hero by the very assertion of her individuality" (184). Furthermore, Haley argues that Medea's actions should be considered heroic because, like male heroes such as Achilles or Odysseus, she challenges injustice and "kills for revenge and honor" (184). Sarah Pomery's study of infanticide in Grecian antiquity shows that during the classical period infanticide was pervasive, especially the murder of girl children. In Hellenistic Greece girls were undervalued and oftentimes mothers would abort, or upon delivery, kill their daughters. If we consider Pomery's findings, it would seem that Medea was derided because she had killed two male children. Although Medea is often referenced in regard to infanticide, she is not the only mythical mother to murder her children.

Procene, for example, also uses infanticide as retribution for her husband's crime. Ovid recounts that after learning that her husband Tereus has abducted, mutilated, and raped her sister Philomela, Procene seeks revenge. Procene mutilates her son's body and serves it to her husband for dinner. For Medea and Procene, spite is the impetus for murdering their children. In *Beloved* Morrison's protagonist is motivated by malice and love.

In Morrison's novel Medea is recast not as the malicious wife who mercilessly kills her children, but as a victimized slave who desperately tries to protect her brood. Morrison transforms Euripides' tale of a domestic dispute into a narrative that investigates the limitations of motherhood for slave women. The major difference between Morrison's modern day Medea and Euripides' ancient heroine is that Morrison's protagonist is enslaved and as a slave she did not have the same rights and responsibilities to motherhood as Medea. Unlike Sethe, Medea was free to rear and nurture her children without fear they would be taken from her. In Euripides' drama little emphasis is placed on Medea's maternal instinct. In contrast, throughout the entire narrative Sethe's maternal bond is reinforced. Morrison illustrates that motherhood was precarious for slave mothers; a slave woman could bear a child but this did not mean she owned her offspring. Legally, Sethe's children were the property of her slave owners. Sethe could never take for granted that her children would remain with her.[6] Sethe's approach to motherhood was unconventional. Despite the obvious limitations of mothering under an oppressive system that literally tried to regulate mind, body, and soul, Sethe took pride in her maternal responsibilities. While many slave women denied attachment to their children because they knew eventually their children would be separated from them, either on the auction block or by death, Sethe creates a strong emotional bond with her sons and daughters. Sethe's lover, Paul D, criticizes Sethe's unyielding "thick" love. But Sethe holds firm to her maternal bond, citing that, "Love is or it ain't. Thin love ain't love at all" (164). Sethe's "thick love" precipitates her act of infanticide.

Sethe's uncompromising love for her children motivates her decision to escape from the Sweet Home plantation. Clearly Sethe wanted freedom for herself, but she also wanted her children to be free of a life of enslavement and abuse. When Sethe escapes from the plantation she is nine months pregnant. Though she is tired Sethe is spurred on by her need to provide breast milk to her newly freed baby girl. Morrison's description of Sethe's heroic travel through the woods in immense pain with swollen bloody feet again reinforces Sethe's "thick love." Leaving Sweet Home gave Sethe the opportunity to care for her children without reserve: "I couldn't love em proper in Kentucky because they wasn't mine to love" (162). Once Sethe arrives in Cincinnati she is free to love her children without restraint.: "there wasn't nobody in the world I couldn't love if I wanted to" (162). By allowing us to witness Sethe's ordeal we can better sympathize with this contemporary Medea. It is difficult to have empathy for Euripides' Medea because throughout the drama Euripides characterizes Medea as a vindictive woman blinded by rage. Euripides recounts that Medea routinely uses her mystical powers to manipulate others and ruthlessly kills her brother and Jason's uncle, Pelias. In contrast, Morrison's reincarnation of the Medea figure is powerless. While at Sweet Home she was victimized sexually and physically. In addition to being sexually molested by White slave holders who defile her body by suckling her breast milk, she was also brutally beaten and disfigured. By stripping Sethe of mystical qualities, Morrison allows us to see a more vulnerable image of Medea.

Euripides' characterization of the mythic Medea demonstrates that pride (more than the desire to protect her sons) accounts for Medea's infanticide. Medea is hurt and humiliated by Jason's betrayal. She kills his sons because she does not want to leave them in an environment where they will be mistreated and because she knows this would be the surest way to make him feel the pain she suffers. In Roche's translation Medea says she kills her sons because "it is the supreme way to hurt my husband" (58). Unlike Euripides, Morrison places a greater emphasis on the fact that, in addition to seeking retaliation, Sethe was trying to protect her children from slavery. It is possible that Morrison could be drawing from Edith Hamilton's rendition of the myth. Hamilton mentions nothing about Medea killing the children out of malevolence. Rather, she shows that Medea believes she has no recourse but to kill her children so that they will be protected from a life of servitude and mistreatment. Just as in Hamilton's narrative, Morrison shows that Sethe's motivations are based on her maternal instinct. The narrator notes that upon seeing the slave catchers Sethe's first thought was to protect her children, put them outside the system of slavery. As the slave catchers approach she picks up an axe and succeeds in maiming her two-year-old "crawling already" daughter. She is stopped before she can wound another. Although Sethe is by far more concerned about shielding her children from a life of enslavement, congruous to Medea she believes killing her children is the ultimate reprisal. In contrast to Medea though, where Medea is certain that killing the children will wound Jason emotionally, Sethe knows that killing her children will hurt the slave owners financially. Also, killing her children (or at least attempting to) is an act of rebellion for she proves that although she has limited power, she can determine her children's fate.

In *Medea* when Jason learns that the children are dead he reminds Medea that she is also hurt by the action. He says, "You are in agony too: you share my broken life" (Roche 75). Jason also questions Medea's justification for killing their sons: "You think it right to murder just for a thwarted bed" (Roche 75). From Jason's perspective the murders were senseless because Medea's irrationality resulted in the loss of her children. In *Beloved*, Paul D also challenges Sethe's act of murder and, like Jason, he suggests Sethe did not gain anything by killing her children. He says, "It didn't work, did it? . . . How did it work? . . . There could have been a way. Some other way" (164–65). Just as in *Medea*, Sethe is clear that she made the correct decision—even though later she was estranged from three of her children: the two boys fled home and another, Beloved, haunts her. She tells Paul D that despite everything her actions were not in vain because she ensured her children would never live a life of enslavement. Sethe's infanticide is a paradoxical act of empowerment: through death her children become free. For both Sethe and Medea the decision to kill their children is bittersweet. Although the women are vindicated, their victory is at the expense of their future happiness. Both women are ousted from their communities, and they suffer criticism that undermines their humanity. Jason calls Medea an animal (tigress) and Paul D tells Sethe she has two feet not four. For both women the men stand in judgment of their actions.

For contemporary readers of *Beloved*, and probably for ancient audiences of Medea, infanticide raises questions about morality. Is it possible for a mother to justify infanticide? In Euripides' narrative Medea kills not because she loves her children, but because she despises her husband. Jason's infidelity and deceit are hurtful but his actions do not seem to warrant infanticide. Moreover, while in part Medea's decision is based upon the future welfare of her children, she is mostly motivated by revenge. So in Medea's case the infanticide might be perceived as immoral. Alternatively, it is more difficult to stand in judgment of Sethe; considering all that she suffered, murder seems almost justifiable. Morrison's rewriting of the Medea story offers a more valid reason for Medea's decision to kill her children. Furthermore, in Morrison's novel perhaps the bigger question is not the immorality of child murder but rather the immorality of slavery. By redirecting our attention from the protagonist to the society at large, Morrison encourages readers to consider how society often plays a role in determining mankind's immorality. In the next novel for discussion Morrison once again forces readers to confront moral truths about our neglect of our communities, our treatment of others, and our promotion of specific cultural values.

The Persephone Myth in *The Bluest Eye*

In *The Bluest Eye*, Morrison appropriates the Persephone and Demeter myth to discuss the sexual and psychological victimization of women. Rape becomes one of the central issues treated in Morrison's narrative. Rape, as Jaffar-Agha concludes, "does not necessarily entail a violent, physical penetration of our bodily integrity. However, it must constitute a violent intrusion into our psyche—an intrusion that transforms us irrevocably and one from which we cannot return" (145). In the novel the white aesthetic violates Pecola's mind and ultimately drives her insane. Pecola is raped twice: first, by the dominant culture's ideology of whiteness that denigrates Blackness and destroys her identity, and later, by her father. Rape and sexual molestation is a prevailing theme in classical mythology. Men whose motivations are capricious routinely rape female characters. Ovid's *Metamorphoses* recounts numerous stories of women who are violated by men who desire them. In today's world Apollo's pursuit of Daphne would be classified as sexual harassment (Daphne literally runs for her life to escape from Apollo's sexual advances). In another case Philomela is unable to defend herself from Tereus' brutal attack.

In addition to raping her Tereus also mutilates her tongue. Jove is perhaps the biggest predator of women's sexuality. A number of mythical stories in Ovid's metamorphosis recount his routine sexual abuse of women like Io, Callisto, and Europa. When *The Bluest Eye* was published it became part of an emerging discourse on sexual violence against women. The Black Arts movement and women's rights movements gave Black women greater publishing opportunities. More than ever before, Black women wrote about incest, rape, insanity, and Black male abuse of Black women. The subject of rape in particular became an important issue tackled by socially conscious Black women writers. Gayle Jones's *Eva's Man* (1976) and Ntozake Shange's *For Colored Girls who have Considered Suicide When the Rainbow is Enuf"* (1974) tell stories about young Black girls who are raped and sexually abused. In addition to writers, social activists also began speaking out against rape. Angela Davis records that during the seventies anti-rape movements emerged. Davis contends that in 1971 "the New York Radical Feminists organized a Rape Speak-Out, which, for the first time in history, provided large numbers of women with a forum in which to relate publicly their often terrifying individual experiences of rape" (*Cornerstones* 799). In the same year a rape crisis center was established in Berkeley California to provide support for rape victims, and Susan Griffin published "Rape: The All-American Crime." The novels, articles, and social activism involving rape discourse attest to the significance of the mythical story for contemporary audiences: rape and violence against women continue to plague women's lives.

Like other women in this study Morrison's goal is to present classical myth from the Black female perspective. So, whereas in the archetypal narrative Persephone's victimization is a result of her gender inferiority—Hades is able to abduct her because she is a helpless female—with Morrison's Persephone figure the intersecting oppressions of race, class, and gender contribute to her subversion. As a poor, Black child, Pecola lives in the margins of society. Pecola is an invisible stain on societies conscience; no one saves Pecola because, like Pepita of Brooks's "In the Mecca," no one cares about her well-being. And unlike the mythic Persephone or Pepita, Pecola has no Demeter figure to rescue her. Similar to "In the Mecca," Morrison's rendition of the Persephone-Demeter myth rewrites the Homeric and Ovidian fairytale ending because in the real world, poor, Black girls who are kidnapped and raped seldom return home.

As discussed earlier, when Brooks wrote "The Anniad" she had clear intentions of writing an epic. Where Brooks is explicit in her use of myth, Morrison often downplays the direct influence of the classics in her story. For example, Elizabeth T. Hayes recounts that when she asked Morrison if she intended to present her own version of the myth, Morrison said others had pointed out the similarities between her story and the Persephone and Demeter myth but "she had most assuredly not set out to create an image of the myth; that is not the way she writes. She allowed, however, that as a classics major, she was certainly familiar with the story, and she concluded that the myth had no doubt influenced her subconsciously on some level as she wrote *The Bluest Eye* (Hayes 173).[7] Morrison's vague retort to Hayes' inquiry raises several questions about authorial intention and audience response.

First, does Morrison intend for readers to relate the Persephone and Demeter myth to her narrative? Second, to what extent is it necessary to know that Morrison alludes to the myth, and if one recognizes that Morrison is appropriating the myth, does the meaning of the narrative change? And third, is the interpretation of the narrative compromised for readers who are not cognizant of a mythic influence present in the text? The title of Brooks' "The Anniad," the esoteric language, and the epic mode are constant reminders of Brooks' classical reference. And in *Mother Love* Rita Dove provides a prefatory statement explaining her appropriation of the Persephone-Demeter myth. In *The Bluest Eye* it is likely that only informed readers of the Persephone and Demeter myth might recognize the mythical allusions. Jacqueline de Weever points out that although Morrison follows the mythic plot, she constantly inverts the myth. The Demeter and Hades characters, for example, are antithetical to their mythic counterparts: Pecola's mother, Pauline, is anything but nurturing and her father, Cholly, lacks Hades' power. Northrup Frye contends that "archetypes of myth are most vividly experienced when they are not directly named, but when they are rediscovered in ordinary experience" (36). In *The Bluest Eye* the mythic proportions of Persephone and Demeter's experiences are rewritten into the average everyday experiences of urban life. Readers who acknowledge the Persephone and Demeter myth are part of what reader response theorist Stanley Fish defines as "interpretative communities."

Interpretive communities are shaped according to cultural factors such as age, race, class, gender, and religious affiliation, which influence how one reads and interprets texts. Readers who are familiar with the vegetation myth are likely to associate the seasonal changes in the narrative with Persephone's death and rebirth. Pecola's rite of passage, menstruation, and rape are also clear intertextual references to the myth. Signification of the myth is also reflected in the narrator's reference to the sterility of the land and Cholly's rape of Pecola is symbolic of Hades' rape of Persephone. Even with these clues, it is still possible that a reader familiar with the Persephone and Demeter myth could read *The Bluest Eye* and not detect that mythic elements are present. In some cases, readers might find other myths at play in *The Bluest Eye*. de Weever, for example, suggests that elements of the Oedipus myth are featured in *The Bluest Eye*: "Claude Lévi-Strauss finds a pattern in the myth, which also appears in Pecola's story, that of difficulties in walking straight. . . . The pattern exhibits a common feature, namely that the characters connected to the story of incest have difficulties in walking or they are lame" (108). Madonne Miner argues that Morrison's narrative can be read as a revision of the mythic story of Philomela. In Ovid's *Metamorphoses*, Philomela is raped and brutally mutilated by her brother-in-law Tereus, who cuts off her tongue. Miner concludes, "individual mythemes from Philomela's story appear, without distortion, in that of Pecola. First, in various ways and at various costs, the female figure suffers violation. . . . Second, with this violation a man asserts his presence as "master," "man-in-control," or "god" at the expense of a young woman who exists only as someone to "impress upon." Third, following the violation/assertion, this woman suffers an enclosure or undesirable transformation; she cowers, shrinks, or resides behind walls of madness. Finally, the most characteristic example of violation/assertion/destruction occurs within the family matrix" Cholly Breedlove rapes his own daughter, violating a standard code of familial relations (178-179).

de Weever's and Miner's interpretations of the texts prove the point that even with a knowledge of classical mythology, one could overlook Morrison's appropriation of the Persephone and Demeter story. For some readers, acknowledging that Morrison has experimented with the Persephone and Demeter myth, or other myths adds a richer dimension to the text and enhances their reading of the story. These readers have the opportunity to read Morrison's narrative alongside the mythic story and to see how she updates the myth to make it relevant for our time. Readers who fail to notice the mythic influence might not see how Western classical myth operates throughout the text, but they are still left with what is most important in the story: that the white aesthetic, internalized racism, and poverty lead to the emotional breakdown of young Black girls.

Morrison's reenactment of the Persephone-Demeter myth follows the same plot as most accounts of the mythic story. Pecola is abducted and raped and then undergoes a transformation of self that results in the creation of two distinct identities. Unlike Persephone who is physically kidnapped, Pecola's abduction is mental rather than physical. Pecola like many young Black girls becomes metaphorically abducted by the image of the white aesthetic. The opening pages of *The Bluest Eye* intimate that Black girls' minds are abducted by primary school texts such as the Dick and Jane primer. The Dick and Jane story, first published in the 1930s as a primer for school-age children, was designed to assist children with their reading development. In addition to aiding children in building their vocabulary and teaching them how to read, the story instilled in its readers the core values to be carried out by the average American family. In the Dick and Jane world the ideal American family is one with two well-behaved children who reside with their two very loving parents, a cat and dog, in a perfect home surrounded by a white picket fence. Morrison deconstructs this myth showing that a family so perfect exists for no one. Morrison presents the Dick and Jane story three times. Each successive telling of the story deviates from the first, thus reflecting the breakdown of this cultural myth and proving that those who attempt to duplicate this fictional family fail. The first rendering of the story is similar to the primer: "Here is the house. It is green and white. It has a red door" (i). This sentence conveys the order and structure of the Dick and Jane world. In Morrison's story the character Geraldine manages to create a household similar to what is presented in the primer. The second version of the story resembles the first, but structurally there are differences. The punctuation is missing and the paragraph reads as one long run-on sentence: "Here is the house it is green and white it has a red door it is very pretty here is the family mother father dick and jane live in the green-and-white house" (ii). The narrator's family, the Macteers, most closely mirrors this Dick and Jane world. Although the Macteer children are reared in a clean and comfortable home, the stability of their lives is marred by poverty and sexual abuse. The third rendition of the narrative is unintelligible, the words collide, and one cannot determine the beginning or ending of the paragraph:

Hereisthehouseitisgreenandwhiteithasareddooritisverypretty-hereisthefamilymotherfatherdickandjaneliveinthegreenandwhite-housetheyreveryhappyseejaneshehasareddressshewantstoplaywho willplaywithjane. (ii)

This is the world occupied by our tragic protagonist whose race and class make it impossible for her to become part of the Dick and Jane world. By the end of *The Bluest Eye* we see that just as Morrison's version of the Dick and Jane narrative fell apart, so too does the mental and emotional state of Pecola Breedlove.

Michael Awkward observes that the Dick and Jane myth is replaced with an alternative story reflective of impoverished Black life. The Breedlove household is dysfunctional. The father, Cholly, is an alcoholic and the mother, Pauline, is a religious zealot who physically and emotionally abuses Pecola. Pecola's home is devoid of love and fraught with abuse. The home itself is not a place of warmth or security. In fact the narrator tells us the Breedlove's dwelling is not a house at all but an abandoned store that once served as a pizzeria and later a bakery. Along with the Breedloves, other families in the narrative endure hardships that restrict them from entering into the Dick and Jane world.

In addition to introducing children to the Dick and Jane primer there are other subtle ways that the white aesthetic infiltrates Pecola's psyche. From candy wrappers, to movie stars and dolls Pecola cannot escape the culturally promoted image of blonde hair and blue eyes. As the narrator concedes bitterly: "the whole world had agreed that a blue-eyed, yellow-haired, pink-skinned doll was what every girl treasured. 'Here' they said, 'this is beautiful, and if you are on this day "worthy" you may have it.'" (20–21). The narrator Claudia tries to resist the white aesthetic. Claudia dismembers the white dolls by breaking the fingers and pushing out the eyes. Later she treats her White playmates in the same violent manner.[8] Claudia, however, is no match for the hegemonic beauty myth defined by Naomi Wolf as "a currency system" and "a culturally imposed physical standard, which is an expression of power relations" (12) where men reign superior. Unfortunately, as Claudia matures she fails to maintain her repudiation of whiteness and learns to love the white dolls as much as Pecola does.

Without the money to purchase skin-bleaching creams or to access colored contact lenses that allow today's Black girls to buy into the fantasy of whiteness, Pecola must find other ways to make the transformation from Black to White. Pecola's resolve is to digest whiteness. She achieves this by eating Mary Jane candy (the candy wrapper features a blonde blue-eyed girl) and frequently drinking from a cup that is stamped with a picture of child icon Shirley Temple. Morrison shows that Pecola's fascination with whiteness is not unique. Pecola's foster sister, Frieda, is also enamored with Shirley Temple. Claudia recounts that both Pecola and Frieda would have loving conversations about how "cu ute Shirley Temple was" (19). Clearly these girls have been held hostage by the white aesthetic. With so many images of White female beauty, Black girls find it difficult to affirm their own beauty; for as bell hooks contends, Black people are "bombarded in the mass media with images that suggest Blackness is not beautiful" (94). Although in contemporary society negative representations of Blackness prevail, hooks' observations are especially true for the 1940s. Where today children can find affirming images of Blackness in a number of children's books, during the 1940s Black children had to contend with *Little Black Sambo* (published at the turn of the century but still widely available during the 1930s and 1940s) a children's book depicting racist caricatures of Black children. The popular syndicated television show *The Little Rascals* also presented denigrating images of Black characters. The show took on the same stereotypical representations of Blackness that were perpetuated in White Minstrel shows. The Black characters in *Little Rascals* spoke in an unintelligible dialect, their skin was greased so as to appear shiny, and their eyes protruded from the sockets. Morrison's novel illustrates that the preoccupation with European standards of beauty is detrimental for Black girls like the protagonist and her friends because they can never escape the superiority of White beauty.

The novel's discussion of color consciousness is a familiar trope in African American women's writing. As noted, Brooks deals with this issue in "The Anniad," and in a later work, *Maud Martha*, Brooks explores fully the struggles of young Black girls who are denigrated not only by Whites, but also Blacks. In addition to Brooks, Dorothy West's *The Wedding* (1995) addresses the subject of colorism, as does Rita Dove's *Through the Ivory Gate* (1992). Morrison shows that while society is guilty of promoting the aesthetic, the African American community is also culpable. The favoritism toward girls with lighter complexions, such as Maureen Peal, reinforce to children with darker complexions that lighter skin affords one the privilege of respect and love.

After deconstructing the Dick and Jane myth Morrison turns her attention to reworking the Persephone and Demeter myth. Morrison's contemporary reworking of the Persephone and Demeter myth diverges from the Homeric and Ovidian narrative in significant ways. First, Morrison alters the sequence of the seasons. The *Homeric Hymn* opens in the springtime when the earth is fecund and the vegetation is ripe. Conversely, in the opening pages of *The Bluest Eye* the vibrant image of spring is replaced with the grayness of autumn. The narrator Claudia recalls the coldness of the autumn weather that brought on sickness and rough blankets. Morrison's change of seasonal cycles not only indicates the despondency of the characters, but the alteration is also "a sign that this text will turn upside down the 'standard' archetype" (Hayes 174).

Morrison's rearrangement of the seasons illustrates that order in the universe has been disrupted. Demeter's separation from her daughter causes her to neglect the land and creates discord on the earth. Here, as in "In the Mecca," Morrison suggests that a steady diet of poverty, self-hatred, and oppression results in an environment that cannot foster life. Maureen Peal, who is described as the "disrupter of seasons" (62), reinforces the chaotic nature of the character's lives. Maureen adds an uncharacteristic warmth to the winter imagery: "There was a hint of spring in her sloe green eyes, something summery in her complexion, and a rich autumn ripeness in her walk" (62). Maureen's association with spring and summer relate her to fertility and life. Her green eyes are representative of green plants budding in the spring and the "ripeness" of walk relates her to nature's harvest. Maureen possesses everything Pecola desires. She has fair skin, green eyes, and wealth. Although she is not White, she has light skin, which for Pecola is closer to White than she will ever be. Maureen is part of the idyllic White world that is juxtaposed against the painful Black world inhabited by Pecola and her friends. Throughout the narrative White and

Black are transformed into binaries of the upper and lower world. The home of the Fishers for whom Pecola's mother works, for example, is emblematic of the utopian White world.[9] The flowers that frame the house symbolize life as well as beauty. In addition, not only the exterior of the house but also the interior décor is blindingly white. The Fisher home is antithetical to the description of Pecola's storefront, which is totally devoid of color, similar to the absence of color that occurs in the fall once the flowers begin wilting. Pecola, throughout the narrative remains locked in the darkness of her reality. It is only when she eats the Mary Jane candy or visits her mother at the Fisher home that she can step out of her darkness.

One of the most significant alterations to the archetypal myth is Morrison's reconfiguration of the death-rebirth motif. Each time Persephone descends into hell or ascends back to earth she experiences a death and rebirth of her identity. On earth Persephone is Demeter's daughter and in hell she is the bride of Hades. Because Pecola remains in hell she does not experience a transformation of self that coincides with the different spaces she inhabits. However, Pecola does experience an emotional death and rebirth. Each time she is demonized by schoolmates, parents, and members of the community she experiences a symbolic death of her Black identity as she rejects her Blackness and renews her wish for blue eyes. Morrison's underworld is characterized in much the same way as the labyrinthian hell of Brooks' "In the Mecca." Just as Brooks portrays pimps, murderers, and the insane, Morrison features prostitutes, pedophiles, and rapists. Morrison's depiction of Pecola's permanent residence in hell is also consistent with Homer's portrayal of Persephone. Gantz notes that each time Persephone is referenced by Homer in the *Iliad* or the *Odyssey* she is featured "always in consort with Hades and the Underworld" (64).

Pecola is literally born into a hellish existence. Her domestic environment is toxic and her parents perpetuate an attitude of internalized racism that teaches Pecola that like her parents she is ugly. The narrator informs us, "[T]heir ugliness was unique. No one could have convinced them that they were not relentlessly and aggressively ugly" (38). The Breedlove's ugliness consumes and defines them: "It was as though some mysterious all-knowing master had given each one a cloak of ugliness to wear, and they had each accepted it without question. The master had said, 'You are ugly people.' They had looked about themselves and saw nothing to contradict the statement, saw, in fact, support for it leaning at them from every billboard, every movie, every glance.... And they took the ugliness in their hands, threw it as a mantle over them, and went about the world with it" (39).

The Breedlove's physical ugliness manifests itself through violent "ugly" behavior. Pauline and Cholly constantly fight and Pecola is routinely beaten without cause, mentally assaulted, and later sexually molested. Pecola thinks if she were White with blue eyes life would be different, she would be loved: "It had occurred to Pecola some time ago that if her eyes, those eyes that held the pictures, and knew the sights—if those eyes of hers were different, that is to say beautiful, she would be different.... If she looked different, beautiful, maybe Cholly would be different, and Mrs. Breedlove too. Maybe they'd say, 'Why look at pretty-eyed Pecola. We mustn't do bad things in front of those pretty eyes'" (46).

In this instance it is clear that Pecola's desire for blue eyes is about more than being deemed attractive; rather, blue eyes would alleviate the chaos in her life and grant her the love and acceptance she craves.

The maternal bond between mother and daughter is integral to the Persephone-Demeter myth, especially the *Homeric Hymn*. Foley states, "the mother-daughter relationship is central to the *Hymn*. The male characters serve as remote and marginal (though critical) catalysts to the action, while the narrative concentrates on the experience of female protagonists in a female world" (123). In the myth, Demeter's love for Persephone is unyielding. When Persephone is abducted her world is shattered; she does not eat or bathe. Likewise, while in hell Persephone grieves and also rejects food. In a major revision of Demeter and Persephone's relationship, Morrison presents a mother and daughter who are estranged. Pecola's detachment from Pauline is emphasized by her impersonal reference to Pauline as Ms. Breedlove. And where Demeter is personified as the ultimate nurturing and adoring mother, Pauline is cruel and abusive toward Pecola. Gloria Wade Gayles notes that African American women writers often characterize Black mothers as unaffectionate and callous because "the exigencies of racism and poverty in White America are sometimes so devastating that the mothers have neither time nor patience for affection" (10). So when Pauline learns that Cholly rapes Pecola, unlike the mythic Demeter, Pauline is not overcome with grief. Instead, Pauline leaves Pecola in a situation where she can be, and is eventually, assaulted again. Moreover, Pecola becomes a victim twice. According to Collins many Black women who are raped suffer a dual victimization as they are abused first, by their rapist and then "are victimized again by family members, community residents, and social institutions" (147) who question their role in the rape. In Morrison's text, when Cholly impregnates Pecola, it is not Cholly but Pecola who is vilified by women in the community who suggest that Pecola encouraged the rape:

"Well they ought to take her out of school."
"Ought to. She carry some of the blame."
"Oh, come on. She ain't but twelve or so."
"Yeah. But you never know. How come she didn't
fight him?"
"Maybe she did."
"Yeah? You never know." (189)

The function of the community in this text operates much the same way as the chorus in Greek tragedy. However, whereas traditionally the chorus serves as an objective commentator, the community stands in judgment of Pecola. Instead of the transition from death to life that Persephone experiences, Pecola remains in a cycle of death. With no Demeter character to save her, Pecola experiences repeated deaths that do not allow her to find liberation from her life in the underworld.

Pauline cannot protect Pecola from emotional abuse nor can she save her from the image of the white aesthetic because she, like Pecola, is also psychologically corrupted by the white aesthetic. The shared experiences of Pauline and Pecola once again links

Morrison's narrative to the archetypal myth. In the ancient myth, Demeter, like her daughter, is also raped. In some accounts Poseidon rapes her and in other versions she claims pirates rape her. Also, in ancient art and literature Persephone's and Demeter's identities are often merged into one identity. The two women's similar experiences of loss and their subsequent transformations present them as "separate-yet-one" (Carlson 23). In *The Bluest Eye*, Pecola relives her mother's experiences. As a young girl, Pauline, like Pecola feels alienated by members of the community. Pauline's Southern mannerisms, her inability to dress as well as other women, and her failure to apply cosmetics tastefully leave her open for ridicule. Pauline is hurt by the women's "goading glances and private snickers at her way of talking (saying 'chil'ren')" (188). Similar to Pecola's fascination with Shirley Temple, Pauline finds her salvation in the movie theater where she escapes to the fantasy of the White world. At the movies she learns to "assign" faces to categories "of absolute beauty" (122), with White faces, like actress Jean Harlow's, occupying the top of the scale.[10] When Pauline secures a job as a domestic she is able finally to leave behind the ugliness and Blackness of her own underworld reality and enter the Dick and Jane world. Pauline desires so much to become part of the order and normalcy of this White world that she neglects her own household as well as her own children in favor of her White charge. Pauline's surrogate motherhood is another play on the mythic theme. After Persephone has been abducted, Demeter becomes a nursemaid for Demophoön. Demophoön offers Demeter the ability to serve as a surrogate mother and subdue her grief. In an effort to make Demophoön immortal, "at night she would bury him like a brand in the fire's might" (qtd. Foley 14). In Morrison's novel Pauline cannot immortalize her charge, but she is able to rear this symbolic Shirley Temple figure as if she were her own daughter.

In addition to the Demeter character, Morrison also depicts a number of Hades-like male characters that engage in verbally or physically abusing Pecola. Each act of abuse is equally damaging.

The first act of abuse against Pecola occurs in autumn when Pecola goes to the store to buy candy. Analogous to the myth, before she is assaulted Pecola stops to admire flowers. Ironically, the flowers Pecola stops to admire are not the beautiful narcissus as in the myth, but dandelions. Here Morrison very clearly signifies on Brooks' *Maud Martha*. In this novel, the protagonist Maud Martha also believes that she is unfavored because of her skin tone and she finds comfort in the dandelion. The narrator of *Maud Martha* explains that Maud "liked the demure prettiness [of the dandelion] second to their everydayness; for in that latter quality she thought she saw a picture of herself and it was comforting to find that what was common could also be a flower" (Brooks 144). Like Maud, Pecola finds beauty in flowers she knows others discard as weeds: "Why, she wonders, do people call them weeds? She thought they were pretty" (47). For a moment Pecola defines beauty according to her own standards, but after going to the store the sentiment is lost. As Pecola enters the store, the owner Mr. Yacobowski, like Hades, appears from below. He "looms up over the counter" (48). To Pecola, Yacobowski is frightening, especially his "lumpy red hand" that "plops around in the glass casing like the agitated head of a chicken outraged by the loss of its body" (49). As Pecola points to the candy she wants to buy, Yacobowski displays his impatience. "Christ. Kantcha talk?" (49). Pecola nods in affirmation yet says nothing. Similar to other female characters, like Niobe or Annie, she is silenced and rendered powerless. Yacobowski does not verbally or physically assault Pecola, but his condescending treatment and unwillingness to acknowledge her presence leave Pecola feeling emotionally disempowered. Although he is an immigrant and has his own issues with marginalization, Yacobowski is a symbol of White male supremacy. Yacobowski's attitude of racial superiority is detected by Pecola who assumes the distaste in his eyes "must be for her, her Blackness (49). Miner reads Yacobowski's refusal to look at Pecola as a symbolic rape: "[M]ale denies presence to female. Pecola cannot defend herself against this denial" (185). Pecola leaves the store feeling "the inexplicable shame ebb" (50).

Morrison shows that in addition to White males, Black males are also guilty of victimizing Pecola. The next instance of assault against Pecola occurs in the second section, Winter. Pecola is invited into the home of playmate Jr. Where the archetypal Persephone is lured to hell by flowers, Pecola is seduced by the promise of a new kitten. Jr.'s home is dark and foreboding. Before entering, Pecola senses danger: "She hesitated there, afraid to follow him. The house looked dark," (89) but she follows him inside. As in the mythic story, before Pecola is attacked she is featured in the midst of vegetation. As Pecola surveys Jr.'s home she notices the "potted plants were on all the windowsills. A color picture of Jesus Christ hung on a wall with the prettiest paper flowers fastened on the frame. . . . There was even a rug on the floor, with enormous dark red flowers" (89). While absorbing the beauty of the flowers, Jr., like Hades, unexpectedly attacks her by throwing a cat in her face. The cat "claws her face and chest" before dropping to the floor. After throwing the cat, Jr. locks her in a dark room. Like Persephone, Pecola become imprisoned. Jr.'s assault on Pecola continues until his mother, Geraldine, comes home. Geraldine heaps more abuse upon Pecola; she calls her a Black bitch and tells her to leave her home. As with Yacobowski, Pecola leaves Geraldine's house with her "held her head down" (93) her confidence shaken.

While Pecola is most closely associated with the vegetation myth, others, like Frieda, also become emblematic Persephone figures. Similar to Annie Allen of "The Anniad," Frieda's fertility is indicated by her "two tiny breasts that like two fallen acorns, scattered a few faded rose leaves on her dress" (99) and by the "tiny bunches of wild roses" (98) imprinted on her dress. While Frieda's parents attend to their gardening, the friendly lodger Mr. Henry sexually molests Frieda by touching her underdeveloped breasts. As Frieda recounts details of the molestation, we learn that Mr. Henry is not the only pedophile in the neighborhood. When Claudia asks Frieda to describe how Mr. Henry touched her, Frieda explains that Mr. Henry did not "pick" at her like Soaphead Church, implying that Soaphead is also guilty of inappropriate sexual behavior. Thus Morrison intimates that, like the young girls featured in Greek myth, all young girls are subject to routine sexual abuse.

Toward the end of *The Bluest Eye* the mythical rape of Persephone is reenacted. Some accounts of the Persephone and Demeter myth suggest that Zeus consents to Hades' rape of Persephone. Gantz notes that in the Homeric Hymn "Hades snatches away his niece with the full permission of Zeus (and without that of Demeter) while she is gathering flowers (in particular the narcissus, grown by Gaia to abet the theft) in the company of the Okeanides in the Nysian Plain" (65).[11] Zeus and Hades' conspiracy to abduct, rape, and marry Persephone, without permission or input from mother or daughter, underscores the patriarchal role of the male characters. And while in the Homeric Hymn Zeus does not rape Persephone, his actions are as egregious as Hades' because, as her father, the man who is supposed to protect her, he allows her to be raped. Cholly's rape of Pecola suggests that Morrison's rendition of the myth likely follows the Orphic texts that recount Zeus' rape of Persephone.[12] The impetus for Cholly's act of rape is similar to Hades'. In the Ovidian myth Ovid reveals that Pluto's actions are motivated by love. After being pierced in the heart by one of Cupid's arrows, Pluto is immediately love-struck. When Cholly rapes Pecola, he is also driven by emotion. Cholly, returning home in a drunken stupor sees Pecola's helpless body at the sink. As he looks at his daughter, Cholly is filled with "revulsion, guilt, pity, then love" (161). At first Cholly wants to find a way to connect with Pecola, but he does not know how. As he thinks about how to console Pecola, first he entertains breaking her neck "tenderly." Once he realizes he can do nothing for her his compassion turns into hatred and then anger. Morrison's description of the rape is graphic. Unlike Brooks, she does not use metaphors or euphemisms to portray Cholly's sexual oppression of Pecola: "He wanted to fuck her—tenderly. But the tenderness would not hold. The tightness of her vagina was more than he could bear. . . . [T]he gigantic thrust he made into her then provoked the only sound she made— a hollow suck of air in the back of her throat. . . . [H]e was conscious of her wet soapy hands on his wrists. . . . Removing himself from her was so painful to him he cut it short and snatched his genitals out of the dry harbour of her vagina. She appeared to have fainted" (163). For some readers this passage is difficult to read. The strong language and depiction of Pecola's helplessness is painful. But Morrison's intention is to ensure that readers respond to the horror of the situation, to re-live it as Pecola experiences it. In this way we relate more closely to Pecola's victimization. In the *Homeric Hymn* Hades rapes Persephone because he can. Not only has he been granted approval from Zeus, but he takes for granted that he will not be challenged. And in the Orphic texts Zeus also uses his power to dominate Persephone. In versions where Hades rapes Persephone, Zeus exerts his power and instructs Hades to return Persephone to Demeter. In contrast to Hades and Zeus, Cholly is powerless. Morrison characterizes Cholly as a weak man who is as racially and economically oppressed as Pecola. As a young boy, two White men humiliate him by demanding that he engage in sexual activity with a young Black girl. The event leaves Cholly feeling powerless and at the same creates his feeling of hatred toward Black women. To be clear, Morrison does not mean for us to empathize with Cholly's own traumatic past. Instead, as Kimberly Drake argues, we are not meant to pity him as a "victim of society nor . . . condemn [him] as inhuman monsters, but . . . locate a space of identification somewhere between these two extremes (63). Although Cholly's act is heinous, after detailing all the other acts of violence against Pecola, Morrison seems to suggest that Cholly's sexual violation is no more damaging than the others. Moreover, rape, as Angela Davis concludes, "is part of a larger continuum of socially inflicted violence, which includes concerted, systematic violations of women's economic and political rights (798). Morrison's description of Cholly as a rapist is provocative because, as Davis and Collins note, the Black male has been stigmatized as the Black rapist. To counter this image of the sexually-deviant male, Morrison shows that the rape is not premeditated, that the act is actually motivated by empathy.

In the mythical story, after the rape Hades devises a plan to ensure that Persephone forever remains his queen of the underworld. He encourages Persephone to eat a pomegranate. Consuming the fruit binds Persephone to Hades for part of the year. Here, unlike the mythic Persephone, who in Ovid's version consumes seven pomegranate seeds, Pecola does not ingest seeds, but Cholly does plant his seed in her womb. Erich Neumann points out, "the redness of the pomegranate symbolizes the woman's womb, the abundance of seeds its fertility" (73). Claudia and Frieda plant seeds in the ground with the hope that their seeds will grow along with the baby in Pecola's body. However, Pecola's womb, like the earth is unproductive. Her baby dies and so do the seeds planted by Claudia and Frieda.

Also, as Awkward notes, "The planting of seeds serves to demonstrate not nature's harmony with humanity and the possibility of preserving (at least the memory of) life, but, rather, a barren earth's indifference to humanity's needs" (91). Pecola, like the seeds in her body, was never nurtured, and so she, like her baby and the seeds, dies.

At the end of the narrative, Pecola experiences a death and rebirth. After the rape she appeals to the local fortuneteller, Soaphead Church, for blue eyes. Just as Hades tricks Persephone and persuades her to eat the seeds, Soaphead deceives Pecola. He promises her that if she successfully carries out his directive she will be granted blue eyes. Pecola's task is to feed poisoned meat to a dog Soaphead loathes. Soaphead tells Pecola that if while eating the meat the dog behaves strangely she will receive her blue eyes. Pecola feeds the dog the poisoned meat. As Soaphead predicts, the dog begins choking, and his body is racked with spasms. Pecola watches in horror. Shortly after the event Pecola is granted blue eyes, but, as we learn, they come with a price: her new blue eyes are at the expense of her sanity. Anias Pratt asserts that in many women's narratives the archetypal "rebirth journey entails risk and psychological danger, as likely to lead to madness as to renewal. Reflecting this fact, fictional heroes often experience surreal images and symbols, disassociated fantasies, and chaotic noises that mimic clinical madness" (Pratt 142–43). At the end of Morrison's novel, Pecola's rebirth is symbolized by her schizophrenic state. Her dual personality is reflective of Persephone's split identities as Demeter's daughter and Hades' wife. Here, however, Pecola's split identity is psychological. Like Hopkins' Sappho Clark, discussed in Chapter 2, Pecola reinvents herself. She is no longer the ugly outcast; instead she has pretty blue eyes that make her the envy of the entire community, including her mother. Coincidentally, Pecola is not completely happy with her blue eyes. Pecola learns that in the end blue eyes do not solve her problems.

She continues to be alienated by others, the rape haunts her, and she is unnerved by the idea that she does not have the *bluest* eyes.

The conclusion of Morrison's revision of the Persephone and Demeter myth is similar to the ending of Brooks' "In the Mecca": the fate that befalls Pecola occurs as a result of the community's failure to protect its own. Morrison shows that the community has lost compassion and communal responsibility. Moreover, like Persephone whose virginity is sacrificed so that humankind could be granted access to the rules of agriculture, Pecola becomes the scapegoat for her community's self-hatred. To quote Elizabeth Hayes, Pecola becomes a "modern wasteland." Claudia reinforces this image of the wasteland: "All of our waste which we dumped on her and which she absorbed. And all of our beauty, which was hers first and which she gave to us. All of us—all who knew her—felt so wholesome after we cleaned ourselves on her. We were so beautiful when we stood astride her ugliness" (205). Morrison's narrative diverges from the mythic story because at the end of her tale order is not restored in the universe and Pecola never surfaces to the upper world. Although she experiences a death and rebirth of self, Pecola remains in the "lower regions" of her fractured mind.

Ironically, Morrison's text about internalized racism was written during a political climate of Black self-empowerment and racial pride. Politicians, writers, and musicians galvanized to promote Black power and Black consciousness. After a legacy of being defined by others, first as slaves and niggers, then Negroes, in the 1970s Blacks were redefining themselves. This move toward self-definition included claiming a Black identity that countered the White ideal. Hair straightening chemical and skin bleaching creams were replaced with Afros and a celebration of dark skin. Gwendolyn Brooks' love letter to Black women, "To Those of My Sister's Who Kept Their Naturals," for example, applauds Black women who did not cave in to the pressure to straighten or color their hair:

> You have not bought Blondine.
> You have not hailed the hot-comb recently.
> You never worshipped Marilyn Monroe.

You say: Farrah's hair is hers.
You have not wanted to be white.
Nor have you testified to adoration of that
State
With the advertisement of imitation
(never successful because the hot-comb is
    laughing too.

But oh the rough dark Other music!
The Real,
The Right.
The natural Respect of Self and Seal!
    Sisters!
Your hair is Celebration in the world! (460)

Brooks sends a powerful message about the politics of beauty; through their natural hairstyles Black women not only affirm beauty for themselves, but they prove their self-respect. Along with Brooks' poem, James Brown's anthem "Say it Loud, I'm Black and I'm Proud," echoed the proclamation of Black pride. *The Bluest Eye* offers a counter discourse to this rhetoric of Black pride and provides the community with an explanation of the origin of its self-hate. Morrison's intention was to show that even if Black was beautiful, for many, slogans, dashiki's, and Afros were not enough to affirm this fact. In an interview she stated, "[N]obody was going to tell me that it had been that easy. That all I needed was a slogan: 'Black is Beautiful.' It wasn't that easy. Being a little Black girl in this country—it was rough. The psychological tricks you have to play in order to get through—and nobody said how it felt to be that" (Neustadt 199). Morrison's novel reveals that a doubly conscious sensibility and a legacy of mental colonization made it challenging for African Americans girls in particular to accept that the world would see dark skin as beautiful.

The Bluest Eye has become a favorite of scholars who have mostly focused on psychoanalytic readings and feminist critiques of the text. Fortunately, Madonne Miner, Elizabeth Hayes, and Jacqueline de Weever have considered examining the mythological aspects of the text. Failure to recognize the myth suggests that scholars are not interested in Morrison's use of Greek mythology in this particular text because cultural myth overshadows classical mythic themes. This has not been the case for Morrison. While there is scant scholarship on the significance of classicism in *The Bluest Eye*, there are numerous articles interrogating the Western classical influence in *Song of Solomon* and *Beloved*. In contrast to Wheatley and Brooks, Morrison has not been harshly judged for her appropriation of myth because she has demonstrated her allegiance to Africa and African American mythology as well as to Western classical myth.

A Universal Approach to Classical Mythology:
Rita Dove's *The Darker Face of the Earth* and *Mother Love*

Of all the writers in this study, Rita Dove has been the most direct about her appropriation of Greco-Roman mythology for two of her major works, *The Darker Face of the Earth* (1994) and *Mother Love* (1995). Both texts adopt thematic and structural elements from Greek mythology. In *The Darker Face of the Earth*, Dove recasts the Oedipus myth into a story about slavery and lost love, and in *Mother Love* the Persephone and Demeter myth is reworked into a narrative about creating and losing identities. A comparative reading of Dove's classical revisions against Brooks' and Morrison's indicates that while the latter two authors' renditions of the Demeter and Persephone myth feature female protagonists who are victims of brutal physical and emotional male assault, Dove depicts an alternative image of the mythic heroine. In *Mother Love*, Dove portrays Persephone as an empowered woman free from male oppression. Where Brooks' and Morrison's adaptations of the myth center on sexual politics, Dove's shifts the focus from male–female conflict to a discussion of the mother–daughter relationship. Dove demonstrates that tension between mothers and daughters is two-fold: in the interest of protecting their children from the world, mothers often stifle their daughters' ability to experience both the hardships and pleasures of life. Consequently, daughters resent their mothers' attempts to shelter them and at their first opportunity go out into the world and leave their mothers traumatized by their departure.

In addition to emphasizing the complexity of the mother–daughter experience, Dove's reprisal of the Demeter-Persephone myth also differs from other versions because she incorporates semiautobiographical details into the narrative. Dove's mythic reconstruction reveals her own epic journey across the world as well as her transition from daughter to wife and mother. The poem, as the dedication indicates, is written FOR Dove's mother and TO her daughter. In addition to conveying to her own mother her struggle for independence, Dove also prepares her daughter, Aviva, for her own potential future mother–daughter battle.

What has been most compelling about Brooks' and Morrison's revisions of Greek mythical narratives is that incorporating the Black female experience into the narrative has been integral to their stories. In contrast, even though in Dove's narrative Persephone and Demeter are at times portrayed as identifiably Black characters, the duo's racial heritage is secondary to the construction of the narrative. While racial themes are present in the text, Dove focuses less on race and more on the universality of the mother–daughter conflict. Dove's universal aesthetic is reflective of her non-racialized and non-gender specified definition of *self*. Although Dove is often categorized as a Black writer, and her works are viewed as part of the African American literary tradition, throughout her career Dove has struggled to forge a personal and artistic identity independent of race and gender. In numerous interviews, Dove explains that she does not write specifically Black poems or female poems because these identifying markers result in dictating how poets should write and what they should write about. Rather than writing Black poems or women-centered poems, Dove seeks to create poems about the human experience relatable to all readers. While Dove might believe her poems evade categorization, texts like *The Darker Face of the Earth* and *Mother Love* emphasize issues of race and gender.

Dove's African American ancestry has made it challenging for her to write from a raceless perspective. Dove recalls that in the 1970s when she first began writing, most Black writers adopted the thematically nationalistic style of the Black Arts Movement. While some writers found the emphasis on Black subjectivity exhilarating, Dove found it too restrictive to write solely about the Black experience. She tells Malin Pereira: "I was terrified that I would be suffocated before I began, that I would be pulled into the whole net of whether this was Black enough, or whether I was denigrating my own people. There is a pressure, not just from the Black Arts movement, but from one's whole life, to be a credit to the race" (159). Unwilling to compromise her artistic integrity, Dove deferred publishing her poetry until she was confident of her own voice.

In addition to resisting being defined exclusively as a Black writer, Dove also dismisses the idea that writers should write for a particular audience. In "A Black Rainbow: Modern Afro-American Poetry," co-written with Marilyn Nelson, Dove acknowledges that some African American writers feel pressured to tailor their art for a specific readership. Dove and Nelson suggest that these writers experience a Du Boisian artistic double consciousness that forces them to choose a target audience or "to combine their audiences, overlooking the differences between them in a hopeful attempt to speak to the whole of the American people" (142–43). Dove and Nelson share that poets such as Robert Hayden and Melvin B. Tolson, who sought to reach a mainstream as well as Black audience, were condemned as the "white man's flunkies" (182). In "Telling It Like It I-S *IS*: Narrative Techniques in Melvin Tolson's *Harlem Gallery*," Dove writes about Tolson's experience as a Black writer caught in the racial divide. She notes, "he was misunderstood by many of those he loved most, by those to whom he dedicated his energies in the creation of his last work—the Black intellectuals" (117). Tolson's struggle to gain acceptance from both Blacks and Whites was a predicament to which Dove was unwilling to be subjected.

In her oft-cited poem "Upon Meeting Don L. Lee, In a Dream," Dove challenged those who sought to dictate what Black artists should write about. The poem relays a surrealistic dream in which the speaker meets iconic Black Arts Movement poet Don L. Lee (Haki Madhubuti). In the poem Lee is described as a robotic-like cult leader, worshipped by robed chanting women who idolize Lee's Black Arts theology. When the speaker and Lee meet, Lee attempts to initiate her into his cult of Black aesthetics. The speaker asks Lee to explain how his rhetoric applies to the current social climate: "Those years are gone— / What is there now?" she inquires, suggesting that Lee's beliefs are anachronistic. The speaker imagines that Lee, unable to defend his position, malfunctions and combusts: "his eyeballs / burst into flame" and "[h]is hair falls out in clumps of burned-out wire" (12). The speaker is amused by Lee's literal meltdown. Savoring her victory over this once great man, she falls to the floor "chuckling as the grass curls around" her. The speaker revels in the fact that, with Lee's destruction, she no longer has to adhere to his definition of Black art. Some read "Upon Meeting" as an indictment of the Black Arts Movement, but in countless interviews Dove insists that the poem is not an attempt to undermine Lee or the movement. In fact, Dove states that she believes the Black Arts Movement was integral to the development of Black poetry: "in order to develop Black consciousness it was important to stress Blackness, to make sure the poems talked about being Black, because it had never really been talked about before" (*Conversations* 22). While Dove may respect the Black Arts Movement, understanding its appropriateness at the time, the movement's tenet of art *for* Black people and *by* Black people, for Dove, is clearly dated and antithetical to her own aesthetic of art for humanity.

The freedom to write on one's own terms, regardless of race, gender, subject, or audience is what Dove admires most about many of the women in this study. Dove relates to fellow poet Phillis Wheatley because in addition to emulating the best poets of the day, Wheatley was not compelled to write about her slave experience. "When I first read Wheatley what impressed me was, here was a Black woman and a slave and she didn't have to write about slavery. She said, I can write like Pope, why not. I can do this, I'm a slave, but I can still imitate Pope and write in the neoclassical tradition" (Walters 167). Writing in the classical tradition, as Wheatley learned, and later Dove learned too, held its consequences for Black writers.

As already noted in Chapter 1, critics like Jefferson insisted that Wheatley's classical paraphrases were poor imitations. Later, contemporary critics like Angelene Jamison argued that Wheatley "wrote to Whites, for Whites and generally in the Euro-American tradition at that time. That is, Phillis Wheatley was influenced by neoclassicism. And much of her poetry reflects various stylistic characteristics of Alexander Pope and his followers" (128). Dove has faced the same kind of indictment that Wheatley encountered: "I've been told that by writing texts, which alluded to classical mythology I am copping out" (Walters 171). But Dove does not allow others to choose her literary inspiration: "I feel you're denying yourself if you don't dig into the cornucopia. . . . I feel you chop your head off by saying something like Blacks shouldn't do this or that because it belongs to a white classical tradition" (Walters 171–72). Dove has also been inspired by Gwendolyn Brooks' artistic choices. Dove compliments Brooks' decision to write poems focusing on "the value of the individual. Her investigations of the interior lives of her subjects probe beyond their skin-deep identities" (Nelson and Dove160).[1] Brooks' occasional endeavor to write beyond the Black subject is a recognizable trait of Dove's own poetry. Dove's task has been to write poems that, as Helen Vendler asserts, betray the concept "that Blackness need not be one's central subject, but equally need not be omitted" (82). So while almost all of Dove's poetry and prose feature Black characters, issues of race do not necessarily drive the narratives.[2]

In her Pulitzer-Prize-winning collection *Thomas and Beulah* (1986), for example, Dove writes about the experiences of her maternal grandparents. The narrative recounts her grandparents' migration from the south to the Midwest. The poems describe her grandparents' lives before meeting, her grandfather's experience working as a riveter in an airplane factory, and her grandmother's experience as a young mother. Although Thomas and Beulah are unmistakably Black characters, their lives are as ordinary as White Americans.[3] However, even though Thomas and Beulah's experiences are as average as any other couple's during the 1920s, Dove does not ignore the realities of racism that the two encountered. For example, in "Magic" Beulah's family is visited by Clan members: "One night she awoke / and on the lawn blazed a scaffolding strung in lights" (176). As terrifying as this event is, Dove does not offer any reflection from Beulah about the incident. By glossing over the incident Dove implies that because hate crimes were an ordinary part of life, Beulah, like many others, learned it was important not to allow these indignities to stop one from living life.

Despite her resistance to categorization, we can link Dove to a tradition of African American women's classical mythmaking. *Mother Love* and *The Darker Face of the Earth* highlight some of the same classical themes appropriated by Wheatley, Brooks, and Morrison. For example, in *Mother Love* and *The Darker Face of the Earth*, Dove features a mother who—like Wheatley's Niobe or Brooks', Ms. Sallie—is traumatized by the loss of her child. And in *The Darker Face of the Earth*, Dove adopts themes of rape and incest that are also addressed by Morrison in *The Bluest Eye*. Similar to Morrison's *Beloved*, Dove situates her mythically revised narrative, *The Darker Face of the Earth*, in slavery, illustrating that the power dynamics between gods and mortals mirrored that of plantation owners and slaves in the antebellum south. Stylistically, Dove's mythopoeic construction is reminiscent of Brooks' "The Anniad." *Mother Love* employs highly sophisticated language and throughout the narrative she incorporates numerous literary allusions and experiments with verse forms. Where Brooks experiments with *ottava rima* and *rhyme royal*, Dove reworks the sonnet. Brooks' contribution to the classical tradition has been recognized by Dove who observes, "[b]efore Gwendolyn Brooks the classics had been used in this country to validate White dominant culture. Brooks shows they could be used for other cultures. I get so angry when people say the classics are not for everybody" (Walters 168). So again, like Wheatley and Morrison, Dove claims the Western classical tradition as part of her own literary heritage.

Dove's iconoclastic approach to writing and her adoption of the classics in texts like *Darker Face of the Earth* and *Mother Love* shows that even works that embrace European literary traditions can still be seen as part of a Black aesthetic. Arnold Rampersad suggests that Dove creates a revisionist Black aesthetic that is radically different from writers of the Black Arts Movement: "Instead of looseness of structure, one finds in her poems remarkably tight control; instead of reliance on reckless inspiration, one recognizes discipline and practice, and long, taxing hours in competitive university poetry workshops and in her study; . . . instead of an obsession with the theme of race, one finds an eagerness, perhaps even an anxiety, to transcend—if not actually to repudiate—Black cultural nationalism in the name of a more inclusive sensibility" (53).

Rampersad infers that Dove's "inclusive sensibility" results in an oppositional view of Black aesthetics that, unlike Black Arts Movement writers, demonstrates that one can write about the Black subject in a way that privileges humanity rather than race.[4] Dove's alternative Black aesthetic calls to mind Trey Ellis', "The New Black Aesthetic" (1989). In the essay, Ellis hypothesizes that artists of the 1980s are part of a New Black Aesthetic that differs from the poetics of the past. Ellis defines artists of the New Black Aesthetic as "cultural mulattos." Cultural mulattos, Ellis explains, have been "educated by a multi-racial mix of cultures that allows them to navigate easily in the white world" (235).

Unlike the Afro-Modernists of the 1940s and 1950s or the Black Arts Movement artists of the 1960s and 1970s, artists of the New Black Aesthetic "no longer need to deny or suppress any part of our complicated and sometimes contradictory cultural baggage to please either White people or Black" (Ellis 235). In many ways, Dove's writing is reflective of Ellis' New Black Aesthetic. Her eclectic writing style, appropriating European as well as the African American tradition, demonstrates that Dove does not write to placate any specific reader. And although in an interview she admits she is uncomfortable with Ellis' definition of "mulatto," she does, as Ellis says of the cultural mulatto, fit comfortably in both Black and White spaces. To borrow from Gates' discussion of Ralph Ellison and Ishmael Reed's literary heritage, Dove, like her two male predecessors, "creates texts that are double-voiced in the sense that their literary antecedents are both White and Black" (Gates xxiii). While Ellis talks primarily about the cultural mulatto's ability to exist effortlessly in both White and Black spaces, Dove is a true cultural mulatto in the sense that she can move in and out of different cultures, not just in America, but across the world. Like Derek Walcott, whom Dove admires because of his international perspective, Dove's writing reflects upon her travels.[5] After graduating from Miami University of Ohio in 1973, Dove traveled to Germany as a Fulbright scholar. Upon returning to America, she took up residence in a number of different states first as a graduate student and then as an academic. Later, in the 1980s she returned to Europe and traveled to Mexico and Jerusalem. While Dove's travels are incorporated into her poetry, so too are her hobbies: Dove is an accomplished musician, she plays the cello and the viola da gamba (cello-like instrument), sings in a choir, and she also speaks German fluently. In many of her poems, the cadences of music and German syntax are present. Dove's rich experiences reflect that she has inherited the best of both Black and White culture. It is not surprising, as Georgoudaki Ekaterini notes, that Dove "often speaks with the voice of a world citizen who places her personal, racial, and national experience within the context of the human experience as a whole, and celebrates its richness and continuity. . . . She is an artist who claims the world's civilizations as her rightful heritage" (216).[6] Dove's cosmopolitanism and her universal approach to literature help explain her affinity for the classics.

Dove's classical training is much like that of the other women of this study. As a young girl she read the Greek narratives that were stacked on her parents' bookshelves. While reading the classical stories Dove was mostly fascinated by the power of the gods and their ability to control the lives of the mortals. Dove says she could relate to how the humans had to defer to the gods who were as fallible as the humans:

> The gods were not perfect. Think of characters like Hera, she was a jealous wife concerned about a husband who was a philanderer. The mortals were subject to the god's whimsy. Sometimes there were not very good reasons for why things happened to the mortals, it was like playing chess. Oftentimes things happened that were not fair. I saw in my own life that people in power were not infallible. As a child, I knew I too had to deal with

things that happened, I knew things were not always going to be fair. What was most interesting to me was, the whole structures of the Greek/Roman myth paralleled the structures in my own life. (Walters 167)

In the 1990s, when Dove published both *The Darker Face of the Earth* and *Mother Love*, many considered the classics to be an outmoded tradition. But Dove believed the classics were as relevant in the nineties as they were in ancient times: "The classics deal with most major human dramas: men returning from war, rape, murder, incest, murdering your own children. They give you a template, scaffolding from which to contemplate your own experience. One could say gods/goddesses we don't believe in these things, but we have celebrities and politicians and other figures of power, the same elements are there" (Walters 169).

Mythic themes of incest, rape, murder, and heartbreak are universal tales that all readers can relate to; and although the classics are set in ancient Greece and Rome, the stories themselves are not just about Greeks and Romans. Rather, the narratives are about the experiences of all mankind. Like other writers in this study, Dove reworks classical narratives because she identifies with the timelessness of these themes.

Dove's revisionist approach to classical myth is analogous to Brooks' and Morrison's. Although the major mythemes are highlighted in Dove's narratives, her intention is not to focus on presenting a contemporary duplication of the original mythical story, but rather to appropriate only those mythic elements that assist in the construction of her narrative. In *The Darker Face of the Earth*, in contrast to Oedipus' predicament of fate versus free will, the protagonist's fate is his birth into slavery. Moreover, rather than emphasizing the horrors of incest, Dove hones in on the love affair between mother and son.

The Darker Face of the Earth

The Darker Face of the Earth, a revision of Sophocles' *Oedipus the King*, was Dove's first full-length classical revision. Dove was inspired to write the play in 1979 after reading the Greek tragedy and pondering what continues to draw readers to the story even though they know the outcome. Dove deduced that readers were intrigued by the fact that Oedipus represents humankind's inability to control our destiny. Bernard Knox contends that Sophocles' play forces us to consider "our own terror of the unknown future which we fear we cannot control—our deep fear that every step we take forward on what we think is the road of progress may really be a step toward a foreordained rendezvous with disaster" (133). As Dove thought about how the play could be appropriated for modern audiences she realized that the antebellum South would serve as the perfect setting for her revision because the patriarchal culture of the plantation society most closely related to the hierarchal system of gods and mortals portrayed in classical myth. Slaves, like the mortals in Greek mythology, had no control over their lives and often faced predicaments similar to those of the tragic figures from Greek mythology.

After writing several drafts of the play, Dove placed the script into a drawer and returned to writing poetry. Dove claims she had no real intention of sending the play out for production. She jokes that at fleeting moments she entertained the idea "that maybe someday when I was dead someone would do it out of pity or whatever" (*Conversations* 148). The play remained untouched for several years until, at the encouragement of her husband, poet Fred Viebahn, she sent it out for review. In 1994, Story Line Press published the first version of the narrative. A year later, Derek Walcott directed a reading of the script at the 92 Street Y in New York City. In 1996, Dove published a revised edition of the play. The play went on to be staged in numerous venues, including the Kennedy Center in Washington, D.C. in 1997. Both the original and revised editions of the play are referenced in this study.

Following in the tradition of Morrison, Dove's classical revision is a fusion of Greek myth and the African American slave narrative tradition. Similar to Morrison's *Beloved*, Dove's story is situated during the antebellum period. *The Darker Face of the Earth* follows the mythic plot detailing Oedipus' attempt to avoid his predicated fate of killing his father and falling in love with his mother.

Sophocles' version of the myth, as Knox observes, emphasizes not what leads Oedipus to his fate (*moira*), but Oedipus' reaction when it is revealed that he fulfilled the oracle's prediction. In the play, an oracle informs King Laius that his unborn son, Oedipus, will kill him. Laius attempts to intercept the curse by binding Oedipus' feet and abandoning him on a mountain, but Oedipus is rescued by a shepherd and is raised as the son of Polybus and Merope, the King and Queen of Corinth. An oracle forewarns Oedipus that he will mate with his mother and kill his father. Fearing that he will kill Polybus and Merope—whom he assumes to be his parents—he leaves Corinth. While on his journey, Oedipus is involved in an altercation resulting in his murder of several men (one of them being his father, Laius). Following the incident, Oedipus reaches Laius' kingdom, solves the riddle of the sphinx, becomes ruler of Thebes, and marries his mother, Jacosta. Later, Oedipus' kingdom is plagued by a curse. He is told that the curse will not cease until Laius' slayer is discovered.

Oedipus zealously works to uncover Laius' murderer. A number of individuals, including Tiresias, the shepherd who saved him at birth, and Jacosta, soon realize that it was Oedipus who killed Laius. On numerous occasions, Tiresias and Jacosta attempt to steer Oedipus away from discovering the truth and give Oedipus the chance to rewrite the script of his life. But Oedipus is unwilling to heed their warnings against gathering more evidence for the case. Finally, at Oedipus' insistence, Tiresias and Jacosta are forced to reveal facts about the past that eventually incriminate him. When Oedipus realizes that the prophecy has come true, he is stunned by the revelation. His initial response is to find Jacosta and kill her, but Jacosta, grieved by what has come to pass, commits suicide. Oedipus gouges out his eyes and goes into exile. Sophocles' story reveals that although Oedipus' fate is predetermined, his free will, his ability to know or not to know the truth, facilitates the eventual outcome of his life.

Dove transforms Sophocles' play by showing her tragic hero's fate is fueled not by his ignorance and refusal to heed the counsel of others, but rather by the constraints of slavery, which account for his tragic circumstance. Dove reworks a number of elements of Sophocles' drama into her own narrative. For example, just as Oedipus' birth was doomed, Augustus is also a fated child. Augustus is the son of a slave, Hector, and a plantation mistress, Amalia LaFarge. His parents' relationship is dangerous as well as illegal because miscegenation laws of the day prohibited Blacks and Whites from engaging in sexual relationships. When it is discovered that Amalia's newborn son, Augustus, is mulatto, she is forbidden to keep him. Just as Laius leaves Oedipus for dead, Amalia's husband, Louis, attempts to kill Augustus, but his plan fails. Twenty years after leaving the plantation, Amalia, not knowing Augustus' identity, purchases Augustus and brings him back home.

Dove begins her story in much the same way as Sophocles'. After Augustus' birth on a South Carolina slave plantation, Scylla, like Apollo's oracle, warns of a curse that will impact Amalia, Louis, Hector, and Augustus: "Black woman, Black man; / white woman, white man: / four people were touched by the curse, / but the curse is still not complete" (DF 31). The curse, as we learn later, involves Augustus' Oedipal mistake of killing his father, Hector, and becoming his mother's lover. Unlike Oedipus, who is warned of the oracle, Augustus is not privy to the fate that befalls him. Whereas Oedipus tries to avoid killing his father, Dove inverts the myth and shows that Augustus *wants* to kill his father. Augustus' motivations are driven by his ignorance of his past. Augustus mistakenly assumes that his father was a slave owner who raped his mother and attempted to kill him. Augustus seeks retribution for his mother's rape and his father's attempted act of murder. Although Augustus' presuppositions about his own conception are false, Dove illustrates that his assumptions are logical because, as the narrative reveals, Amalia's husband frequently raped his female slaves. In scene one, Amalia confronts her husband Louis about his abuse of power and violation of young slave girls "in the name of ownership" (DF 16). Here, Dove fails in her quest to avoid emphasizing racial and gender concerns and underscores the racial and gendered discourse of victimization. Like her literary predecessors, Dove shows that the race and gender of slave women made them powerless against the onslaught of male abuse.

Like Oedipus, Augustus returns to the plantation as a mysterious, courageous, well traveled, intelligent stranger. Unlike other slaves on the plantation he is highly educated. We learn that his former slave master exposed him to the poetry of Milton, the Bible, and Greek literature. Augustus' strength of character and erudition is admired by most on the plantation—including Amalia. The attraction between Amalia and Augustus is instantaneous. She admires his fearlessness and he is attracted to her beauty and shared sense of rebelliousness.

Dove's portrayal of Amalia and Augustus' romance is one of the most significant revisions of Sophocles' drama. Although in Sophocles' drama Oedipus and Jacosta are married, their romance is not emphasized. In *The Darker Face*, prior to the revelation that Augustus and Amalia are mother and son, the two engage in a blossoming incestuous romance. While Augustus is enamored with Amalia, unbeknownst to him he is actually caught in a love triangle. One of his fellow slaves, Phebe, also vies for his affection. Dove's focus on the relationship between Augustus and Amalia offers an alternative view of the typical plantation mistress and slave relationship. Rather than see these two individuals in their traditional binaries of the victimizer and the oppressed, Dove presents Augustus as a man in love, rather than a slave fleeing persecution. Amalia on the other hand is a lover and mother rather than a ruthless slave driver. And whereas typically slaves were often forced into sexual engagements with their masters or mistresses, Dove flirts with the idea that a plantation mistress and a slave could indeed fall in love. The developing relationship between Augustus and Amalia is complicated by the fact that Augustus and other slaves have been planning a coup to overturn the plantation. In order for the seditionists to execute their plan successfully, Amalia, along with Louis, must be killed. Once the relationship between Amalia and Augustus begins to develop, Augustus loses sight of his responsibilities to the cause, and he is ultimately forced to make a choice between Amalia and the salvation of his people. Just as Oedipus is blinded by denial, Augustus is blinded by love.

Mirroring Oedipus, Augustus commits patricide: Augustus has an altercation with Hector resulting in Hector's death. Shortly after killing Hector, Augustus is coerced by the leaders of the slave revolt to carry out the plan to kill Amalia and Louis. Before Augustus can kill Louis, Louis reveals to Augustus that Amalia is his mother. Augustus, like his mythic predecessor, is shocked by the revelation and confronts Amalia. In the original version of Dove's play, right as Amalia learns that Augustus is her son, she, along with Augustus, is shot and killed by revolutionaries. In an image reminiscent of Othello and Desdemona of Shakespeare's *Othello*, the two lay dead together. In the revised edition of Dove's play, Amalia, grieved by the revelation that Augustus is her son, commits suicide. The coup leaders mistakenly assume Augustus killed Amalia, and Augustus is heralded as a hero. Dove's decision to change the ending in the revised edition actually occurred after her daughter suggested it would be better for Augustus to be alive and in misery rather than dead. Thus in the revised edition, Augustus, like Oedipus, does not die but instead lives with the painful reality that Amalia was both his mother and lover. Both versions of Dove's narrative present tragic circumstances for the characters. Due to the institution of slavery Amalia and Augustus are restricted from loving each other either as lovers or as mother and son.

The mythic themes in *The Darker Face of the Earth* are coupled with other elements of classical mythology. For example, most of the slaves in the story are given ancient Greek and Roman names. Dove says she did not set out to give her characters classical names, but while searching through slave records she encountered virtually all of the names (Phebe, Hector, Augustus, Scylla) she had adopted for the enslaved characters in the play. Dove surmises that slave owners found it ironic to name their powerless slaves after strong mythic figures from antiquity. Dove also discovered that she could make connections between the Greek chorus and the oral tradition of the slave community. The slave community in *The Darker Face of the Earth* functions in the same way as the community in Brooks' "*In the Mecca*" or Morrison's *The Bluest Eye* and *Beloved*. The community, like the Greek chorus, comments on events in the play and the actions of the characters. Dove tells Robert McDowell:

Using the ancient Greek dramatic form, with its infamously difficult to handle master chorus, proved less problematic than I anticipated. I'd grown up in the Black church, where call-and-response
was part of the ritual. The Black community extends beyond
immediate family and even the neighborhood; it's a community
that holds itself responsible for each member's actions and will feel
free to voice its opinions—often loudly and with great sarcasm. So
the type of running commentary provided by the Greek Chorus
sounds "down home" to me! (175)

Dove's statement echoes Morrison's earlier discussion concerning
the relationship between the Greek chorus and the African American
oral tradition. The call-and-response pattern usually involves a
lead orator and an audience. The orator presents the call/state-
ment, and the audience responds with verbal and non-verbal affirmation. In scene one of the revised edition, for example, Scylla is
portrayed as the lead orator who presents the mythic plot and
foreshadows the impending curse. The other slaves punctuate
statements:

SCYLLA   Hector, son of Africa—
                stolen from his father's hut,
                sold on the auction block!
SLAVES   Black man.
SCYLLA   Hector was a slave in the fields
                until Miss Amalia took him up
                to the house. He followed her
                like her own right shoe . . .
SLAVES   Black woman, Black man—
                both were twisted
                when the curse came over the hill
SCYLLA   While the slave turned to grief,
                the master turned to business.
                Miss Amalia hiked up her skirts
                and pulled on man's boots.
SLAVES   White woman.
SCYLLA   And Massa Louis . . . Massa Louis
                Took off his riding breeches—
SLAVES   White man. (*DF* 39–40)

Dove's appropriation of the call-and-response convention is one of many African American tropes present in the play. Dove's troping of this African American convention illustrates her ability to move "from the language of the European classic, substituting and reorganizing its elements, employing the African American vernacular trope" (Carlisle 137). Dove's use of a number of tropes and motifs from the slave narrative tradition also serves as evidence of her marriage of the Western classical and African American literary tradition.

Dove's use of sorrow songs, songs that expressed the slaves' "sorrow" for their physical and mental bondage, serve as an example of the African American folkloric traditions reworked in the narrative. Along with sorrow songs, Dove also incorporates *signal* songs. Signal songs used double entendres to signal plans for escape. For example, in the eighth scene, the slaves sing "Steal Away to Jesus":

> Steal away, steal away,
> Steal away to Jesus;
> Steal away, steal away home,
> I ain't got long to stay here. (*DF* 85)

Historians explain that although this song was often sung to signal an impending escape, in Dove's play the slaves use the song to signal an uprising.

Other elements from the slave narrative tradition include major motifs such as the theme that knowledge and education can liberate the slaves from physical and mental bondage. Augustus, having traveled with his master on a ship, can read and write. In the vein of Fredrick Douglass' *Narrative of The Life of Frederick Douglass, An American Slave Written By Himself* (1845), Augustus' education leads to his self-empowerment and freedom. When Augustus arrives at the plantation, he uses his knowledge to mobilize other slaves to gain their emancipation. One of the most remarkable aspects of *The Darker Face of the Earth* that should be noted is that throughout the narrative Dove cites a number of well-known slave revolts including the Haitian Revolution, the Cinque-lead mutiny of the Amistad, and the 1822 Denmark Vesey's conspiracy. Dove's reference to these transatlantic slave revolts both records history and educates audiences about the Western hemisphere's colonial legacy. Dove also makes intertextual references to David Walker's revolutionary treatise, *Appeal: To the Coloured Citizens of the World* (1829) as well as Martin Delany's political pan-African novel, *Blake: or the Huts of America (1859)*.[7] In *The Darker Face of the Earth*, Delany's protagonist Henry Blake appears in Dove's narrative as one of the seditionists.[8]

In addition to reworking elements of the slave narrative into her classical revision, true to the African American women's tradition of mythmaking, Dove presents a female perspective to Sophocles' play.[9] While in Sophocles' drama much of the narrative centers on Oedipus' tragic circumstances, in Dove's narrative, Amalia is as tragic as Augustus. Dove shows that despite her position of power, in some ways Amalia is as oppressed as her slaves. As a young girl she is forced into the standard arranged marriage, which results in a loveless and sexless union. Rather than adhering to the cult of womanhood and playing the role of sexually-frustrated plantation mistress, Amalia defies convention and empowers herself sexually, first by seeking out her own sexual partner and second by defying the laws of the day and engaging in an affair with a slave. Once she gives birth to Augustus, Amalia's relationship with Hector ends. Louis immediately assumes Amalia has been raped, but she quickly corrects him and lets him know that she willfully engaged in a sexual relationship with one of her slaves: "so you can stroll out by the cabins / any fine night you please, / but if I summon a buck / up to the house I'm a bitch? Well then, I'm a bitch" (*DF* 15), she says exposing Louis' infidelity and claiming her own. As Pauline Hopkins does in *Contending Forces*, Dove reveals the hypocrisy of slave owners who enforced laws forbidding miscegenation but who did not uphold them themselves. Augustus' birth is a tragic moment for Amalia because in addition to losing Hector (the relationship ends after Hector thinks Augustus is stillborn) she also loses her son. Like the women featured in Wheatley's "Niobe" or

Brooks "In the Mecca," Amalia is depicted as the grieving mother who suffered separation from her child.

In the rrevised edition of *The Darker Face of the Earth*, Amalia recounts that she never reconciled herself with the pain of being separated from Augustus: "It was like missing an arm or a leg / that pains and throbs, even though / you can look right where it was / and see there's nothing left (*DF* 147). Typically, slave narratives focus on slave mothers who are separated from their children, but here Dove reverses the traditional story to show that plantation mistresses might have endured similar circumstances. As Steffen notes, "the irony of Dove's play is in the role reversals of the main characters, for it is the white woman who has deliberately pro- duced a child by a Black slave, in defiance of convention" (128). In the Dovesian tradition of focusing on our commonality, our human traits, Dove de-emphasizes the fact that Amalia is a slave owner and instead highlights her experience as a woman, a mother, and lover. Amalia experiences traumatic heartbreak twice—once with Hector's father and again with Augustus. The tragic circumstance of Augustus and Amalia's relationship is revealed at the end of the play when they both learn of their rela- tionship. As Dove notes, "in a different world, Amalia (the Jacosta figure) might have been a woman of independent means and Augustus (who recalls Oedipus) a poet" (qtd. Pereira 37). But these individuals are living during a time period when Whites and Blacks could not engage in romantic relationships, and so the union between Augustus and Amalia is doomed before it begins.

Some of the themes presented in *The Darker Face of the Earth* resurface in *Mother Love*, Dove's other mythical adaptation. *Mother Love* also deals with the themes of maternal trauma and female self-empowerment.

Mother Love: From Daughter to Poet to Mother

Brooks' "The Anniad" and Morrison's *The Bluest Eye* offer no con- crete evidence to prove that the texts are appropriations of the Demeter and Persephone myth. But with *Mother Love*, Dove is clear about her invocation of the myth. In her foreword to Mother

Love, "An Intact World," Dove explains her reasons for adapting the myth and her decision for writing the narrative as a sonnet sequence. She explains that she rewrites the myth because it presents "a modern dilemma" concerning the forced or voluntarily separation between mother and daughter: "there comes a point when a mother can no longer protect her child, when the daughter must go her own way into womanhood" (i). The modern dilemma of which Dove speaks relates not only to the mythic tale but also to Dove's maturation as a poet. When Dove writes *Mother Love*, she becomes the rebellious poetic daughter who "goes her own way into womanhood," refusing to conform to convention by bastardizing the sonnet. The traditional Petrarchan or Shakespearean sonnet (fourteen lines of iambic pentameter), she explains, is a conventional literary mode that represents order and structure: "The sonnet is a *heile Welt*, an intact world where everything is in sync, from the stars down to the tiniest mite on a blade of grass" (i). Despite its presumed "fixed" state, like all things, the sonnet can be manipulated. Dove continues, "any variation from the strictly Petrarchan or Shakespearean forms represents a world gone awry" (i). Dove's break from the traditional sonnet illustrates that just as the sonnet cannot be protected from modification, relationships between mothers and daughters are also prone to transformation.

In the African American literary tradition, the sonnet has been adopted for aesthetic, and political functions. Steffen observes that for poets like Wheatley, Countee Cullen, Claude McKay, and Langston Hughes, the sonnet "marked momentous personal and public turning points" in their careers (128). Dove's sonnet sequence does not highlight a defining moment in her career, but her use of the form does align her with Brooks, whose own experimentation with the sonnet and the epic challenged the expected genres and rhyme styles emblematic of Black poetry. Susan Van Dyne suggests that Dove's sonnet sequence is an "emphatic challenge in the 1990s to the critical expectation that the only or most authentic voice for the Black poet is a street-wise or folk-inflected free verse" (81). In addition to defying expectation, Dove's appropriation of the sonnet is political because it serves as "an audacious confirmation of her place as a Black woman within a classical tradition," which displays "her wish to continue that tradition rather than simply repudiate it" (Van Dyne 80). In some sections of *Mother Love*, detecting the sonnets requires careful reading because the traditional fourteen lines of iambic pentameter are often fused to create double sonnets.

The title poem "Mother Love," for example, is divided into two stanzas of twelve and sixteen iambs. As Stephen Cushman notes, "the key to Dove's sonnets lies not in accentual-syllabic meter or regular rhyming but in their various arrangements based on the number fourteen" (132). He adds, "The sonnets of *Mother Love* are relentlessly metrical, for Dove counts lines and stanzas and strophic groupings" (132).[10] So again, Dove's experimentation with the sonnet symbolizes her attempt to deviate from conventional poetic modes to create a new sonnet form independent from the established tradition.

Dove is one of a number of contemporary African American women poets writing about the mother–daughter experience. Lucille Clifton, Alice Walker, and Audre Lorde all wrote poems about mothers and daughters. Andrea Rushing observes that the mother is a prominent figure in African American women's poetry that is often mythologized into a complimentary view of the mother that rarely calls out her flaws. According to Rushing, "in almost all the mother poems, mother is above criticism, the almost perfect symbol of Black struggle, suffering, and endurance" (76). In *Mother Love*, Dove avoids mythologizing Demeter as the ideal mother; instead she portrays her Demeter character as an overbearing woman who projects her insecurities on to her daughter. Fabian Worsham contends that African American women poets who have written about mother–daughter relationships "are creating a poetics of matrilineage," which shows "mothers and their daughters as unique, individual women within a larger community of women" (129). As part of this poetics of matrilineage, Dove's interpretation of the Persephone and Demeter myth presents mothers and daughters as individuals and universalizes their experience. Dove's multidimensional perspective of the mother–daughter conflict distinguishes her reworking of the

Demeter-Persephone narrative from Brooks' and Morrison's. Brooks divides the Persephone and Demeter story into two separate poems: in "The Anniad" she presents Persephone's journey to the underworld and in "In the Mecca" she features Demeter's search for her daughter. In *The Bluest Eye* Morrison focuses solely on Persephone's experience.

Motherhood is a perennial theme in Dove's work. In *Thomas and Beulah*, poems such as " Motherhood" and "Daystar" convey a mother's fears and frustrations with motherhood, and in the collection *Grace Notes* (1989) Dove devotes several poems about her maternal experience with daughter, Aviva. Surprisingly, however, although Dove had written frequently about motherhood, she had not written about her own mother before *Mother Love*. Here, for the first time, Dove writes about her mother as well as about her experience as her mother's daughter. In addition to the distinctions mentioned, Dove's version of the Persephone and Demeter myth stands apart from other contemporary African American women's adaptations for four distinct reasons. First, she revises the image of the African American Persephone from a victimized protagonist into a liberated woman whose transition to womanhood occurs in spite of her relationship with Hades. Second, where other renditions of the Persephone and Demeter myth show that Hades is primarily responsible for the estrangement between mother and daughter, Dove illumines that the separation between mother and child occurs not because of Hades but because of Persephone's struggle for independence. Third, Dove incorporates autobiographical details into the poem, writing as daughter, mother, and poet—a similar convention featured in Brooks' *Annie Allen*. Last, *Mother Love* differs from other Persephone and Demeter stories because Dove offers a closer examination of the emotional anguish Demeter experiences as she fights to come to terms with her own death and rebirth from mother to mother-in-law.

Dove's version of the Persephone and Demeter myth draws from Ovid's *Metamorphoses* as well as the *Homeric Hymn*. *Mother Love* is divided into seven sections "mirroring the seven seeds of the pomegranate" (Steffen 131) that Persephone eats in the underworld. Each section plays out in a call-and-response pattern, first presenting Persephone's experiences followed by Demeter's response. Dove features multiple Persephones and Demeters, but in *Mother Love* sometimes the pair is specifically African American and other times the women are not. Throughout the narrative Dove shifts back and forth between the mythic world of the ancient tale and contemporary settings in the United States, Mexico, and Europe. The mythic tale is repeated several times and each telling remains incomplete. The fragmented nature of the narrative reflects the divided relationship between Persephone and Demeter. When Persephone and Demeter are separated, each loses a part of herself that can only be regained once the two are reunited as mother and daughter.

The Persephone and Demeter myth in the *Homeric Hymn* (and in Brooks' and Morrison's adaptations of it) almost immediately characterizes Persephone as an innocent young maiden who is defenseless against Hades' attack. Contrastingly, Dove inverts Persephone's role as victim and instead portrays *her* as the victimizer. Consistent with mythical accounts, in the opening poem, "Heroes," Persephone sees a wilting poppy and picks it to save it from dying, even though she knew "it was going to die" (*ML* 4).[11] Here Dove alludes to Ovid's tale of Proserpine. According to Graves, Ovid recounts that Core (Persephone) was picking poppies, rather than the narcissus featured in the other versions. He notes, "Core picks or accepts poppies because of the soporific qualities, and because of their scarlet colour which promises resurrection after death" (96). In *Mother Love*, after picking the poppy, instead of being abducted and victimized by Hades, Persephone engages in a violent encounter with the owner of the poppy field who reprimands Persephone for taking her last poppy. In an unexpected turn of events, Persephone accidentally kills the woman. With this initial poem, Dove prepares us for a new telling of the myth that, like her sonnets, will defy convention.

The next poem, "Primer," again presents a different image of Persephone. This time Persephone *is* subject to attack:

> I was chased home by
> The Gaitlin kids, three skinny sisters

In rolled-down bobby socks. Hissing
Brainiac! And *Mrs. Stringbean!*, they trod on my heel. (*ML* 7)

Before the Gaitlin sisters can inflict violence, Demeter appears
ready "to shake them down to size" (7), but Persephone rejects her
mother's offer of protection. Rather than seeking refuge in her
mother's car she walks home determined she would "show them
all: I would grow up" (7). Here again, Dove offers a portrayal of
Persephone differing from other representations of the mythic
heroine. Persephone will not depend on her mother to rescue her,
for she is determined to fight her own battles.

In most ancient versions of the Persephone and Demeter
myth and in contemporary versions by Brooks and Morrison,
Persephone's puberty signals her fertility, her subsequent rape by
Hades, and transition to womanhood. In *Mother Love*, as in
Jamaica Kincaid's *Annie John* (another book about mother–daughter conflict that is referenced in the epigraph to section four),
Persephone's puberty marks her rite of passage and her initial
desire to create an independent identity. In "Party Dress for a First
Born," Persephone reflects on a time when her mother was the
center of the earth. "When I ran to my mother, waiting radiant / as
a cornstalk at the edge of the field, / nothing else mattered: the
world stood still" (8). The use of past tense suggests Persephone no
longer feels the strong attachment that she once held with her
mother. It should be mentioned that Persephone's description
of Demeter "as radiant as a cornstalk" establishes another link
between the Persephone and Demeter myth and *Mother Love*. In
the Eleusinian Mysteries Demeter reportedly showed Triptolemus
how to sow corn seeds. In the second stanza, Persephone reveals
her maturation and budding sexual awakening. As she dresses for
a party, she envisions the mating dance of the men, who "stride
like elegant scissors across the lawn / to the women arrayed there,
petals waiting to loosen" (8). Persephone imagines that when she
enters the party, she will solicit the attention of the male guests:
"When I step out, disguised in your blushing skin, / they will
nudge each other to get a peek / and I will smile, all the while wish-
ing them dead" (*ML* 8). Whereas in Brooks' and Morrison's texts

Persephone's sexuality oppresses her, here Persephone recognizes that her sexuality is empowering, for with her body she can control male desire.

While Dove portrays strong, independent images of Persephone, she also features the more familiar image of the violated daughter who is raped and abducted. In "Persephone Falling," the traditional mythic story emerges. Persephone is mesmerized by a narcissus and reaches down to pluck it from the earth. Just as the flower loosens from the soil Hades "sprung out of the earth / on his glittering terrible / carriage, [and] he claimed his due" (9). As Hades carries Persephone away, Demeter's unheeded directive echoes in response to Persephone's scream for help: "(Remember: go straight to school. / This is important, stop fooling around! Don't answer to strangers. Stick / with your playmates. Keep your eyes down / This is how easily the pit / opens. This is how one foot sinks into the ground" (9). Here, Dove presents the chilling reality about child abduction: despite a mother's best intensions to give her daughter the tools for survival, "there comes a point when a mother can no longer protect her child" (i).

Persephone's abduction is followed by several poems outlining Demeter's reaction to her daughter's kidnapping. Similar to the *Homeric Hymn*, Demeter is devastated when she learns Persephone has been captured:

> Blown apart by loss, she let herself go—
> wandered the neighborhood hatless, breasts
> swinging under a ratty sweater, crusted
> mascara Blackening her gaze. (10)

In contrast to Brooks' "In the Mecca" where it is not until the end of the poem that readers are given a true sense of Ms. Sallie's response to loosing Pepita, here Demeter's devastation is immediately evident. Dove's employment of strong language to describe Demeter's unkempt appearance clearly intimates how deeply she is impacted. Dove's description of Demeter's eyes smudged with mascara and her braless breasts are also significant for they create a realistic image of the inconsolable mother that is identifiable to the contemporary reader.

In "Protection," Demeter tries to resign herself to the fact that Persephone has disappeared, but she is constantly reminded of her: "Everywhere in the garden I see the slim vine / of your neck, the stubborn baby curls . . . / I know I'm not saying this right. / "Good" hair has no body / in this country; like trained ivy, / it hangs and shines"(11). This quote is significant because it is one of three direct indications of Persephone and Demeter's African American heritage. Dove's description of Persephone's tightly coiled hair, or as she says, "stubborn baby curls," versus the European-like bodiless "good hair," returns us to the intraracial politics discussed in Brooks' and Morrison's narratives. By virtue of how she characterizes her daughter's hair, Demeter, like Pecola and Annie, has clearly fallen victim to the White aesthetic. While Dove's treatment of colorism is subtle in comparison to Brooks' and Morrison's, it is equally relevant because Dove draws attention to the issue of colorism experienced by African American women.

In both the archetypal myth and in Brooks' "*In the Mecca*," individual women, (Hecate in the mythic story and Aunt Dill in Brooks' narrative) offer consolation to Demeter. In "Grief: The Council," Dove presents a community of women who stage an intervention to coax Demeter back to life. Much like the community of women in Euripides' *Medea* and Morrison's *Beloved* who assemble to assist the grieving mothers during their emotional crises, the women in *Mother Love* function in the fashion of a Greek chorus providing both assistance and commentary on the events: "Sister Jefferies, you could drop in / tomorrow morning, take one / of your mason jars, something / sweetish, tomatoes or bell peppers . . . Miz Earl can fetch her later to the movies— / a complicated plot should distract her, something with a car chase through Manhattan / loud horns melting to a strings-and-sax ending" (16). The characters' vernacular and, as Steffen notes, colloquialisms and double negations (67)[12] betray once again that the characters in the narrative are African American. Although the women are intent on helping Demeter, they are slightly impatient with her reaction to Persephone's captivity:

I told her: enough is enough.
Get a hold of yourself, take a lover,
help some other unfortunate child.
Yes, it's a tragedy, a low-down shame,
but you still got your own life to live. (15)

The women talk as though Demeter overreacts to Persephone's disappearance. Here Dove deconstructs what Michele Wallace refers to as "the myth of the Black superwoman." This myth centers on the notion that Black women are emotionally and physically equipped to handle racism and sexism and any other challenges. The women expect Demeter to accept her loss because, like most Black women, they have learned to bear the brunt of their adversity. But Demeter's uncombed hair and braless breasts indicate her refusal to acquiesce to her prescribed role of the resilient Black woman. Thus Dove continues in the tradition of Black women writing against the controlling image of Black womanhood and presents an alternative view of the "strong Black woman" to show that Demeter, as a woman, can be vulnerable. When the speaker notes that Demeter has to live for herself, she makes a crucial statement. Demeter stopped living for herself long before Persephone is kidnapped. Like many mothers she loses herself in her role as mother. Despite the tragic circumstance, she now has the opportunity to experience her own rebirth and begin her own life, for as the leader of the women's group notes, it seems unlikely that Persephone will return: "I thought of those blurred snapshots framed / on milk cartons, a new pair each week" (15). The "blurred snapshots" on the milk cartons again puts the narrative in its modern context and serves as a haunting reminder that Dove's narrative is not just a mythological tale but contemporary reality too.

At the women's urging, Demeter decides not to wallow in despair. She recognizes that although her own child is gone she can pass on her "mother love" to another. Demeter becomes an "othermother": "women who assist blood mothers by sharing mothering responsibilities" (Collins 47). As an othermother, Demeter experiences a rebirth. As Jaffar-Agha notes, "the death of the old Demeter presages the birth of the new: her movement from mother to crone. But acknowledgement that she has passed from one phase to the next does not necessarily mean that Demeter has internalized or reconciled herself with the changes that have been forced upon her" (120). Demeter realizes that although she still grieves, her mother's instinct is still intact: "Who can forget the attitude of mothering?" she says (17). Similar to the Demophoön episode in the archetypal narrative, Demeter is persuaded to become a surrogate mother for a baby boy. She selfishly attempts to make her ward immortal by placing "him on the smouldering embers, / sealing his juices slowly so he might / be cured to perfection." (17). Before long Demeter is caught trying to make the child immortal. But whereas in the *Homeric Hymn* Demeter is outraged by the mother's horrified response to Demeter's attempt to immortalize her son, Dove's Demeter is empathetic: "Oh, I know it / looked damning at the hearth a muttering crone / bent over a baby sizzling on a spit / as neat as a Virginia ham. Poor human—" (17). Dove's mythic mother can identify with Demophoön's mother because she understands the painful experience of knowing the helplessness one feels when she cannot protect her child.

Following Persephone's abduction Dove breaks from the mythic plot and describes Persephone's sexual defloration, first by rape and then through a series of consensual relationships. Dove's description of the rape is couched in the metaphoric language of Brooks' "The Anniad."

And though nothing could chasten
The plunge, this man
Adamant as a knife easing into
The humblest crevice, I found myself at
The center of a calm so pure, it was hate. (12)

Brooks' and Morrison's versions of the story, and the *Homeric Hymn* show that Persephone's descent to hell and cyclical death and rebirth is dependent on Hades' abduction and rape. Alternatively, Dove imagines that Hades bears no responsibility for Persephone's departure: she leaves on her own terms. Moreover, unlike Morrison's

Persephone, Dove's mythic daughter experiences an emotional and physical descent into hell.

The third section of *Mother Love* features Persephone's sojourn to hell. Persephone's descent to the underworld occurs on both a vertical and horizontal axis.[13] Persephone moves horizontally across the globe, first stopping in Paris and then traveling to Germany and Mexico. In this section of the narrative, myth and autobiography merge as Dove plays out her grandmother Beulah's dream that "she would make it to Paris one day" *(Selected Poems 176)*. [14] Moreover, considering Dove's own travels abroad, it is likely that descriptions of Persephone's experiences in Europe are also slightly based on Dove's experience as a Fulbright scholar in Tubingen, Germany. Persephone's vertical descent is featured in several poems describing her downward journey into the heated and dark depths of hell. In "Persephone in Hell," for example, she goes "down into the stone chasms of the 'City of Lights'" (23), and down again into the oppressive heat of the metro station. Here the "chasm" is reminiscent of the opening left by Hades' entry and exit on earth. As Persephone walks through the darkened Paris streets, Persephone sees an object "throbbing with neon tubing / like some demented plumber's diagram / of a sinner's soul" (29).

In Paris Persephone experiences her archetypal death and rebirth. Although she is not imprisoned nor longing to go home, she sheds her youthful innocence and becomes an independent self. Paris, a city usually associated with romance, art, and culture, is the perfect locale for Persephone's new life. Like many young people who travel to Europe to discover themselves, Persephone is "not quite twenty" when she travels to Paris. She dwells in communal "loveless facilities shared by / the shameful poor and shamelessly young" (23). Occasionally Persephone thinks of her mother; but whereas Homer's Persephone yearns for her mother to rescue her, Dove's Persephone rejoices in the fact that she has limited interaction with her mother. Reflecting on her mother's naïveté, Persephone scoffs at her mother's request for daily phone calls:

Mother with her frilly ideals
gave me money to call home every day,

but she couldn't know what I was feeling;
I was doing what she didn't need to know.
I was doing everything and feeling nothing. (25)

Like any overprotective mother, Demeter gives Persephone money to call home not only because she wants to be sure of Persephone's well-being but also because she wants to maintain the close ties she has with her daughter. But Persephone rejects her mother's attempt to keep the relationship as it once was. In *Of Woman Born*, Adrienne Rich suggests that daughters at some stage of their lives become matrophobic and fearful of becoming as subverted as their mothers. Rich maintains: "The mother stands for the victim in ourselves, the unfree woman, the martyr. Our personalities seem dangerously to blur and overlap with our mothers'; and in a desperate attempt to know where mother ends and daughter begins, we perform radical surgery" (236). In an effort to divorce herself from any sense of victimization and to create her own sense of identity, Persephone drowns her anxieties in sexual escapades. Dove inverts the mythic story showing that her Persephone figure is not a victim of sexual abuse for she freely makes her own sexual choices:

There was love of course. Mostly boys:
A flat-faced engineering student from Missouri,
A Texan flaunting his teaspoon of Cherokee blood.
I waited for afterwards—their pale eyelids, foreheads
Thrown back so the rapture could evaporate.
I don't believe I was suffering. I was curious, mainly:
How would each one smell, how many ways could
He do it?
I was drowning in flowers. (25–26)

Here, Dove's Persephone regards her deflowering as a learning experience that teaches her about her own sexuality and the sexual prowess of her male suitors. Hades' rape of Persephone is crucial to the *Homeric* myth because his rape signifies the rupture of the mother–daughter relationship as well as his sexual and physical oppression of Persephone. The decision to take Persephone to the underworld is made by Zeus and Hades, two representatives of male power. Neither Persephone nor Demeter is in a position to stop the rape from occurring. Christine Downing offers a different reading of the rape. Downing argues that Hades and Zeus are "playing culturally approved roles" that aide in Persephone's transition from child to woman and therefore the abduction can be seen "not as violation but as initiation" (161). In accordance with ancient tradition, "initiations typically mark the transition from one life stage to another in dramatically violent ways and often involve a figurative death experience" (161). In *Mother Love*, Dove's protagonist experiences a sexual initiation that does not render her powerless. Unlike the mythic figure, because Persephone is sexually independent, Hades cannot victimize her. By the time the two meet, Persephone is an experienced lover and therefore has become a woman in spite of Hades. Unlike other characterizations of Persephone by the women in this study, when Persephone meets Hades she freely enters into the relationship. In contrast to the mythic story where Persephone is seduced by the narcissus, here Hades confronts Persephone directly:

> If I could just touch your ankle, he whispers, there
> on the inside, above the bone—leans closer,
> breath of lime and peppers—I know I could
> make love to you. She considers
> this, secretly thrilled, though she wasn't quite
> sure what he meant. (37)

As Persephone entertains Hades' offer she wonders if she really likes him or if she is looking for a new adventure: "Was she falling for him out of sheer boredom— / cooped up in this anything-but-humble dive, stone / gargoyles leering and brocade drapes licked with fire? / Her ankle burns where he described it" (37). Persephone is intrigued by Hades and allows for the sexual encounter. As he "drives home his desire" (37), in the upper world "her mother aboveground stumbles, is caught / by the fetlock—bereft in an instant—" (*ML* 37). At this moment, Persephone's loss of innocence, and subsequent transition from child to woman, corresponds with Demeter's symbolic "stumble" or loss of control over her daughter and her own life. As Persephone develops her sexual self, Demeter embarks on a journey to find her. As Steffen suggests, "The two wondering heroines—Demeter who searches worldwide for her lost daughter, and Persephone who waxes and wanes between upper- and underworld—not only represent a perennial dimension of the mother-daughter-consort triangle. They also personify an ethic and aesthetic rendition of the political experience of exile and self-reflexive discussion of the void that constitutes the essence of love and loss" (239).

In the archetypal myth, Persephone departs from hell only when her mother intercepts and saves her. Dove's Persephone is not restricted from leaving at will. When she is ready to return to America, Persephone contacts her mother and requests a wire transfer. Persephone's dependence on her mother's financial assistance hints at the fact that although she might wish to be independent Persephone is still very much dependent on her mother, at least financially.

The *Homeric Hymn* characterizes the reunion between Demeter and Persephone as blissful; mother and daughter are relieved to be together again. But in *Mother Love* the reunion is marred by tension. In the preface, Dove foreshadows the reality that once the mother–daughter bond is destroyed the relationship could never be recreated: "But ah, can we every really go back home, as if nothing had happened," she muses (*ML* ii). The poem "The Bistro Styx" uncovers Demeter and Persephone's estrangement. Like the Orphic hymn, which describes Demeter going down to Hades to retrieve her daughter, instead of being reunited in the upper world, in *Mother Love* Demeter and Persephone meet in the lower world of Paris. Similar to the archetypal narrative, Persephone's relationship with Hades stands between daughter and mother. Demeter is resentful of Persephone's relationship with Hades. She is also disturbed by the realization that Persephone is no longer a naïve innocent child that she can protect, for Persephone is now a woman. When Demeter and Persephone meet for lunch, Demeter is unprepared to see how Persephone has matured into a sophisticated woman. Demeter notes that "she was dressed all in gray, / From a kittenish cashmere skirt and cowl / down to the graphite signature of her shoes" (40). During the luncheon Demeter is cautious about what she says to Persephone. She wants to offer motherly advice and persuade Persephone to leave Hades, but she resists, realizing that her words of wisdom would be unwelcome:

> "How's business?" I asked, and hazarded
> a motherly smile to keep from crying out:
> Are you content to conduct your life
> as a cliché, and what's worse,
> an anachronism, the brooding artist's demimonde? (40)

Demeter is frustrated by what she sees as Persephone's naïveté. Like most mothers, Demeter wants to save Persephone from heartache but knows she must allow Persephone to make her own mistakes. In *Sister Outsider*, Audre Lorde maintains, "All mothers see their daughters leaving. Black mothers see it happening as a sacrifice through the veil of hatred hung like sheets of lava in the pathway before their daughters" (158). "The Bistro Styx" reads much like Dove's poem "In a Neutral City" from *Grace Notes*. In this poem a mother imagines that one day when her daughter matures she will be able to revive the maternal bond: "In rain / over lunch we will search for a topic / only to remember a hill, a path hushed / in some waxen shade of magnolias. / Someday we'll talk because there'll be little else to say: and then the cheese and pears will arrive" (Dove *GN* 56). Ironically, in *Mother Love* when the cheese and pears arrive the conversation ceases. As the two eat, Demeter acknowledges Persephone's insatiable appetite: "Nothing seemed to fill / her up: She swallowed, sliced into a pear, / speared each tear-shaped lavaliere / and popped the dripping mess into her pretty mouth" (42). And as Persephone bites into the "starry rose of a fig," a symbolic replacement for the pomegranate, Demeter admits, *"I've lost her"* (42). Demeter realizes that Hades does not keep Persephone captive; that Persephone remains in Paris by her own volition. Here Dove offers a play on Ovid's narrative.

In the *Metamorphoses*, after Persephone mistakenly eats the pomegranate, she compromises her ability to return permanently to earth. Eating the fruit results in her having to divide her time between hell and earth. Dove rewrites the myth to show that Persephone has no desire to return to the upper world, and so during the luncheon she devours each course that is set before her.

In "The Anniad" Brooks shows that each time Tan Man returns and departs, Annie experiences a metaphorical death and rebirth. Dove presents a similar scenario. Although Demeter knows Persephone will never return home, every time Persephone visits from one of her trips and then departs, Demeter experiences her own death and rebirth. Like Niobe, Demeter is portrayed as the perpetually grieving—and perhaps depressed—mother. Downing says that in the myth Demeter's depression is evidenced by "her unwillingness to allow anything to flourish, her mourning for a year, her unwillingness to be active in any form other than wandering for almost a year" (175–76). Dove's Demeter is equally as despondent. In "Demeter, Waiting" Demeter expresses her inability to cope with Persephone's absence: "She is gone again and I will not bear. / it, I will drag my grief through a winter / of my own making and refuse / any meadow that recycles itself into / hope" (*ML* 56). Demeter's refusal to deal with Persephone's absence reflects her narcissism. Downing observes that when Persephone goes to hell Demeter does not consider that a "change in relationship" (176) might be vital for Demeter nor does she "support her daughter to take an independent step" (176). Rather, she "selfishly uses her powers to get her daughter back" (176). In *Mother Love* Demeter also refuses to acknowledge that Persephone is her own woman and must live her own life. At one point Demeter becomes the stereotypical overbearing mother who tries to make Persephone feel guilty by telling her that expensive gifts cannot replace Persephone's physical presence:

> Nothing can console me. You may bring silk
> to make me sigh, dispense yellow roses
> in the manner of ripened dignitaries.
> You can tell me repeatedly
> I am unbearable (and I know this):
> Still nothing turns the gold on corn,
> Nothing is sweet to the tooth crushing in. (48)

Demeter admits that her behavior is a little melodramatic, but she believes that she cannot change her feelings. But there is hope for Demeter. She surmises that in the future, "I may laugh again at / a bird, perhaps, chucking the nest— / but it will not be happiness, /

for I have known that" (48). Demeter has difficulty coping with Persephone's absence because she defines herself and her self-worth through her ability to mother Persephone. Without Persephone, Demeter does not have a sense of identity. Rich argues that motherhood is an institution defined by patriarchy, and thus the roles of motherhood are socially constructed and oppressive. Demeter is a victim of this socially constructed role of mother. In order to reconcile with Persephone's departure, Demeter must realize that her life extends beyond her title as mother. Toward the end of the poem, Demeter resigns herself to the fact that Persephone has become a woman and is the wife of Hades. She appeals to her son-in-law (Hades) to protect her daughter: "This alone is what I wish for you: knowledge. / To understand each desire has an edge, / to know we are responsible for the lives / we change" (63).

The mythic theme of death and renewal plays out through Demeter's loss of self worth and Persephone's development of self. As Demeter experiences her own gradual descent into an emotional hell, Persephone blossoms into a woman, an artist, and mother. Persephone's many travels across the globe to Germany, Mexico, and Sicily contribute to her personal as well as artistic development. de Weever notes that in African American women's literature, there are numerous examples of "the theme of the artist, who grows or does not grow through the relationship to the mother, the ultimate creative force" (151). Dove picks up on this theme of the mother–daughter conflict and the development of the artist, showing that as tensions between Persephone and her mother climax, Persephone's development as an artist flourishes.

One of the distinctions between Dove's contemporary reworking of the myth, and Brooks' and Morrison's renditions of it, is Dove's discussion of the cyclical nature of the mother–daughter relationship. Dove reinforces the fact that as daughters become women they inevitably become mothers themselves, thus resulting in the overlapping of identities. Jung posits: "We could therefore say that every mother contains her daughter in herself and every daughter her mother, and that every woman extends backwards into her mother and forwards into her daughter. This participation and intermingling give rise to that peculiar uncertainty as regards *time*: a woman lives earlier as her mother, later as a daughter" (162).

In *Mother Love* the mother–daughter relationship revolves around this cyclical tension as mothers and daughters become one and the same. The blending of identity is conveyed in the seventh part of "Persephone in Hell." This poem features both mother and daughter speaking individually and at the same time, their voices in concert overlapping:

If I whispered to the moon	
if I whispered to the olive	I am waiting
which would hear me?	you are on the way
the garden gone	I am listening
the city around me	I am waiting
	(33)

Here, readers must rely upon the typographical format of the poem to distinguish between Persephone's voice and Demeter's. As each woman speaks it is difficult to discern who is speaking, thus reestablishing the cyclical nature of the mother–daughter relationship.

When Persephone becomes a mother she has the opportunity to relive Demeter's fears and anxieties. Dove draws from her own personal experience to write about Persephone's bout with motherhood. She tells Pereira, "The mother daughter poems in *Mother Love* were a product of my life, obviously, with a daughter growing up" (166). In *Grace Notes* Dove writes extensively about her experience with motherhood. Many of the mother poems capture the maternal bond between mother and child. "Pastoral," for example, highlights the pureness of mother love:

I liked afterwards best, lying
Outside on quilt, her new skin
Spread out like meringue. I felt then
What a young man must feel
With his first love asleep on his breast:
Desire, and the freedom to imagine it. (38)

In contrast to *Grace Notes*, in *Mother Love* Dove reveals a less utopian view of motherhood. Dove illustrates that while motherhood may be rewarding, mothers must make physical, emotional, and professional sacrifices for their children. In "Used," for example, Persephone laments the postnatal consequences of weight gain and diminishing altered sexual libido:

> The conspiracy's to make us thin. Size threes
> Are all the rage, and skirts ballooning above twinkling knees
> Are every man-child's preadolescent dream.
> [w]e've earned the navels sunk in grief
> when the last child emptied us of their brief
> interior light. Our muscles say We have been used.
>
> Have you ever tried silk sheets? I did,
> Persuaded by postnatal dread
> And a Macy's clerk to bargain for more zip.
> We couldn't hang on, slipped
> To the floor and by morning the quilts
> Had slid off, too. Enough of guilt—
> It's hard work staying cool. (60)

Along with frustration about body image, Dove writes about how children impede on one's ability to find the space and time to be creative. Speaking candidly with Richard Peabody, Dove confesses that having a child meant she had "little concentrated time [...] Time gets really broken up into snippets and it's extremely frustrating" (*Conversations* 31). Dove echoes Virginia Woolf's oft-cited statement regarding the female artist's need to have a "room of one's own" to indulge in the creative process. Dove's confession also brings to mind the frustration experienced by the mother in the poem "Daystar." In this poem the character Beulah feels overwhelmed by her mothering duties: "She wanted a little room for thinking: / but she saw diapers steaming on the line, / a doll slumped behind the door" (*Selected Poems* 188). As she looks around at her children, she waits until they are sleeping to steal some time for herself: "She had an hour, at best, before Liza appeared / pouting from the top of the stairs" (188). Perhaps the biggest lesson that Persephone must learn, which Dove grappled with herself, is that maternity is volatile: "I hadn't anticipated the vulnerability of being a mother; the vulnerability of accepting that there are things you can't do anything about in life; that you can't protect another person completely; that in fact when you were the daughter, you didn't want to be protected" (Steffen 130). In time, Persephone, like her mother before her, will also learn this lesson.

Mother Love culminates with Persephone/Dove's trip to Sicily to visit the ancient site of Persephone's abduction. Here again Persephone's ethnicity comes into view. Persephone remarks that the tour guide is intrigued by her Blackness. She remarks, "[t]he way he stops to smile at me / and pat my arm, I'm surely his first / Queen of Sheba" (*ML* 70). As Dove/Persephone, her husband, and the tour guide search for the ancient site, Persephone takes note of the neglected earth.

> . . . we climb
> straight through the city dump,
> through rotten fruit and Tampax tubes
> so our treacherous guide can deliver us into
>
> what couldn't be: a patch of weeds sprouting six—no seven—
> columns, their Doric reserve softened by weather
> to tawny indifference. (72)

While we have the same kind of wastelandic imagery presented in Brooks' and Morrison's texts, here the earth has been neglected not because of social bankruptcy but rather because history has been forgotten. The mythical past has been buried and replaced with modernity. When Persephone and company finally reach the site, what they find is not temples or a shrine but instead a racetrack: "Bleachers, Pit stops. A ten-foot fence / plastered with ads—Castrol, Campari— / and looped barbed wire; no way to get near" (*ML* 75). The circular form of the racetrack symbolizes the cyclical nature of life and repetitive theme of birth and renewal in the archetypal myth. At the poem's conclusion Dove offers no resolution for Persephone and Demeter:

No story's ever finished; it just goes
on unnoticed in the dark that's all
around us: blazed stones, the ground closed. (*ML* 77)

This conclusion is consistent with the ending of the mythical story, which also shows Persephone and Demeter in a constant cycle of reconciliation and departure. Dove's duo will continue with their symbiotic relationship and if and when Persephone becomes a mother she will engage in the same conflicts that she had with her own mother.

Written forty-six years after Brooks' "The Anniad" and twenty-five years after Morrison's *The Bluest Eye, Mother Love* is a powerful story about motherhood and self-identity that finally rewrites the image of Persephone as the victimized subject. Dove plays the archetypal myth against a contemporary version of the narrative to show that although rape and abduction do happen to young women, female growth and development does not have to be contingent upon the violent actions of a male predator. Rather, she shows that Persephone is an empowered woman who makes her own choices in life. . Dove's 1990s depiction of Persephone differs from Brooks' and Morrison's because she has created a character whose attitude is consistent with many of the young women of the decade. A legacy of feminism and other movements taught young girls to be independent and strong, and they heeded this advice. So whereas Annie of Brooks' "The Anniad" is docile and voiceless, Dove's Persephone asserts her authority. Dove's narrative also demonstrates that while the maternal bond that mothers have for their daughters is unyielding, daughters do not necessarily reciprocate the same emotional attachment to their mothers. In fact, daughters often find their mother's love to be stifling and oppressive. Dove reveals that ultimately, either by force or by choice, all daughters leave their mothers, and unlike the mythic story they do not always return home.

Brooks, Morrison, and Dove are three writers who are rarely studied collectively. Bringing these writers together enables readers to acknowledge that these three mid-western Pulitzer and (or) Nobel prize winning authors have much in common. In addition to sharing similar biographical histories, they are drawn to the classics for the same reasons, they produce literary works that reflect a number of thematic parallels, and they provide new ways to read and interpret ancient classical myths about motherhood and the female rite of passage. By focusing on issues of race and gender these women offer contemporary perspectives of ancient myths that highlight the oppression and the empowerment of African American women. Just as the ancient narratives provide a useful resource for modern writers to adapt, in time the classical revisions of Brooks, Morrison, and Dove will serve as the narratives that inspire generations to come.

The classical revisions by these women also serve as a reminder that African American writers claim the classics as part of their own literary heritage. By writing the classics Black, these writers establish a new tradition of classicism that is Black centered. *African American Literature and the Classicist Tradition: Black Women Writers from Wheatley to Morrison* is only as a launching point for the study of Black writers and the classicist tradition. As the field of *Classica Africana* continues to develop, classicists and scholars of Black literature will expand their critical analysis of Black writers and classical mythology. Other studies might consider, for example, how African American male writers rework the classics.

Another possible study might focus on how Black writers from across the globe, namely Caribbean poet Derek Walcott, Black British writer Bernadine Evaristo, and African poet/novelist Wole Soyinka, have appropriated classical mythology. Walcott's *Omeros* (1990), Evaristo's *The Emperor's Babe* (2001), and Soyinka's *The Bacchae of Euripides: A Communion Rite* (1974) reveal that, similar to the African American women writers discussed in this work, writers from across the African Diaspora use the classics as a blueprint for the creation of their narratives and marry classical mythology with myths specific to their own cultures. Recognizing that Black writers have made a contribution to the Western classical tradition is significant for scholars of Black literature and classicists. Scholars of Black literature who are already investigating the relationship between the Western classical tradition and Black literature can place their scholarship under the specialized field of

Classica Africana. As for classical scholars, acknowledging the scholarship and the creative reworking of classical narratives by Black writers allows for a more inclusive approach to the discipline—one that recognizes the contributions not only of Black writers but other groups as well.

Notes

Introduction

1. Ronnick also as Vice Chair of the National Committee for Latin and Greek, an organization that promotes and encourages classical studies.
2. Ronnick says Scarborough felt that as times changed he experienced a hostile reception from new members of the APA, 267. *The Autobiography of William Sanders Scarborough: An American Journey from Slavery to Scholarship*. Detroit: Wayne State UP, 2005.
3. See Robert Fikes, Jr., "African American Scholars of Greco-Roman Culture" (2002), an historical documentation of classical scholars from the nineteenth century to contemporary times published in *The Journal of Blacks in Higher Education*.
4. In the preface to Wheatley's *Poems on Various Subjects, Religious and Moral*, Wheatley's slave master, John Wheatley, notes, "she has an inclination to learn the Latin Tongue, and has made some Progress in it," (Mason, 1989, 47).
5. In her discussion of African American poets and classical mythology Christa Buschendorf observes that in African American poetry "a particular myth is juxtaposed, combined, or even merged with other myths, while the importance of the individual myth diminishes. Rather than [aim] at revision, syncretism aims at recreation." Christa Buschendorf, "White Masks: Greek Mythology in Contemporary Black Poetry." *Crossing Border: Inner- and Intercultural Exchanges in a Multicultural Society*. Ed. Heinz Ickstadt. Germany: Peter Lang, 1997, 76.
6. Elizabeth Hayes' article, "Like Seeing you Buried": Persephone in *The Bluest Eye, Their Eyes Were Watching God* and *The Color Purple*," *Images of Persephone: Feminist Readings in Western Literature* Gainesville: University Press of Florida, 1994, discusses how Zora

Neale Hurston, Alice Walker, and Toni Morrison adapt the Persephone and Demeter myth.

Chapter 1

1. For Foley's complete list of ancient sources see Foley, Helene P. Ed. *The Homeric Hymn to Demeter: Translation, Commentary, and Interpretive Essays.* New Jersey: Princeton UP, 1994.
2. Other Homeric Hymns include Hymns to Apollo and Hermes.
3. For an in-depth discussion of the Mysteries see Foley and Kerényi, Carl *Archetypal Image of Mother and Daughter.* Trans. Ralph Manheim, New York: Pantheon Books, 1967.
4. Although she is not featured as a significant character in the Homeric Hymn, Hecate is an important Goddess. In pre-Olympian times she was a triple goddess, ruler of Earth, Sky, and Underworld. She also makes up the triad Maiden (Core), Nymph (Persephone), Hecate (Crone). In some versions she serves as Persephone's companion. In art she is often featured alongside Persephone and Demeter.
5. See Foley for more about the various witnesses of Hades' rape of Persephone 99–100.
6. In most versions, after Ceres is reunited with Proserpine she rejuvenates the earth. In Graves' interpretation, when Ceres learns that Proserpine will have to return to hell, she refuses to restore order to the land and threatens to return to Olympus. Graves, Robert. *The Greek Myths.* New York: Penguin Books, 1960.
7. See Nancy Chodorow's psychoanalytic reading of the mother-daughter relationship, *The Reproduction of Mothering: Psychoanalysis and the Sociology of Gender.* Berkeley: Univ. of California Press, 1978.
8. Niobe is mentioned in one of Sappho's poems. *Gantz, Timothy. Early Greek Myth: A Guide to Literary and Artistic Sources.* Baltimore: The Johns Hopkins UP, 1993.
9. Parthenius' story is influenced by the myths of Cinyras and Adonis, see Graves 1960, 260.
10. The last stanza of Wheatley's poem features Niobe as a stone figure. There is some debate about the last stanza. The editor of Wheatley's poem includes a notation claiming Wheatley did not write this ending. Wheatley, Phillis. *The Poems of Phillis Wheatley.* Ed. Julian D. Mason. Chapel Hill: Univ. of North Carolina Press, 1989.
11. A Corinthian work prior to ca 430 shows Medea on a "Chest of Cypselus" and on a Lekyuthos of ca 530. Nussbaum, Martha.

"Serpents in the Soul: A Reading of Seneca's Medea." *Medea: Essays on Medea in Myth, Literature, Philosophy, and Art.* Ed. James Clauss and Sarah Iles Johnson. New Jersey: Princeton Univ. Press, 1997, 262.

Chapter 2

1. John C. Shields' article "Phillis Wheatley's Use of Classicism" provides an in-depth discussion of the neoclassical influence on Wheatley's poetry. *American Literature: A Journal of Literary History, Criticism and Bibliography* 52 (1980): 97–111.
2. As Helen Burke notes, Wheatley had "an [u]nderstanding of how the process of poetic legitimization works in the Western European literary tradition. Wheatley accepts, as does for example, her predecessor Alexander Pope, that the individual writer has significance strictly in relation to this tradition." Burke, "Problematizing American Dissent: The Subject of Phillis Wheatley." *Cohesion and Dissent in America.* Ed. Carol Colatrella and Joseph Alkana. New York: State University of New York Press, 1994, 33–34.
3. We can credit Susannah Wheatley for introducing Phillis to Terence. Susannah may have intended to show Phillis that other Africans had risen above their station in life. In the eighteenth century Terence's story was well known. As Paula Bennett notes: "[A]ccording to an anonymous biography prefixed to Donatus's commentary on Terence's works, Terence was manumitted as a reward for his literary achievements. . . . This information was a regular part of eighteenth-century biographies of Terence, which group him with a select number of other figures from antiquity, such as Plato's Phaedo, whose intellectual accomplishments earned them their freedom. . . . Given that Terence was standard reading for intermediate Latin, . . . not only Wheatley but many in her audience as well were probably aware of his history." Bennett, "Phillis Wheatley's Vocation and the Paradox of the 'Afric Muse.'" *PMLA* 113 (1998): 67.
4. John Shields suggests that Wheatley referred to one of George Sandy's translations of the *Metamorphoses*. Sandys' editions of the *Metamorphoses* were published from 1628 to 1690. Though it is unlikely, Wheatley's Niobe poem could have been drawn from Aischylos' play. As noted in chapter 1, there are a number of similarities between Wheatley's version of Niobe and Aischylos' version.
5. See Betsy Erkkila's discussion of Wheatley's use of irony and double meaning. Erkkila, Betsy. "Phillis Wheatley and the Black American

Revolution." *A Mixed Race: Ethnicity in Early America*. Ed. Frank Shuffleton. New York: Oxford University Press, 1993, 231.

6. Alicia Ostriker observes that the Niobe poems "may be a veiled portrait of her own powerlessness—or even, more radically, a lament on behalf of the mother from whom she herself had been torn." Ostriker, "The Thieves of Language: Women Poets and Revisionist Mythmaking." *The New Feminist Criticism: Essays on Women, Literature, and Theory*. Ed. Elaine Showalter. New York: Pantheon Books, 1985.

7. Ovid's *Metamorphoses* was quite popular during the nineteenth century and most would have been familiar with the story. Ovid, *Metamorphoses*. Trans. A. D. Melville. Oxford: Oxford University Press, 1986.

8. Judith P. Hallet supports duBois' assertion, maintaining: "[T]he prevalent modern impression that Sappho was a lesbian, that she herself took part in homosexual practices is not based on ancient testimony. . . . [T]he ancient sources who as much as mention Sappho's reputation for physical homoerotic involvement, the earliest of which post dates her lifetime by at least 300 years describes this reputation as nothing more than a wholly disgraceful accusation." Hallet, "Sappho and Her Social Context: Sense and Sensuality." *Reading Sappho: Contemporary Approaches*. Ed. Ellen Greene. Berkeley: U of California P, 1996, 130.

9. Kate McCullough observes: "Whether we read the original Sappho as the forerunner of the modern lesbian or merely as the leader of a spiritual community of women, Hopkins' use of the name to signify friendship, love, and community among women is explicit. Indeed, throughout the novel, Sappho and Dora trust in and support each other, in the face of duplicitous lovers and blackmailers." McCullough, Kate. "Slavery, Sexuality, and Genre: Pauline Hopkins and Representation of Feminine desire." *The Unruly Voice: Rediscovering Pauline Elizabeth Hopkins*. Ed. John Cullen. Urbana U of Illinois P, 1996, 21–49.

Chapter 3

1. See Bell's quote on pages 11–12 in this book's introduction.
2. According to D. H. Melhem, in "The Anniad" Brooks employs "an elaborate scheme of rhyme and half-rhyme, a tetrameter line . . . using three or four rhymes per stanza, varying greatly the initial *a b (a) c (a) b (a) d d c* with closing couplets and other modifications" (62).

3. For a discussion of the epic-like qualities of "The Anniad," see Tate, "Allegories of Black Female Desire; or, Rereading Nineteenth-Century Sentimental Narratives of Black Female Authority." *Changing Our Own Words. Essays on Criticism, Theory, and Writing by Black Women.* Ed. Cheryl Wall. New Jersey: Rutgers University Press, 1989, 98–126; Seligman, "The Mother of Them All: Gwendolyn Brooks's *Annie Allen.*" *The Anna Book: Searching for Anna in Literary History.* Connecticut: Greenwood Press, 1992, 131–38, and my own essay, "Gwendolyn Brooks' 'The Anniad' and the Indeterminacy of Genre," *CLA* 44 (2001), 350–66.

4. See Harry B. Shaw, "Perceptions of Men in the Early Works of Gwendolyn Brooks." *Black American Poets Between Worlds, 1940–1960.* Ed. R. Baxter Miller. Knoxville: University of Tennessee Press, 1986, 136–59.

5. See Anne Folwell Stanford, "An Epic With a Difference: Sexual Politics in Gwendolyn Brooks' 'The Anniad.'" *American Literature* 67 (1995): 290.

6. As Stanford argues, "The dreams and images by which Annie lives—drawn from [W]hite European myth and fairy tale—emphasize female passivity, [W]hite Euro-American notions of beauty, and highly romanticized conceptions of love" 285.

7. Interestingly, as Melhem points out though, Tan Man is also a victim of romanticism. When Tan Man goes off to war he, like Annie, is "victimized . . . by illusions of male supremacy, he has obeyed a romantic code, replete with the false glamour of war" 66.

8. Gertrude Reif Hughes asserts that as a solider Tan Man feels more empowered than he does in his position as Annie's husband. Hughes, "Making it *Really* New: Hilda Doolittle, Gwendolyn Brooks, and the Feminist Potential of Modern Poetry." *On Gwendolyn Brooks: Reliant Contemplation.* Ed. Stephen Caldwell Wright. Ann Arbor: The University of Michigan Press, 1996, 198.

9. See Arthur P. Davis' "Black and Tan Motif in the Poetry of Gwendolyn Brooks." *College Language Association Journal* 6 (1962): 90–97.

10. Jimoh points out that Annie is angry because her black hair is "not blond—and 'boisterous' not straight hair," which serves "as a symbol of the falsity of the prevailing beauty fictions." Jimoh, "Double Consciousness, Modernism, and Womanist Themes in Gwendolyn Brooks's 'The Anniad.'" *Melus* 23 (1998): 5.

11. Bolden notes, "The reality of her [Annie's]" "fate" as a black woman in the urban ghetto of Bronzeville is visibly signaled by the absence of

mythological illusions in her new world vision and the discarded lofty diction and complex wordplay of earlier stanzas." Bolden, *Urban Rage in Bronzeville: Social Commentary in the Poetry of Gwendolyn Brooks, 1945–1960*. Chicago: University of Illinois Press, 1994, 112.

12. Some critics marveled at Brooks' use of language and theme. In a 1950 *New York Times* book review, Phyllis McGinley says, "'The Anniad' is unmatched by any of the other pieces, or so it seems to me. Full of insight and wisdom and pity, technically dazzling, it is a surprising accomplishment in combining storytelling with lyric elegance" (7). Others disagreed with McGinley. Some felt the language was a turn-off to readers. For example, in a review for *The Nation*, Rolphe Humphries wrote: "Her weakness lies in streaks, as it were, of awkwardness, naiveté, when she seems to be carried away by the big word or the spectacular rhyme; when her ear, of a sudden, goes all to pieces. The first two sections of the present collection [*Annie Allen*] contain much more of this kind of work than does the third" (8).

13. Erkkila also says Brooks "rewrites and blackens the Demeter and Persephone myth as a black mother-centered resurrection myth." Erkkila, "Phillis Wheatley and the Black American Revolution." *A Mixed Race: Ethnicity in Early America*. Ed. Frank Shuffleton. New York: Oxford UP, 1993, 214.

14. In "Define the Whirlwind Gwendolyn Brooks's Epic Sign for a Generation" R. Baxter Miller examines the relationship between "In the Mecca" and "The Wasteland."

15. Tanya Wilkerson writes: "The first stage of Demeter's journey reflects a descent into the underworld of primal loss. The victim can sometimes continue wandering and ceaseless calling for that which is lost, never reaching out for the connection and sustenance available in the here and now. In this state a person may become saturated, not just with his or her own helpless grief, but by the grief of the world as well." Wilkerson, *Persephone Returns: Victims, Heroes, and the Journey from the Underworld*. California: Page Mill Press, 1996, 33–34.

16. Brooks' portrayal of Sallie is consistent with Wilkerson's discussion of Demeter. In "In the Mecca," Sallie is also consumed by the grief of her uncompassionate neighbors.

Chapter 4

1. See Marilyn Mobley's article on the role of myth in Morrison's *Song of Solomon*. Mobley, *Folk Roots and Mythic Wings in Sarah Orne Jewett and Toni Morrison*. Baton Rouge: Louisiana State University Press, 1991.

2. If Morrison is referencing Phaeton, it could be because he is associated with flying and he is supposedly responsible for giving Ethiopians black skin.

3. There have been a number of articles discussing the flying motif in *Song of Solomon*. See Bruck, "The Returning to One's Roots: The Motif of Searching and Flying in Toni Morrison's *Song of Solomon*," *The Afro-American Novel Since 1960*. Eds. Peter Bruck and Wolfgang Karrer. Grüner: Amsterdam, 1982, 289–305; Ousseynou, "Creative African Memory: Some Oral Sources of Toni Morrison's *Song of Solomon*." *Of Dreams Deferred, Dead or Alive: African Perspectives of African American Writers*. Ed. Femi Ojo-Ade. Westport: Greenwood Press, 1996, 129–41; Clark, "Flying Black: Toni Morrison's *The Bluest Eye, Sula*, and *Song of Solomon*," *Minority Voices* 4 (1980): 51–63; and Tidey, "Limping or Flying? Psychoanalysis, Afrocentrism, and *Song of Solomon*." *College English* 63 (2000): 48–70.

4. In an interview with Kathy Neustadt, Morrison said that Pilate's song in *Song of Solomon* is similar to a song sung by members of her family. "I don't know all the lyrics but it starts with a line like 'Green, the only song of Solomon,' and then some words I don't understand, but it is a genealogy. I made up the lyrics in the *Song of Solomon* to go with the story." Neustadt, "The Visits of the Writers Toni Morrison and Eudora Welty." *Conversations with Toni Morrison*. Ed. Danielle Taylor-Guthrie. Mississippi: UP of Mississippi, 1994, 90.

5. The ancient historian Didimus reports that Medea leaves her sons with Jason. After she leaves Corinth, in retaliation for what Medea did to Glauce, Creon's family kills Medea's children.

6. In antiquity mothers did not hold rights to their children. Children were the property of their fathers. In the *Medea* though, Medea had the option of taking her children with her.

7. Hayes is incorrect. Morrison's minor was in classical studies. Hayes, "Like Seeing You Buried": Images of Persephone in *The Bluest Eye, Their Eyes Were Watching God*, and *The Color Purple*. *Images of Persephone: Feminist Readings in Western Literature*. Gainesville: University Press of Florida.

8. Donald Gibson suggests that Claudia's attempt to dismember the dolls is also an attempt to dismember dismember the myth of White beauty. Gibson, "Text and Countertext in Toni Morrison's *The Bluest Eye." Literature, Interpretation, Theory* 1 (1989): 21.

9. The Fishers give Pauline a sense of self-worth.

10. A similar idea is featured in *Maud Martha*.

11. Zeus did not want to anger Demeter or disappoint Hades, so he neither gave nor witheld his consent.

12. See Gantz, *Early Greek Myth: A Guide to Literary and Artistic Sources.* Baltimore: The Johns Hopkins UP, 1993, 69.

Chapter 5

1. Dove also admires Al Young's universal approach to poetry. She notes, "he didn't write about just being Black—he wrote about a grandmother, an aunt, he wrote about simply being in love" 188.

2. In addition to Wheatley and Brooks, Dove has also been inspired by Toni Morrison, whose regional works situated in the Midwest offered a view of Black life with which Dove could identify. In a 1991 interview with Mohamed B. Taleb-Khyar, Dove shared, "I practically considered Toni Morrison a personal savior. When her first novel, *The Bluest Eye*, came out, I thought, finally, someone who's writing about where I come from. It was a break though that a Black writer was writing about growing up in a Midwestern town, rather than dealing with the south or with urban decay" 86. Following in the tradition of Morrison, Dove's Pulitzer-Prize-winning first collection, *Thomas and Beulah* (1986) is also situated in the Midwest.

3. See Vendler, *The Given and the Made: Strategies of Poetic Redefinition.* Cambridge: Harvard University Press, 1995, 78.

4. For a more in depth discussion of Dove's aesthetics, see Pereira, *Rita Dove's Cosmopolitanism*. Illinois: University of Illinois Press, 2003, 9.

5. Dove writes about Walcott's cross-cultural poetics in "Either I'm Nobody or I'm a Nation." *Parnassus Poetry in Review* 14 (1987): 49–76.

6. See Pereira for a full-length discussion of Dove's cosmopolitanism.

7. Dove first writes about Walker in the poem "David Walker (1785–1830)," published in *The Yellow House on the Corner* (1980).

8. For a more expansive discussion of Dove's reference to slave revolts, see Steffen, *Crossing Color: Transcultural Space and Place in Rita*

Dove's Poetry, Fiction, and Drama. New York: Oxford University Press, 2001, 125.

9. Adrienne Kennedy also wrote a play based on Oedipus titled *Oedipus Rex* 2001.

10. For more about Dove's use of the sonnet, see Steffen and Lofgren, "Partial Horror: Fragmentation and Healing in Rita Dove's *Mother Love*. *Callaloo* 19 (1996) 135–42.

11. Steffen observes that Dove's reference to the poppies is an intertextual reference to Rainer Maria Rilke's *Sonnets to Orpheus*, which Dove admits influenced her own sonnet sequence, 132–33.

12. A similar occurrence of communal rescue is featured in Morrison's *Beloved*. When Sethe's dead daughter returns to reunite with her mother and destroy her, a group of women in the community gather to help her.

13. See Steffen, 131.

14. Van Dyne makes a similar argument in "Siting the Poet; Rita Dove's Refiguring of Traditions." *Women Poets of the Americas: Toward a Pan-American Gathering*. Ed. Jaqueline Vaught-Brogan and Candelaria Cordelia-Chavez. Notre Dame: University of Notre Dame Press, 1999, 76.

Works Cited

Awkward, Michael. *Tradition, Revision, and Afro-American Women's Novels: Inspiriting Influences.* New York: Columbia UP, 1989.

Baker, Houston A., Jr. "The Achievement of Gwendolyn Brooks." *A Life Distilled: Gwendolyn Brooks, Her Poetry and Fiction.* Ed. Maria K Mootry and Gary Smith. Urbana: U of Illinois P, 1987. 21–29.

Bannerman, Helen. *The Story of Little Black Sambo.* New York: Harper Collins, 2003.

Behrendt, Stephen. "Introduction: History, Mythmaking, and Romantic Artist." *History and Myth: Essays on English Romantic Literature.* Ed. Stephen Behrendt. Detroit: Wayne State UP, 1990.

Bell, Bernard. *The Afro-American Novel and Its Tradition.* Amherst: U of Massachusetts P, 1987.

Bennett, Paula. "Phillis Wheatley's Vocation and the Paradox of the 'Afric Muse.'" *PMLA* 113 (1998): 64–76.

Berger, Anne Emmanuelle. "The Latest Word from Echo." *New Literary History: Literature, Media, and the Law* 27 (1996): 621–40.

Bernal, Martin. *Black Athena: The Afroasiatic Roots of Classical Civilization.* New Jersey: Rutgers UP, 1987.

Bolden, Barbara Jean. *Urban Rage in Bronzeville: Social Commentary in the Poetry of Gwendolyn Brooks, 1945–1960.* Chicago: U of Illinois P, 1994.

Booth, Alison. "Abduction and Other Severe Pleasures: Rita Dove's *Mother Love.*" *Callaloo* 19 (1996): 125–30.

Braxton, Joanne M. and Sharon Zuber. "Silences in Harriet "Linda Brent" Jacobs's *Incidents in the Life of a Slave Girl.*" In *Listening to Silences: New Essays in Feminist Criticism.* Ed. Elaine Hedges and Shelley Fisher Fishkin. New York: Oxford UP, 1994. 146–55.

Brooks, Gwendolyn. "Why Negro Women Leave Home." *Negro Digest* (March 1951): 26–28.

———. *Selected Poems.* New York: Harper Row, 1963.

———. *Report From Part One.* Detroit: Broadside Press, 1975.

———. *Blacks.* Chicago: Third World Press, 1994.

———. *Report From Part Two.* Chicago: Third World Press, 1996.

Bruck, Peter. "The Returning to One's Roots: The Motif of Searching and Flying in Toni Morrison's *Song of Solomon.*" *The Afro-American Novel Since 1960.* Eds. Peter Bruck and Wolfgang Karrer. Amsterdam: Grüner,1982. 289–305.

Bulfinch, Thomas. *Mythology.* New York: Dell, 1959.

Burke, Helen M. "Problematizing American Dissent: The Subject of Phillis Wheatley." *Cohesion and Dissent in America.* Ed. Carol Colatrella and Joseph Alkana. New York: State U of New York P, 1994. 193–209.

Buschendorf, Christa. "White Masks: Greek Mythology in Contemporary Black Poetry." *Crossing Border: Inner- and Intercultural Exchanges in a Multicultural Society.* Ed. Heinz Ickstadt. Germany: Peter Lang, 1997. 65–82.

Bushe, Vera. "Cycles of Becoming." *The Long Journey Home: Re-visioning the Myth of Demeter and Persephone for Our Time.* Ed. Christine Downing. Boston: Shambhala, 1994. 187–90.

Calame, Claude. "Sappho's Group: An Initiation into Womanhood." *Reading Sappho: Contemporary Approaches.* Ed. Ellen Greene. Berkeley: U of California P, 1996. 113–24.

Campbell, Jane. *Mythic Black Fiction: The Transformation of History.* Knoxville, The U of Tennessee P, 1986.

Campbell, Joseph. *The Hero with a Thousand Faces.* New Jersey: Princeton UP, 1972.

Carby, Hazel. *Reconstructing Womanhood: The Emergence of the Afro-American Woman Novelist.* New York: Oxford UP, 1987.

Carlisle, Theodora. "Reading the Scars: Rita Dove's *The Darker Face of the Earth. African American Review* 34 (2000): 135–50.

Carlson, Kathie. *Life's Daughter/Death's Bride: Inner Transformations Through the Goddess Demeter/Persephone.* Boston: Shambhala, 1997.

Carretta, Vincent, Ed. *Unchained Voices: An Anthology of Black Authors in the English-Speaking World of the 18TH Century.* Kentucky: The UP of Kentucky, 1996.

Clark, Norris. "Flying Black: Toni Morrison's *The Bluest Eye, Sula,* and *Song of Solomon.*" *Minority Voices* 4 (1980): 51–63.

Collins, Patricia Hill. *Black Feminist Thought: Knowledge, Consciousness, and the Politics of Empowerment.* New York: Routledge, 2000.

Chodorow, Nancy. *The Reproduction of Mothering: Psychoanalysis and the Sociology of Gender.* Berkeley: U of California P, 1978.

———. "Feminism and Difference: Gender, Relation and Difference in Psychoanalytic Perspective." *Socialist Review* 46 (1979): 51–69.

Cooper, Anna J. *A Voice From the South*. New York: Negro UP, 1969.

Corti, Lillian. "Medea and Beloved: Self-Definition and Abortive Nurturing in Literary Treatments of the Infanticidal Mother." *Disorderly Eaters: Texts in Self-Empowerment*. Eds. Lillian R. Furst and Peter W. Graham. Pennsylvania: Pennsylvania UP, 1992. 61–77.

Croxall, Samuel. "Book Six." *Ovid's Metamorphoses in 15 Books Translated by the Most Eminent Hands*. London, 1717.

Cushman, Stephen. "And the Dove Returned." *Callaloo* 19 (1996): 131–34.

Cutter, Martha J. *Unruly Tongue: Identity and Voice in American Women's Writing, 1850–1930*. Jackson: UP of Mississippi, 1999.

Davis, Arthur P. "Gwendolyn Brooks." *On Gwendolyn Brooks: Reliant Contemplation*. Ed. Stephen Caldwell Wright. Ann Arbor Michigan: U of Michigan Press, 1996. 97–105.

Davis, Angela. *Women, Race & Class*. New York: Vintage. 1983.

———. "We Do Not Consent: Violence Against Women in a Racist Society." *Cornerstones: An Anthology of African American Literature*. Ed. Melvin Donalson. New York: St. Martin's Press, 1996. 795–805.

Davis, Cynthia. "Self, Society, and Myth in Toni Morrison's Fiction." *Contemporary Literature* 23 (1982): 335.

de Weever, Jacqueline. *Mythmaking and Metaphor in Black Women's Fiction*. New York: St. Martin's Press, 1991.

Dove, Rita. "Telling It Like It I-S IS: Narrative Techniques in Melvin Tolson's *Harlem Gallery*." *New England Review and Bread Loaf Quarterly* 8 (1985): 109–17.

———. *Thomas and Beulah*. Pittsburgh: Carnegie-Mellon UP, 1986.

———. "Either I'm Nobody, or I'm a Nation." *Parnassus Poetry in Review* 14 (1987): 49–76.

———. *Grace Notes*. New York: W. W. Norton & Company, Inc., 1989.

———. *The Yellow House on the Corner*. Pittsburgh: Carnegie-Mellon UP, 1989.

———. *Selected Poems*. New York: Vintage Books, 1993.

———. *The Darker Face of the Earth*. Story Line Press: Brownsville, 1994.

———. *Mother Love*. New York: W. W. Norton & Company, 1995.

———. *The Darker Face of the Earth*. Revised. Story Line Press: Ashland, 2000.

Downes, Jeremy M. *Recursive Desire: Rereading Epic Tradition*. Tuscaloosa: The U of Alabama P, 1997.

Downing, Christine. *The Long Journey Home: re-visioning the Myth of Demeter and Persephone for Our Time.* Boston: Shambhala, 1994.

Drake, Kimberly. "Rape and Resignation: Silencing the Victim in the Novels of Morrison and Wright." *Literature Interpretation Theory* 6 (1995): 63–72.

duBois, Page. Introduction. *The Love Songs of Sappho.* Trans. Paul Roche. New York: Prometheus Books, 1999.

Eliot, T. S. *The Complete Poems and Plays: 1909–1950.* New York: Harcourt, Brace & World, Inc., 1952.

Ellis, Kate. "Text and Undertext: Myth and Politics in Toni Morrison's *Song of Solomon." Literature, Interpretation, Theory* 6 (1995): 35–45.

Ellis, Trey. "The New Black Aesthetic." *Callaloo* 12 (1989): 233–43.

Erkkila, Betsy. *The Wicked Sisters: Women Poets, Literary History, and Discord.* New York: Oxford UP, 1992.

———. "Phillis Wheatley and the Black American Revolution." *A Mixed Race: Ethnicity in Early America.* Ed. Frank Shuffleton. New York: Oxford UP, 1993. 225–40.

Euripides. *Medea. Three Plays of Euripides: Alcestis, Medea, The Bacchae.* Trans. Paul Roche. New York: W. W. Norton and Company, 1974.

Fikes, Robert, Jr. "African American Scholars of Greco-Roman culture." *Journal of Blacks in Higher Education* 35 (2002): 120–24.

Foley, Helene P. Ed. *The Homeric Hymn to Demeter: Translation, Commentary, and Interpretive Essays.* New Jersey: Princeton UP, 1994.

Foster, Frances Smith. *Written By Herself: Literary Production by African American Women, 1746–1892.* Bloomington: Indiana UP, 1993.

Frazier, E. Franklin. *The Negro in the United States.* New York: McMillan, 1957.

Frye, Northrup. "Literature and Myth." *Relations of Literary Study: Essays on Interdisciplinary Contributions.* Ed. James Thorpe. New York: MLA, 1967. 27–55.

Gantz, Timothy. *Early Greek Myth: A Guide to Literary and Artistic Sources.* Baltimore: The Johns Hopkins UP, 1993.

Gates, Henry Louis, Jr. "Phillis Wheatley and the Nature of the Negro." *Critical Essays on Phillis Wheatley.* Ed. William H. Robinson. Boston: G. K. Hall & Co., 1982. 215–33.

———. "Authority, (White) Power and the (Black) critic: Or, It's All Greek to Me." *Cultural Critique: The Nature and Context of Minority Discourse II.* 7 (1987): 19–46.

———. *Figures in Black, Words, Signs, and the "Racial" Self.* New York: Oxford UP, 1987.

————. *The Signifying Monkey: A Theory of African-American Literary Criticism.* New York: Oxford UP, 1988.

Gelles, Richard. "Power, Sex, and Violence: The Case of Marital Rape." *The Family Coordinator.* 26 (1977): 339–347.

Georgoudaki, Ekaterini. *Race, Gender, and Class Perspectives in the Works of Maya Angelou, Gwendolyn Brooks, Rita Dove, Nikki Giovanni, and Audre Lorde.* Thessaloniki: Aristotle University of Thessaloniki, 1993.

Gibson, Donald. "Text and Countertext in Toni Morrison's *The Bluest Eye.*" *Literature, Interpretation, Theory* 1 (1989): 19–32.

Graf, Fritz. "Medea, The Enchantress from Afar: Remarks on a well-known Myth." *Medea: Essays on Medea in Myth, Literature, Philosophy, and Art.* Eds. James Clauss and Sarah Iles Johnson. New Jersey: Princeton UP, 1997. 21–43.

Graves, Robert. *The Greek Myths.* New York: Penguin Books, 1960.

Grimstead, David. "Anglo-American Racism and Phillis Wheatley's "Sable Veil," "Length'ned Chain," and "Knotted Heart." *Women in the Age of the American Revolution.* Eds. Ronald Hoffman and Peter J. Albert. Virginia: UP of Virginia, 1989. 338–443.

Gutherie, Taylor. *Conversations with Toni Morrison.* Mississippi: UP of Mississippi, 1994.

Haley, Shelley P. "Black Feminist Thought and Classics: Re-membering, Reclaiming, Re-empowering." *Feminist Theory and the Classics.* Ed. Nancy Sorkin Rabinowitz and Amy Richlin. New York: Routledge, 1993. 23–43.

————. "Self Definition, community and resistance. Euripides' *Medea* and Toni Morrison's *Beloved.*" *Thamyris: Mythmaking from Past to Present* 2 (1995): 177–206.

Hallet, Judith. "Sappho and Her Social Context: Sense and Sensuality." *Reading Sappho: Contemporary Approaches.* Ed. Ellen Greene. Berkeley: U of California P, 1996. 125–42.

Hamilton, Edith. *Mythology.* Boston: Little, Brown and Co., 1969.

Hansell, William. "Gwendolyn Brooks's 'In the Mecca': A Rebirth into Blackness." *Negro American Literature Forum* 8 (1974): 199–209.

Harman, Karin Voth. "Immortality and Morality in Contemporary Reworkings of the Demeter/Persephone Myth." *From Motherhood to Mothering: The Legacy of Adrienne Rich's Of Woman Born.* Ed. Andrea O'Reilly. New York: State U of New York P, 2004. 137–57.

Hayden, Lucy K. "Phillis Wheatley's Use of Mythology." *CLA* 35 (1992): 432–47.

Hayes, Elizabeth T. "Like Seeing You Buried": Images of Persephone in *The Bluest Eye, Their Eyes Were Watching God*, and *The Color Purple*. *Images of Persephone: Feminist Readings in Western Literature*. Gainesville: UP of Florida, 170–94.

Henderson, Mae Gwendolyn. "Speaking in Tongues: Dialogics, Dialectics, and the Black Women Writer's Literary Tradition." Feminists Theorize the Political. Ed. Judith Butler and Joan W. Scott. New York: Routledge, 1992. 144–166.

Helgerson, Richard. *Self-Crowned Laureates: Spenser, Jonson, Milton and the Literary System*. Berkeley: U of California P, 1983.

Homer. *Iliad*. Trans. Stanley Lombardo. Indianapolis: Hackett Publishing Company, Inc., 1997.

hooks, bell. *Sisters of the Yam: Black Women and Self-Recovery*. Boston: South End Press, 1993.

Hopkins, Pauline E. *Contending Forces: A Romance Illustrative of Negro Life North and South*. New York: Oxford UP, 1988.

Hughes, Reif Gertrude. "Making it *Really* New: Hilda Doolittle, Gwendolyn Brooks, and the Feminist Potential of Modern Poetry." *On Gwendolyn Brooks: Reliant Contemplation*. Ed. Stephen Caldwell Wright. Ann Arbor: The U of Michigan P, 1996. 186–212.Ingersoll, Earl. *Conversations with Rita Dove*. Jackson: UP of Mississippi, 2003.

Humphries, Rolfe. "Verse Chronicle." *On Gwendolyn Brooks: Reliant Contemplation*. Ed. Stephen Caldwell Wright. Ann Abor: The U of Michigan P, 1996. 8.

Ingersoll, Earl G. Ed. *Conversations with Rita Dove*. Jackson: UP of Mississippi, 2003.

Jaffar-Agha, Tamara. *Demeter and Persephone: Lessons from a Myth*. North Carolina: McFarland & Co, Inc. Publishers, 2002.

Jamison, Angelene. "Analysis of Selected Poetry of Phillis Wheatley." *Critical Essays on Phillis Wheatley*. Ed. William H. Robinson. Boston: G. K. Hall, 1982. 128–35.

Jimoh, Yemisi. "Double Consciousness, Modernism, and Womanist Themes in Gwendolyn Brooks's 'The Anniad.'" *Melus* 23 (1998): 167–86.

Johnsen, Gretchen, and Richard Peabody. "A Cage of Sound." *Conversations With Rita Dove*. Ed. Earl Ingersoll. Mississippi: UP of Mississippi. 2003. 15–37.

Jones, Gayle. "Community and Voice: Gwendolyn Brooks's 'In the Mecca.'" *A Life Distilled: Gwendolyn Brooks, Her Poetry and Fiction*. Ed. Maria K. Mootry and Gary Smith. Chicago, U of Illinois P, 1987. 192–204.

Jung, C. G. "The Psychological Aspects of the Kore." *Essays on a Science of Mythology*: *The Myth of the Divine Child*. Eds. C. G. Jung and C. Keréyni. New Jersey: Princeton UP, 156–77.

Keith, Verna M. and Cedric Herring. "Skin Tone and Stratification in the Black Community." *The American Journal of Sociology*. 97 (1991): 760–778.

Kincaid, Jamaica. *Annie John*. New York: Farrar, Straus and Giroux, 1997.

Kerényi, Carl. *Archetypal Image of Mother and Daughter*. Trans. Ralph Manheim, New York: Pantheon Books, 1967.

Khyar-Taleb, Mohamed. "Gifts to Be Earned." *Conversations with Rita Dove*. Ed. Earl G. Ingersoll. Jackson: UP of Mississippi, 2003. 74–87.

Knox, Bernard. Introduction. *The Three Theban Plays*. Sophocles. Trans. Robert Fagles. New York: Penguin Books, 1982.

Lander, Byron G. "Group Theory and Individuals: The Origin of Poverty as a Political Issue in 1964." *The Western Political Quarterly* 24 (1971): 514–526.

Laurence, Patricia. "Women's Silence as a Ritual of Truth: A Study of Literary Expressions in Austen, Bronte, and Woolf." *Listening to Silences: New Essays in Feminist Criticism*. Ed. Elaine Hedges and Shelley Fisher Fishkin. New York: Oxford UP, 1994. 156–67.

Locke, Alain. "Self-Criticism: The Third Dimension in Culture." *Phlyon* 11 (1950): 391–94.

Lofgren, Lotta. "Partial Horror: Fragmentation and Healing in Rita Dove's *Mother Love*. *Callaloo* 19 (1996) 135–42.

Logan, Shirley Wilson. Ed. *With Pen and Voice: A Critical Anthology of Nineteenth-Century African American Women*. Carbondale: Southern Illinois UP, 1995.

Lord, Mary Louise. "Withdrawal and Return: An Epic Story Pattern in the Homeric Hymn to Demeter and in the Homeric Poems." *The Homeric Hymn to Demeter: Translation, Commentary, and Interpretive Essays*. Ed. Helene P. Foley. New Jersey: Princeton UP, 1994. 181–89.

Lorde, Audre. *Sister Outsider*. New York: Crossing Press, 1984.

Lowney, John. "A Material Collapse that is Construction": History and Counter Memory in Gwendolyn Brooks' 'In the Mecca.'" *MELUS* 23 (1998): 3–19.

Martin, Karin A. *Puberty, Sexuality, and the Self: Boys and Girls at Adolescence*. New York: Routledge, 1996.

Mason, Julian D. *The Poems of Phillis Wheatley*. Chapel Hill: The U of North Carolina, 1989.

McCullough, Kate. "Slavery, Sexuality, and Genre: Pauline Hopkins and Representation of Feminine desire." *The Unruly Voice: Rediscovering Pauline Elizabeth Hopkins.* Ed. John Cullen. Urbana U of Illinois P, 1996. 21–49.

McDowell, Robert. "Language is Not Enough." *Conversations with Rita Dove.* Ed. Earl Ingersoll. Mississippi: UP of Mississippi, 2003. 174–79.

McGinley, Phyllis. "Poetry for Prose Readers." *The New York Times Book Review.* 23 Jan. 1950: 7.

McManus, Barbara F. *Classics and Feminism: Gendering the Classics.* New York: Twayne Publishers, 1997.

Melhem, D. H. *Gwendolyn Brooks: Poetry and the Heroic Voice.* Lexington: U of Kentucky P, 1987.

Miner, Madonne. "Lady No Longer Sings the Blues: Rape, Madness, and Silence in *The Bluest Eye. Conjuring: Black Women, Fiction, and Literary Tradition.* Eds. Marjorie Pryse and Hortense Spillers. Bloomington: Indiana UP, 1985. 176–91.

Mobley, Marilyn. *Folk Roots and Mythic Wings in Sarah Orne Jewett and Toni Morrison.* Baton Rouge: Louisiana State UP, 1991.

Morrison, Toni. *Song of Solomon.* New York: Alfred Knopf, 1977.

———. *Beloved.* New York: Plume, 1988.

———. *The Bluest Eye.* New York: Plume, 1993.

———. "Unspeakable Things Unspoken: The Afro-American Presence in American Literature." *Within the Circle: An Anthology of African American Literary Criticism for the Harlem Renaissance to the Present.* Ed. Angelyn Mitchell. Durham: Duke UP, 1994. 368–98.

Mukhtar, Ali Isani. "The British Reception of Wheatley's *Poems on Various Subjects.*" 66 (1981): 144–49.

Nelson, Marilyn and Rita Dove. "A Black Rainbow: Modern Afro-American Poetry." *Poetry After Modernism.* Ed. Robert McDowell. Oregon: Story Line Press, 1998. 142–98.

Neumann, Erich. "The Woman's Experience of Herself and the Eleusinian Mysteries." *The Long Journey Home: Re-visioning the Myth of Demeter and Persephone for Our Time.* Ed. Christine Downing. Boston: Shambhala, 1994. 173–76.

Neustadt, Kathy. "The Visits of the Writers Toni Morrison and Eudora Welty." *Conversations with Toni Morrison.* Ed. Danielle Taylor-Guthrie. Mississippi: UP of Mississippi, 1994. 84–92.

Newlands, Carole E. "The Metamorphosis of Ovid's Medea." *Medea: Essays on Medea in Myth, Literature, Philosophy, and Art.* Ed. James

Clauss and Sarah Iles Johnson. New Jersey: Princeton UP, 1997. 178–208.

Nussbaum, Martha. "Serpents in the Soul: A Reading of Seneca's *Medea.*" *Medea: Essays on Medea in Myth, Literature, Philosophy, and Art.* Ed. James Clauss and Sarah Iles Johnson. New Jersey: Princeton UP, 1997. 219–49.

Ostriker, Alicia. "The Thieves of Language: Women Poets and Revisionist Mythmaking." *The New Feminist Criticism: Essays on Women, Literature, and Theory.* Ed. Elaine Showalter. New York: Pantheon Books, 1985. 314–38.

Ousseynou, Traore. "Creative African Memory: Some Oral Sources of Toni Morrison's *Song of Solomon.*" *Of Dreams Deferred, Dead or Alive: African Perspectives of African American Writers* Ed. Femi Ojo-Ade. Westport: Greenwood Press, 1996. 129–41.

Ovid. *Metamorphoses.* Trans. A. D. Melville. Oxford: Oxford UP, 1986.

———. *Heroides.* Trans. Harold Isbell. New York: Penguin, 1990.

Pearson, Carol, and Katherine Pope. *The Female Hero in American and British Literature.* New York: R. R. Bowker Company, 1981.

Pereira, Malin. *Rita Dove's Cosmopolitanism.* Illinois: U of Illinois P, 2003.

Pomery, Sarah. "Infanticide in Hellenistic Greece." *Images of Women in Antiquity.* Ed. Averil Cameron and Amelie Khurt. Detroit: Wayne State UP, 1983. 207–22.

Pratt, Annis. *Archetypal Patterns in Women's Fiction.* Bloomington: Indiana UP, 1981.

Ray, Henrietta C. *Sonnets.* New York: J. J. Little & Co., 1893.

———. *Poems.* New York: The Grafton Press, 1910.

Rampersad, Arnold. "The Poems of Rita Dove." *Callaloo* 9 (1986): 52–60.

Rankine, Patrice. *Ulysses in Black.* Wisconsin: Wisconsin UP, 2006.

Reynolds, Margaret. *The Sappho Companion.* New York: Palgrave, 2001.

Rich, Adrienne. *Of Woman Born: Motherhood as Experience and Institution.* New York: Norton, 1986.

Robinson, Tracy and Janie Victoria Ward. "A Belief in Self Far Greater Than Anyone's Disbelief: Cultivating Resistance Among African American Female Adolescents." *Women, Girls and Psychotherapy: Reframing Resistance.* Ed. Carol Gilligan, Annie G. Rogers, et al. New York: Harrington Park Press, 1991. 87–103.

Ronnick, Michele Valerie. "After Bernal and Mary Lefkowitz: Research Opportunities in Classica Africana. *Negro History Bulletin* 60 (1997): 1–12.

———. "A Look at Booker T. Washington's Attitude Toward the Study of Greek and Latin by People of African Ancestry." *The Negro Educational Review* 53 No 3 (2002): 59–70.

———. "A Lesson in Biomythology: The Classical Origin of Audre Lorde's 'Nom de Plume "Rey Domini"'." *Classical and Modern Literature* 24 (2004) 149–51.

———. Ed. *The Autobiography of William Sanders Scarborough: An American Journey from Slavery to Scholarship.* Detroit: Wayne State UP, 2005.

———. "Epic Imagery in Gwendolyn Brooks' *Annie Allen.*" E-mail to the author. 23 Apr. 2006. 1–8.

Rushing, Andrea Benton. "Images of Black Women in Afro-American Poetry." *The Afro-American Woman: Struggles and Images.* Ed. Sharon Hartley and Rosalyn Teborg-Penn. New York: National U Publications-Kennikat P, 1978. 74–84.

Sandys, George. *Ovid's Metamorphosis Englished by George Sandys.* 8th ed. London, 1690.

Seligman, Dee. "The Mother of Them All: Gwendolyn Brooks's *Annie Allen.*" *The Anna Book: Searching for Anna in Literary History.* Connecticut: Greenwood Press, 1992. 131–38.

Sertima, Ivan Van. *Black Women in Antiquity.* New Brunswick: Transaction Publishers, 1997.

Shaw, Harry B. "Perceptions of Men in the Early Works of Gwendolyn Brooks." *Black American Poets Between Worlds, 1940–1960.* Ed. R. Baxter Miller. Knoxville: U of Tennessee P, 1986. 136–59.

Sherman, Joan. *Invisible Poets: Afro-Americans of the Nineteenth Century.* Chicago: U of Illinois P,1989.

Shields, John C. "Phillis Wheatley's Use of Classicism." *American Literature: A Journal of Literary History, Criticism and Bibliography* 52 (1980): 97–111.

Shinn, Thelma. *Worlds Within Women: Myths and Mythmaking in Fantastic Literature by Women.* Connecticut: Greenwood Press, 1986.

Snowden, Frank, Jr. *Blacks in Antiquity: Ethiopians in the Greco-Roman Experience.* Cambridge: Harvard UP, 1970.

Stanford, Anne Folwell. "An Epic With a Difference: Sexual Politics in Gwendolyn Brooks' 'The Anniad.'" *American Literature* 67 (1995): 283–301.

Steffen, Therese. *Crossing Color: Transcultural Space and Place in Rita Dove's Poetry, Fiction, and Drama.* New York: Oxford UP, 2001.

Stipes, Emily Watts. *The Poetry of American Women from 1632 to 1945.* Austin: U of Texas P, 1977.

Terrell, Mary Church. *A Colored Woman in a White World.* Washington, D.C.: Ransdell, Inc. Publishers, 1940.

Tate, Claudia. "Allegories of Black Female Desire; or, Rereading Nineteenth-Century Sentimental Narratives of Black Female Authority." *Changing Our Own Words. Essays on Criticism, Theory, and Writing by Black Women.* Ed. Cheryl Wall. New Jersey: Rutgers UP, 1989. 98–126.

Tidey, Ashley "Limping or Flying? Psychoanalysis, Afrocentrism, and *Song of Solomon.*" *College English* 63 (2000): 48–70.

Van Dyne, Susan. "Siting the Poet; Rita Dove's Refiguring of Traditions." *Women Poets of the Americas: Toward a Pan-American Gathering.* Ed. Jaqueline Vaught-Brogan and Candelaria Cordelia-Chavez. Notre Dame: U of Notre Dame P, 1999. 68–87.

Vendler, Helen. *The Given and the Made: Strategies of Poetic Redefinition.* Cambridge: Harvard UP, 1995.

Walker, George. "Phillis Wheatley a Study." *The Colored American,* June 7, 1904. 440–42.

Walker, Margaret. *On Being Female, Black, and Free: Essays by Margaret Walker, 1932–1992.* Knoxville: The U of Tennessee P, 1997.

Walters, Tracey L. *Reclaiming the Classics: The Emancipatory Strategy of Selected African American Women Poets—Phillis Wheatley, Henrietta Cordelia Ray, and Gwendolyn Brooks.* Diss. Howard University, 1999.

———. "Gwendolyn Brooks' 'The Anniad' and the Indeterminacy of Genre." *CLA* 44 (2001). 350–66.

———. "Rita Dove's *Mother Love*: Revising the Black Aesthetic Through the Lens of Western Discourse." *August Wilson and Black Aesthetics.* Ed. Dana Williams and Sandra Shannon. New York: Palgrave, 2004. 37–48.

Weisenburger, Steven. *Modern Medea: A Family Story of Slavery and Child-Murder from the Old South.* New York: Hill and Wang, 1998.

Wade, Gloria. "The Truths of Our Mothers' Lives: Mother-Daughter Relationships in Black Women's Fiction. *SAGE* 1 (1984): 8–12.

Wheatley, Phillis. *Poems on Various Subjects Religious and Moral.* London, 1773.

———. *The Poems of Phillis Wheatley.* Ed. Julian D. Mason. Chapel Hill: The U of North Carolina P, 1989.

Williams, Kenny J. "The World of Satin-Legs, Ms. Sallie and the Blackstone Rangers: The Restricted Chicago of Gwendolyn Brooks." *A*

Life Distilled: Gwendolyn Brooks, Her Poetry and Fiction. Ed. Maria K. Mootry and Gary Smith. Chicago, U of Illinois P, 1987. 47–70.

Wilkerson, Tanya. *Persephone Returns: Victims, Heroes, and the Journey from the Underworld.* California: Page Mill Press, 1996.

Williamson, Margaret. *Sappho's Immortal Daughters.* Massachusetts: Harvard UP, 1995.

Wisker, Gina. "Weaving Our Own Web: Demythologising/Remythologising and Magic in the Work of Contemporary Women Writers. *It's My Party: Reading Twentieth-Century Women's Writing.* Ed. Gina Wisker. London: Pluto Press, 1994. 104–28.

Wolf, Naomi. *The Beauty Myth: How Images of Beauty Are Used Against Women.* New York, William Morrow and Company, Inc., 1991.

Wolf, Amy. "Virtue Housekeeping, and Domestic Space in Pauline Hopkins Contending Forces." *Domestic Goddesses.* Ed, Kim Wells. August 23, 1999. Online. Internet. June 2007.http://www.womenwriters.net/domesticgoddess/Woolf.htm.

Worsham, Fabian Clements. "The Poetics of Matrilineage: Mothers and Daughters in the Poetry of African American Women, 1965–1985." *Women of Color: Mother Daughter Relationships in 20th Century Literature.* Ed. Elizabeth Brown-Guillory. U of Texas P, 1996.

Index